The sun was rema~~rkably~~ ~~warm for England~~ in the early days of summer. The lady's skin was uniformly tinted an almost dark brown; she lay upon her back, her eyes closed, so there was no reason for me to refrain from a closer inspection of her person than I would have made had she been aware of it. Her shoulders were slim and her arms beautifully turned, her breasts, while perfectly full and luscious when she was standing, now fell into the lines of gently swelling hillocks, each tipped by a tiny, darker brown pinnacle. The entire sight was a most beguiling one, my heart was in my mouth with admiration; I shifted uneasily upon the grass through the effect her beauty had had, inevitably, upon me. As I did so, she opened her eyes and raised her head . . .

Also available from Headline

Eros in the Country
Eros in Town
Eros on the Grand Tour
Eros in the New World
Eros in the Far East
The Eros Collection
Eros in High Places
Eros in Society
Eros off the Rails
The Ultimate Eros Collection
Eros Strikes Gold
Eros in Springtime

Eros in Summer

Anonymous

First published in Great Britain in 1994
by HEADLINE BOOK PUBLISHING

A HEADLINE DELTA paperback

10 9 8 7 6 5 4 3 2 1

ISBN 0 7472 4463 4

Typeset by CBS, Felixstowe, Suffolk

Printed and bound in Great Britain by
Cox & Wyman Ltd., Reading, Berks

HEADLINE BOOK PUBLISHING
A division of Hodder Headline PLC
338 Euston Road
London NW1 3BH

**For the convenience of the reader
we here record a note of
IMPORTANT PERSONS APPEARING IN
THE NARRATIVE
in the order of their appearance**

Andrew Archer Esq, MP, our hero.

Mrs Sophia Nelham, our heroine.

Jack, a postilion.

Arthur Fennel Esq, a retired gentleman.

Margaret, his supposed daughter.

A working man.

Señor Angel Ganivet, a guitarist.

Mrs Emily Twyce-Knightley, a complaisant wife.

Captain George Twyce-Knightley, a complaisant husband.

Lieutenant Fenwick and Mrs Penelope Marjoribanks, of a
   similar disposition.

The Hon. Rupert Montjoy, a masquerader.

Mlle Desirée Beauregard.

Sir Harry Vane, a young gentleman.

Mrs Clara Carclase, an actress.

Sir Herbert Taylor, a servant of His Majesty.

Sir Tunbridge Waller, a private gentleman.

Xavier Tanoski Esq, another.

Josiah Flaxman Henby Esq, MA (Oxon), a headmaster.

Mrs Prudence Henby, his wife and helpmeet.

A number of their pupils.

A rustic onanist.

M. Charles Tronc (so-called).

Mally, a milkmaid.

Mrs Emmeline Winthrop, a widow.

Percival Jameson Esq, a businessman.
Miss Emma X, a young lady.
Jack Y, Esq, a young gentleman.
Mrs Emmeline Possett, an accommodating lady.
Mrs Rosabel Esdaile, an unwise lady.
Anthony Furness Esq, a miscreant.
Jack Fitton, a page.

Chapter One

The Adventures of Andy

The adventures which I and my friend Mrs Nelham will narrate in the following pages occurred as the result of a request made to me by a number of gentlemen engaged in a speculation, the nature of which was unusual: it was consequent upon the spreading of the railways throughout the country – which, soon after the earliest years of that remarkable invention the steam engine, took place with an acceleration almost as rapid as that of the engines themselves!

It had been rumoured that a line was soon to be laid down from the metropolis to the coastal town of Brighthelmstone, or Brighton as the vulgar now began to call it; and it was considered as probable that upon its becoming an easy, speedy and inexpensive matter to make one's way from London to the coast, there would undoubtedly be an increased demand for accommodation where the moneyed classes could take their ease in the summer months – for it was the case that the reduction of the time taken upon the journey to between one and two hours would make it possible even to live upon the coast of Sussex, and spending several hours of the day at work in London, to return to the coast for the night's slumber, at the same time setting aside the weekends for relaxation in an air considerably more salubrious and healthful than that available within the sooty confines of the city.

A band of gentlemen was considering the establishment of an entirely new village or town somewhere on the southern coast, particularly designed for the use of those metropolitans to whom the idea might appeal; and such a speculation being (as they believed) capable of returning a considerable profit, it was decided to send some gentleman forth to examine the entire coast between Rye in the east and Arundel in the west, to discover the place best suited by situation for the establishment of just such a new town. My friend the Viscount Chichley having put forward my name as a responsible and acute person who might be trusted with the endeavour, I had been commissioned to perform it – and my friend Mrs Sophia Nelham (whose personal narrative, as is usual with us, shares these pages) decided that, weary of the heat of London, she would accompany me at least as far as Brighton, where she might spend some weeks enjoying the sea air.

There being at least thirty coaches running daily between London and Brighton we had no difficulty in taking places in one of them on the day upon which we wished to travel over the fifty and eight miles which connected the two places (by the direct route through Croydon, Riegate and Cuckfield).

It may be too easy for travellers of a later age to suppose that such a journey, by road, was of ineffable tedium; yet this was by no means the case, provided one had the means to travel by the best equipage – which (in the case of the coach in which we reserved our seats) was both commodious and elegant, adorned with taste, drawn – or rather, carried away! – by four beautiful horses, all alike, all with the same pace, who devoured the distance, champing bits of the most splendid polish, and starting and snorting under a harness of a rich and noble simplicity while being driven by a coachman in livery and urged on by a handsome, neat postilion. Every two leagues, more postilions – attentive, civil, neither impertinent nor in liquor – brought out fresh horses just like the first, which, as we came to the staging points, we could see striking the ground at a distance as though eager and impatient to take their places.

Upon our drawing into the courtyard of an inn at Riegate, an officious major-domo introduced us into a magnificent salon in which were served all sorts of refreshments – limpid tea which sparkled in china, frothy porter which foamed in silver, and on a side table choice, copious, varied dishes. I reflected as we took our lunches that at best England was surely the first country in the world for its horses, public carriages and inns, for those of which I had had experience in France and Germany, though pleasant enough, were certainly less well ordered than here – just as the roads were more pock-marked with holes and ruts than our own. How fortunate, I reflected, were those foreigners whose means enabled them to travel in our country.

Sophie, on my repeating my emotions aloud, agreed – though, she said, it was to be regretted that in England strict attention to morality, which (she opined) was the result of the reaction from the looseness of the reign of the second Charles, too often prevented travellers from enjoying those forms of sensual recreation open, on the Continent, no less to ladies than to gentlemen, and which lightened the most tedious journey.

On my enquiring precisely her meaning, she freely admitted

(for we were friends of long standing who needed to conceal nothing from each other) that she referred to the possibility of an *amour en passage* which was perfectly possible in France, Germany, Italy – as will be recognised by those readers of an earlier volume of our reminiscences[1], a book, however, not to be recommended to those who shrink from frank expositions of sensuality.

I took leave to differ from her. It might not be the case, for instance, that in English inns one was offered such services with the freedom with which they were made available in Paris or Brussels; but to those capable of reading the meaning in a lively eye, there was no difficulty in making an alliance with an agreeable maid.

'But my dear Andy,' she said, 'it must always be – in the female case at all events – that we must make the first move; while abroad a likely young fellow will offer himself as freely and inoffensively as he will agree to clean one's boots; will perform with the greatest adequacy if the offer is accepted; and yet will accept a refusal with grace. I have never, I think, known such an arrangement to be made in this country without my first signalling that I was in need of it!'

I must accept her opinion, not being a female; but, as I said, I found it difficult to believe that my friend, if in need of corporeal comfort, need remain bereft of it, given the contiguity of a handsome fellow susceptible to female charms!

Sophie smiled at this, and even nodded; but at the same time insisted that her former statement was correct.

Having partaken of refreshment, we asked to be ushered to the rooms set aside for travellers to refresh themselves, two

[1]*Eros on the Grand Tour*

of which lay side by side at the top of a staircase; and on being shown up by the young postilion from our own carriage, who had stood beside my chair to serve us, I could not resist enquiring *sotto voce* whether he had overheard our conversation. After some persuasion – for he did not wish it to be thought that he had been listening – he admitted to it; and seeing that he was an upright lad who seemed likely to be able and willing, I could not but suggest that it was a duty on him to prove that English lads were no less forward, at the right time, than the Continentals – and emphasised my argument with a guinea piece.

He hesitated, for (as he said in a low voice) strict rules on such matters were laid down by his masters, who were doubtless of the opinion that the pleasure given to some ladies by an offer from such an upstanding young fellow was necessarily outweighed by the offence which might be taken by the minority. Besides which, it seems that one such offer made by another chap a few years previously had resulted in a complaint of rape. However, I encouraged Jack (which was his name) to believe that no such complaint would be made by my friend – and that in the event of her not wishing to take advantage of his offer, she would merely decline in the most polite manner possible, and without taking the least offence in the world.

This argument, together with the guinea, sent him off in search of Sophie, while I set about refreshing myself by making use of a bowl of warm water accompanied by several clean towels, and made use of the chamber-pot set upon the floor by the bed (nearby there being a notice displayed with the legend: 'Please do not place beneath the bed after use, for the steam rusts the springs').

I had just completed my toilet, when I became conscious of noises from next door which were suggestive in the extreme; and I trust the reader will not condemn me for wishing to satisfy my curiosity as to what they signified. I therefore slipped quietly from my room – and on turning towards the neighbouring door, to whose keyhole (I will not disguise it) I thought of applying my eye, I was rewarded by the sight of a chambermaid whose own was already occupying the said aperture! That she was intrigued by what she saw was evident not only from her complete obliviousness to my presence, the ruddiness of her cheeks and her panting breath, but from the fact that her hand was thrust beneath her skirts, where her fingers seemed busily occupied.

The opportunity was one which was not to be missed by any young man of spirit, and pausing only to unloose my breeches I stepped behind her and throwing up her skirts disclosed a handsome white arse, with, at its centre, a triangular aperture which upon thrusting my prick into it embraced the invading article with the warmest affection. Able then to take possession of the young lady with an ease almost surprising (through, I suppose, the lubricity of her own actions), I was pleased to discover by a little wriggle of pleasure that she was by no means averse to my impertinence; indeed, she did not even remove her eye from the keyhole through which (I believed) she was observing my friend receiving the attentions of Jack the postilion!

Not having the advantage (though in the case of a gentleman it can, through speeding the process, be a disadvantage) of any titillation of a similar kind, I was able without difficulty (and despite her wriggling, which I confess was almost excessively charming) to maintain my composure for as long as was needed to bring madam to her apogee, carried out with an easy, swinging motion which, though it was without urgency, at each separate movement brought my belly with a smack against the delightfully firm, rounded cheeks of her bottom, which motion finally reduced her to such ecstasy that she was bound to screw her eyes shut and exchange the prospect of others' pleasure for the reality of her own. This completed, she straightened herself and her clothing, turned, and, with a saucy wink and a curtsy which seemed as appreciative as it was respectful, left the scene without a word.

My own clothing adjusted, I knocked upon the door and at once entered – finding both my friend and Jack now fully dressed, the latter already taking up the small bag which was Sophie's only travelling luggage (but at the same time, unobserved, giving me a look which confirmed my suspicion that he had fully performed that function I had suggested). Sophie said nothing as to her adventure – neither did I attempt to draw her out; for though we were perfectly frank one with another, there was no necessity for everything to be held in common between us. She did at last, however, remark that upon reflection she believed that the verdict she had passed upon English servants, at luncheon, might have been too severe – at which I could not but burst into laughter; whereupon I believe she understood the situation entirely, striking me lightly upon the cheek with her hand – though still without saying anything.

Inns of a very respectable character occur in every direction in Brighton, and we had no difficulty in obtaining rooms at the Albion Hotel. This is a large town, now of some twenty-five thousand people inhabiting some eight thousand houses, besides upwards of one thousand included in the adjoining parish of Hove – a proportion to the inhabitants far greater than in London and other large towns, the obvious reason for which is that about one-third are constantly occupied by visitors, at least one hundred thousand of whom come there during the year for some space of time, not less than a week.

The sea line of Brighton already extends beyond the western esplanade a full three miles from the eastern extremity of Kemp Town. Nearly in the centre, but rather inclining towards the west, is the opening of the Steyne, with a prospect of the Downs behind it – a fine expanse equally conducive to health and to pleasure. A little before the Pavilion is reached, the old North Street, which is in fact the High Street of Brighton, runs up a hill, eventually attaining the height of one hundred and fifty feet; and on the opposite side of the Steyne, St James's Street rises with a slighter elevation towards Kemp Town; this may be termed the local Bond or Regent Street.

Sophie announced her intention of remaining in Brighton while I ventured forth on my peregrination along the coast. We would meet, as she said, when we wished or when circumstance allowed; though always glad of her advice, I did not find it a positive necessity that she should travel with me, and she was of the opinion that a stay of some month or six weeks in Brighton would relax and recreate her.

So we said goodbye on the very morning after our arrival, and I set off to the eastward, having hired a carriage and driver to take me upon the first leg of my journey – for it would be cheaper for me to hire, or even buy, a horse somewhat out in the country than in Brighton (not that the hiring charges were by any means exorbitant, the cost for a first-class carriage being but one shilling and six pence for the

8

first mile, and nine pence for each additional mile).

My first stop was intended to be at Newhaven, some five miles along the coast from Brighton. On leaving the Signal House to the right beyond Kemp Town, the road continued in a straight direction to Rottingdean – a distance of four miles or so – passing over one or two hills, with no material objects except good sea and coast views when looking back upon Brighton. This road has within a few years been diverted to a greater space from the edge of the cliff than it formerly occupied, but my driver (a pert young man whose enthusiasm seemed fortunately to be matched by skill) still drove rather too fast and too near the cliff for me to be entirely comfortable – and told rather too many stories of the lamentable accidents that had occurred along the road as a consequence of rash driving on dark evenings.

Rottingdean is a neat and pleasant village, with one street running up into the country from an opening in the cliff, which affords convenient facilities for bathing. We ascended the hill and proceeded along the pretty road towards Newhaven. No villages are to be met with here; the road ascends and descends several steep eminences, but has nothing interesting beyond a quiet and pastoral appearance, the dark green of the South Downs diversified by the appearance of many sheep, while on the right, cliffs often bold with many inequalities of height, may be seen.

Few houses came into view – but by a stroke of fortune we had just passed the gate to one, when, by the driver's momentary inattention, a wheel of the carriage ran into the ditch, and in a moment we were overturned! It was no remarkable sideshow, but enough to throw me from my seat and quite over the hedge, and on my attempting to rise I found my right ankle unable to bear me, through being broken, or, more likely – as I gingerly inspected it – badly sprained.

My driver, who had escaped uninjured, was in some panic, though on my assuring him that the accident had not slain me, he recovered somewhat, his confusion reduced simply to the state of standing scratching his head as to how the carriage could be righted (which, though small, was too heavy for him). My suggestion that he should try at the house nearby was met with such expressions of wonder at my intelligence and quickness of mind that they would have been a compliment to the mental powers of Mr Isaac Newton, and within five minutes he had gone and returned with an amiable gentleman accompanied by two servants, who, in a moment, had both righted the carriage and – despite my assurances that I would be capable of continuing my journey – escorted me into the house.

There, Mr Arthur Fennel, evidently a gentleman of some means, busied himself fetching brandy and water and summoning a young lady of rather fewer years than might have been expected, from the age of her father. On my removing my shoe and stocking, a foot already swelling and changing colour was revealed, and the young lady, immediately taking charge, insisted on my being helped to a chamber upstairs, where she sent for cold water and kneeling at my feet insisted on bathing my foot and ankle, then placed a cold compress upon it, secured by a neat bandage. The coolness was (as I readily admitted) most soothing and comforting. She insisted – as did her father, who addressed her by the name of Margaret – that I must make no effort to continue my journey that night, and in order that it might prove impossible gave instructions in my hearing that my driver should be dismissed and my portmanteau brought to the room – which was immediately done by a servant.

Although it was barely six o'clock, the young lady insisted that I should take to my bed; the placing of my foot upon a level with the rest of my body would enable the blood (as she argued) to circulate more freely, and thus hasten the repair of any damage done to its tissues. I rose, hopped towards the bed, and sat upon the edge of it, whereupon, with great kindness, she knelt at my feet and began to undo my second shoe.

I must confess that it has often been my experience that the infliction of pain or discomfort has had the result – once the immediate shock is over – of heightening my sensual emotions. I can offer no explanation for this, though those gentlemen who make it their business to examine the workings of the human mind and body suggest that any pain brings about an automatic suggestion of the idea of death, to which we react by recalling our only means of immortality – that is, the generation of children; and therefore results in the heightening of the instinct which, when put into action, has that result.

However that may be, I became conscious at that moment of the truth that Miss Margaret was a most attractive young lady. She was dressed in a gown which I supposed to be kept for her leisure, for it eschewed the decoration and over-elaboration of day-gowns, but was simpler than the current fashion, and more revealing of a figure which, while not voluptuous, was sufficiently full to be entirely feminine. As she leaned forward somewhat below me, I could not but be conscious that her bosom was almost freely displayed, the entire upper halves of the globes upon view, the nipples only just concealed by the line of her bodice – indeed, I fancied

11

that I glimpsed for a moment the edge of a darker circlet just where cloth met skin. Her arms were naked, and beautifully shaped, suggesting the presence of slim, rounded shoulders; and I could not but remark, through the thinness of the material of her dress, the exquisite line of her hips and thighs.

Despite any embarrassment that might be caused, I could do nothing to prevent my body from reacting as might be expected by any gentleman in such a situation, and had the young lady carefully observed the bifurcation of my breeches, she might have seen a swelling arise there which would have revealed, to a more experienced woman, my admiration. However, my natural good manners came to my rescue before I could make any motion which might have been misconstrued by the innocent child (who could surely not have been above the age of fifteen); and I requested her to send for one of the male servants, who could help me to undress – for, I said, I was in doubt that I could remain sufficiently steady upon one leg to enable me to remove my breeches without falling over, and possibly exacerbating the damage to my ankle.

'Alas!' she said, 'John has driven with Mr Fennel into Rottingdean to fetch an ointment, and the only person left in the house is the cook. But if you would not be offended, I will be happy to take your arm . . .'

She looked up at me with a glance which in a more experienced woman would have been taken for a libidinous offer, but which in so young and charming a girl could surely have been nothing of the sort! I should, of course, have declined the offer; but to be frank, the idea of the young lady's hands about my limbs was such that, whatever the danger, I could not persuade myself to do so.

I therefore rose to my feet – or rather, my foot – and

steadying myself upon her arm, attempted to undo my belt. This proved difficult enough, and after some fumbling she suggested that I should confine my efforts to steadying myself by clutching at the bedpost; and on my doing so, released my belt with such an expertise that one might almost have thought her practised in the action! She then, without hesitation, drew my breeches down over my hips, and I was able to step out of them.

Though the idea of drawers had now begun to come in, and they were embraced by (or rather, they embraced the persons of) the fashionable, I still clung to the notion that no such fripperies were necessary provided sufficient attention was paid to cleanliness. I will not conceal that in some situations a freedom from undergarments is an advantage in amorous affairs, lending a convenient speed (as in the little adventure at Riegate); on the other hand, on the present occasion I could have wished for some concealment other than my shirt, for this having ridden up, upon the young lady drawing down my breeches, my admiration for her person was clearly evidenced, since upon the waistband passing below my belly an engorged prick stood at attention but a few inches from her eyes. With perfect self-control, she took no notice of this – or at least, did not do so at the first moment; but on my releasing the bedpost with one hand in order to tuck the tail of my shirt uncomfortably between my legs, she reached out a hand to stop me, remarking that it were a pity to conceal so admirable an instrument – and in an action which seemed to me an instant confession of experience, laid her hand beneath the limb and with an inexpressible effect lifted it to a position more convenient for placing a kiss upon its tip!

Ignoring the pain in my ankle consequent upon the action, I now entirely released the bedpost, and clutching at her shoulders raised the young lady to her feet, and drawing her to me kissed her lips with the utmost enthusiasm – at which, to my delight they parted with the most accessible gesture, positively instructing me to insert my tongue between them and meet her own, which played about it with a freedom which would have been sufficient confirmation of her womanhood even had she not at the same time drawn up my shirt still further and placed the palms of her hands firmly upon the cheeks of my arse, in order to press our very centres together.

My balance lost, I reluctantly released her as I fell upon the bed; where, before I could move, she placed one knee between my thighs, tight up against my bollocks, and for a moment knelt there while she drew her dress above her head and threw it with a delightful freedom across the room – revealing a body, which, in its firm and willowy lubricity, was all I could have guessed, or wished for, from those signs I had already seen.

I half sat, to turn her to my purpose; but with a gesture, she stayed me, whispering that I should not engage in any action which might bring me pain, and thrusting me backwards she now knelt astride, lowering herself so that she sat upon my riding-muscle, which lay right along the crack of her arse, and to which, by a charming wriggling motion, she conveyed a most delightful sensation. I did not hesitate now – for it was clear that she was no tyro – to test with my palms the jaunty curves of her breasts, even attempting to raise myself sufficiently to take my lips to those pink buds which knotted suggestively beneath my fingers; but I could not reach them –

at which my disappointment must have been clear, for I was offered another prize when, rising upon her knees, the lady brought within reach of my lips that aperture, wreathed in tight chestnut curls, where I cordially hoped eventually to come to anchor.

In the meantime, however, I was happy to pay it the tribute of a kiss, and to seek out with my tongue that firm module of flesh which stood out at its apex, my attentions to which resulted in the young lady throwing back her head with a little mew and an unmistakable gesture of amorous pleasure, while at the same time she reached behind her and, seizing my cock, began to smooth and tease it with such dexterity that in a moment I must catch at her wrists in order that she should not bring me off too soon.

Immediately taking my point, she now once more retired, and pausing only to part with her fingers those coral lips which lay within the chestnut curls, brought the tip of my prick within them and sank slowly upon it until her hair and my own met and kissed.

It would be impertinent of me to paint a more particular picture of the scene, for some privacy must ever be preserved where the meeting of the sexes is concerned. Suffice to say that our meeting was neither too brief nor too drawn out, my staff, shining with the joint effusions of our enthusiasm, being first revealed then concealed by the rise and fall of her body, until unable further to resist the mounting tide of pleasure, I at last allowed my emotions to relieve themselves in the conventional fashion; ensuring at the same time, by the attention of a forefinger to a cavity not too far removed from the centre of her being, that she enjoyed the same relief.

It was almost at that moment, or not more than a minute

later, that, the noise of a carriage being heard on the gravel outside, I remarked that Miss Margaret's father had returned; whereupon replacing her dress, she had only time to remark that Mr Fennel was her guardian rather than her father, before withdrawing – the gentleman in question appearing only a few moments later with an ointment of arnica.

My thanks were, he assured me, superfluous; adding to the kindness he had already shown by remarking that Miss Margaret would be glad to apply the ointment, and with only some slight hesitation, and in so many words, offering me her services in any other manner which would comfort me. Needless to say, I was happy to accept so generous a gesture, and the young lady's offices were so full and so energetic that before morning the pain in my ankle had quite subsided, and upon my being greeted in the drawing room at breakfast time with an excellent dish of freshly grilled fish from the Newhaven boats, I was able to assure Mr Fennel that I was perfectly recovered.

Chapter Two

Sophie's Story

Since it has already been narrated, I need scarcely reiterate the circumstances of our setting out for Brighton. Nor need I detain the reader with a fuller exposition of the little scene devised for my entertainment at Riegate, other than to say that the postilion proved as adept in the bedroom as in the saddle, and as dextrous in the deployment of his riding-muscle (in this case a sufficiently apt term) as at cracking that other whip with which he encouraged the steeds in his command.

My decision to remain for a week or so at Brighton was the result of a winter and spring season somewhat over-busily spent, first in the metropolis, and then engaged in the distant county of Cornwall upon a task for my brother Sir Franklin Franklyn, Bart., (of which the curious may read in our volume entitled *Eros in Springtime*); after which a month or so in a pleasant seaside town equipped with the usual civilised amenities – viz., libraries, baths, assembly and concert halls – could be nothing but restorative.

As it happened, the day upon which Andy set off on his peregrinations, and I found myself alone, was the very one upon which their majesties King William and Queen Adelaide made their first most welcome entry into Brighton, with a view to establishing there an annual residence (as did their predecessor, first as the Prince Regent, then as His Majesty King George IV).

On such an auspicious occasion the feelings of the inhabitants were pleasurably excited, and were displayed (upon Their Majesties' arrival at Preston) by the line of several hundred carriages filled with well-dressed and gratulating spectators.

Near the northern entrance of the Pavilion – that remarkable building erected by the late King – stood a temporary triumphal arch constructed of timber, fifty feet high, with an aperture of twenty-five feet, covered to the summit with greens and flowers, decorated with many flags, and comprising three or four galleries in which were ranged charity children and seamen in their holiday dress. Beside this arch ran two additional galleries or ranges of seats raised upon wooden scaffolding, upon one of which I was able (on payment of a certain sum) to secure a seat convenient for viewing the procession, the others being occupied by tradesmen, their wives, and even servants.

As is the case in many provincial towns, a lack of proper organisation meant that the preparations for greeting the royal party had been considerably delayed, and up until the very last moment there was a noise of hammering as workmen adjusted the wooden struts of the scaffolding. Indeed, from time to time I could see movements as workmen passed to and fro in the gloom beneath my seat.

The day was beautifully warm, and by eleven o'clock the heat was such that several ladies about me, dressed in the height of fashion, were upon the edge of fainting. I had taken the precaution of dressing myself as lightly as possible, with the result that I was quite comfortable – but what I had not, however, taken account of (and who can blame me?) was that I would be placed on an elevation, seated upon a narrow plank below which workmen were free to walk. Had I realised that this would be the case, I would perhaps have considered my position more carefully; for I now realised – rather with interest than either embarrassment or fear – that anyone who had the occasion to pass immediately beneath my seat would be regaled with a clear (though no doubt shadowy) view of my lower limbs – and indeed considerably more!

It was not surprising then that one of the young men engaged on ensuring the stability of the scaffolding which supported the galleries should, upon noting my state of dress, have been drawn to a closer examination of the interesting phenomenon immediately above him – though only a man of some assurance would have gone as far as he did: that is, to grasp one of the wooden bars of the scaffolding, and by means of his simple strength raise himself until his face was so close that he was able to plant a kiss upon each of my ankles.

A woman more nervous than myself might have been shocked and made an outcry; but to be honest, I had heard a certain stirring beneath me, and on glancing down had seen the whitened knuckles of a pair of hands clutching the strut at my knees, and therefore was well able to withhold any exclamation which might have disturbed my neighbours.

No doubt inflamed by the success of his adventure, my secret assailant now lifted himself even further, so that I felt a head positively raised between my thighs – and feeling that the effort required a reward, edged myself somewhat forward so that his lips could reach that part of my anatomy which, I had no doubt, was in one way or another the goal at which he aimed. His kiss was so deliberate, so warm, and, despite the muscular effort required to sustain him in his present position, so tender that – the afternoon in addition being warm enough to heighten my usual receptivity to the attentions of the other sex – I could not resist a forceful expiration of breath, at which my neighbour, a lady's maid of moderate but not overwhelming intelligence, was kind enough to enquire whether I was in health.

I had only a moment in which to reply that I was feeling somewhat faint (no less than the truth) when cheering from close by signalled the approach of the royal carriage.

The gentleman whose compliments had so far aroused me now lowered himself, and, placing his hands about my ankles, was so kind as to indicate, by a warming pressure, that he would find a closer acquaintance rewarding; and I can only admit that the prospect of welcoming Sailor William and his spouse was quite outweighed by the prospect of myself being welcomed by what must surely be one of the town's more vigorous citizens. So, without so much as an apology to my neighbours, I slipped my feet below the board which supported me, and allowed myself to sink between the seats and into the arms of an aspiring member of the labouring class.

The man whose embrace I now received was, as I had supposed, of uncommon strength, for he carried me down as easily and gently as any nursing mother would carry a babe; but there the similitude ended, for upon my body being pressed against his own, I found that in the matter of brawn, he was broad and firm, his arms and breast (which were unclad, no doubt due to the exertions of the past hour) hard with the muscle which is only formed by physical labour, while on my passing my hands about him, I discovered (through touch alone, for it was excessively dark in the space in which I now found myself) his back to be no less brawny and covered, to boot, with a thick matting of wiry hairs, often in my experience – though by no means invariably – indicative of physical might.

I lost no time, since his appetite was strong and my own was growing, in loosening the thick leather belt at his waist and baring his lower limbs, my hand now falling upon a baton which seemed no less sturdy than the wooden struts which he had spent his morning in fixing; but was allowed no time in which either to examine or compliment him upon the weapon, for my companion drew me immediately to the ground where the grass which normally formed a part of the Pavilion gardens received us. There, throwing me upon my back and placing his knees between my thighs, he fell upon me and in a moment was engaged in that activity natural to the position, his piston plumbing deeply into my person, and affording me the opportunity to confirm that the power already demonstrated by his arms was equally efficacious in that part of his body which he now directed his energy in using.

I cannot pretend that my situation was comfortable; but as is often the case under such circumstances, what was lacking in luxury was certainly compensated by pleasure, and in short I found myself roused to a degree comparable to that of my assailant, and found myself joining him in a cry of triumph – fortunately just as the crowd above us greeted with a great hubbub the passage of the royal carriage, from which the

King and Queen evinced the most satisfying affability and the most affecting pleasure in the scene before them.

As I lay for a moment exhausted by the experience, I could not but notice (flat upon my back as I was below the crowd) how many of the fashionable fair of Brighton followed my own example in rejecting the foreign taste for undergarments; and was happy to recognise that I had been paid a considerable compliment by my new friend, in his choosing of me from the many young ladies whose charms were so freely displayed above us.

His amorous energies for the time expended, he now rose and handed me to my feet, kissing my hand with rustic charm and apologising should he have disturbed my sensibilities by an over-familiar roughness. I was able to comfort him upon that point – but he still seemed uneasy, and insisted that on our meeting again he would be happy to show greater consideration for my comfort. Indeed, he invited me to take a stroll with him that very evening, and I was happy to accept. On hearing my voice for the first time, he was clearly somewhat taken aback, realising that I was a lady rather than the servant for whom he had taken me (through my being seated among the poorer classes). However, I immediately showed him I was no snob, and agreed to present myself upon the chain pier at nine o'clock – when, he said, there would be fireworks (an interesting remark).

The chain pier is a great feature of Brighton, being (as I believe) the first edifice of its kind in England to be constructed on piles, the efficacy of which at first excited some doubt, though confidence was secured by information obtained that the batteries erected on piles by the Czar Peter at Cronstadt remained unimpaired to the present day.

The length of the pier is one thousand one hundred and thirty feet – exactly six-sevenths of a quarter of a mile – and it has a width of thirteen feet. The platform is supported by the chains, which at the south end are strongly bolted into the cliff. They then pass with alternate dips over the towers to descend into the sea at the furthest extremity, where they are embedded in the rock. The towers, of cast iron, each weighing fifteen tons, are twenty-five feet high from the platform, which is itself thirteen feet above high-water mark.

The colours were flying from the flagstaff upon the platform, in honour of the royal visit, and it was below that staff that I found my companion waiting just as the sun began to set. He was evidently dressed in his best clothing, and looking sufficiently uncomfortable in such garb to suggest that he wore it only on high days and holidays – indeed, so pitiful was I of his evident discomfort that my first act, having greeted him, was to suggest that he should remove the high collar into which he had forced himself – which he did with the utmost relief.

We walked for some time upon the pier, but it was clear from my companion's demeanour that polite conversation was the last thing on his mind – indeed, while I had hoped to glean from him some information about the town and its inhabitants, the manner in which he lowered his hand from my waist to my bum whenever it was convenient to do so, and the manner in which his brown eyes continually played upon my own, signalled clearly what he wished for – and that such was the case was no surprise to me; for now that I saw him it was clear that he was of an age not far removed from twenty years, and thus only just past that peak at which it is possible for the young male to engage in copulation three or four times a day without either physically or emotionally repining!

I might take the opportunity at this point of recording the unusual fact – observed by a friend of mine who has spent a lifetime in research upon the question – that one boy of sixteen was recorded as performing the act of onanism to the point of paroxysm no less than twenty and four times in a row; and if it is argued that this was an artificial measurement, for no expenditure of energy upon a partner was involved, my friend will produce upon request a carefully compiled record which shows that a gentleman of her acquaintance performed the act three times a day for thirty years, while another was observed to enjoy the same pleasure thirty and three times each week over the same period of time.

It was therefore no surprise to me that my friend Tom (as his name proved to be) was so soon intent on again enjoying me – and on his suggesting that he should show me the gallery below the pier head, I was perfectly willing to be escorted down some metal stairs to that place – a sort of ledge above the waves which, since it was low tide, was undisturbed by spray, and was occupied only by a few dark figures engaged in the sort of activity only to be expected of the young in so convenient a spot.

The only light which fell upon the gallery was shed from above, where that of a lamp fell between the slats of wood which formed the floor of the pier; and on my turning to my companion, I found myself confronted by a strange similitude of a tiger – for he had lost no time in divesting himself of his clothing (unlike the more modest gentlemen around him, most of whom retained some if not all of their own) and stripes of light fell across his naked body! My own clothing was not so elaborate that it took me long to place myself in a state equally ready for familiar congress; and upon our embracing, and there being time for a little more examination by me of his person, I had the opportunity to confirm that this was in all respects as powerful as those shoulders and that chest with which I was already familiar – his thighs, back and arse being as thickly covered with hair as the rest of his body – so that, striped as he was, our embrace was almost that of a lady and a wild animal!

Upon my gently nipping his flesh with my teeth, he coughed and hawed a little, as though about to make some kind of request; but unable or unwilling to articulate it, merely indicated his meaning by pressing his hands upon my shoulders; whereupon I had no hesitation in falling to my knees and saluting a prick which, alas, could not clearly be seen – but which, dim sight being aided by digital and oral exploration, proved comparable as to size and muscularity to the rest of his person.

Though it was indeed a fact that we had no need to hurry our embraces, as had been the case at our earlier meeting, I will not say that the circumstances of the present encounter were even slightly more comfortable: indeed, I soon found that the kneeling position which I maintained as I saluted my friend was more than a little painful, the boards beneath me being of hard wood. Indeed, shortly I found I must raise myself – however disappointed the gentleman might be at my relinquishing an occupation which clearly delighted him; but on my explaining the reason, he was all sympathy, and rather than laying me down upon those same boards, bid me place my arms around his neck, and by the simple expedient of placing his hands beneath my buttocks, hoisted me easily into such a position that, embracing him with my thighs, I was able to welcome that sturdy prick once more into the aptest receptacle; whereupon placing my back against a convenient pillar, he exercised the prerogative of the male and thrust home with a will.

I will not affirm that this posture was particularly agreeable: I have found it inspiriting upon occasion – always supposing that the male protagonist is sufficiently strong to ensure that no feeling of nervousness detracts from the experience; but on this occasion, though the evening was a warm one, the situation itself was less than charming – though the place was clearly commonly used for just the sort of activity in which we were engaged, for all around us were ladies of Brighton in much the same attitude (though some preferred to lean their heads against the pillars, lifting their rumps to their energetic assailants, and the exclamations falling from their lips were of pleasure rather than of reproach.

Happily, the vigorous nature of my companion's love-making was a considerable compensation for any mild discomfort, which in the end gave way to enjoyment; and I could not but laugh when, upon reaching my apogee – a moment before the cry of 'I come!' announced the height of my friend's pleasure – a series of explosions and a great sheet of sparkling stars announced – as he had forecast – fireworks, but those of a public rather than a private nature!

The reader may be surprised that I should so readily have succumbed – and for the second time in a day! – to the attentions of a member of the lower orders; but I must confess first that I have never acknowledged that belief common among the so-called upper classes that they have the advantage in any other way than in wealth and formal education, and that in the second place I find the unaffected vigour of the peasant a happy contrast to the over-nice attentions of those gentlemen from whom the determination always to be well-mannered removes that natural fervour which is a necessary concomitant of the achievement of satisfaction.

I shortly made my excuses and left, the gentleman all profuse thanks and myself all condescension. I will not pretend that the experience had been more than merely animal in its nature; but I have found that from time to time an encounter of this sort is a salutary reminder of what the great part of female humanity must regard as the chief end of romantic attachment!

The Albion Hotel, where I had taken rooms, was an establishment sufficiently attractive to the affluent to be a prospective source of income for those professional men and women of the town who relied upon the patronage of guests looking for some means of filling idle hours. On my descent for breakfast on the morning after my inaugural adventure I found at the porter's desk a collection of cards advertising (among others) *Signor* Pozzi of Marine Street, teacher of singing; Mr Louis Parez of Regency Street, publisher of a volume of paintings of 'The Banks of the Loire' and a teacher of drawing; *Signor* Frederic Amati, Mr Charles de Cothi and the Baron de Fabeck, teachers of languages, and Mr Claudius Michelet, fencing master – together with *Señor* Angel Ganivet, a Spanish gentleman and a tutor of the guitar.

As readers of our previous journals will perhaps remember, my friend Andy is something of an expert upon that instrument; and I had often envied him his expertise. Here, it may be, was an opportunity secretly to learn at least the rudiments of the guitarist's art, and to surprise him at our next meeting.

I therefore sent a boy around to Clarence Place with a note inviting *Señor* Ganivet to call at my rooms when it was next convenient, and almost immediately received the reply that he would attend on me at noon that day. He was announced by one of the servants with a flourish which seemed somewhat upon the ironic side, but presented an attractive figure, inspiring confidence by a carriage which was at once elegant and manly – too elegant, I supposed, to please those not conversant, as I was, with European manners, which tend to be somewhat more flowery than our own – and it may be this which placed him under suspicion to the servants at the hotel.

Señor Ganivet was perhaps in his middle twenties, with flowing black hair which hung in ringlets to his collar; finely drawn black eyelashes which closed upon a brown cheek, and the lids beneath them now veiled, and now disclosed sparkling dark eyes. His features were finely drawn, his mouth slimly curved and pretty almost to excess in a young man; his hands I noticed immediately as having the most refined, slim fingers, with the nails beautifully, though a little curiously, shaped, those upon the right hand long, while those upon the left were cut exceedingly short. He carried a case which, upon his setting it down on a side table and opening it, disclosed a handsome, small guitar.

On my exclaiming with pleasure at the sight of such a beautiful object, the *Señor* was quick to correct me: a guitar, he said, was always referred to in the feminine case – because (he said) she had a beautiful voice, and because her body was so similar to that of a woman – with a slender neck, an equally slim waist, and a handsome ... his voice tailed off as his hands, which he had moved over each portion of the instrument as he spoke of it, passed over the curved bottom of the guitar. It was clear to me that if he was devoted to his instrument, he was certainly equally devoted to the female figure it resembled.

I smiled warmly to show that there was no offence; and he asked whether I had played the instrument before.

On my admitting that that was not the case, he placed it in my hands and attempted to show me how to hold it.

This proving difficult, he requested that I move from the chair in which I was sitting, and place myself upon a lower stool, so that, passing behind me, he could more easily show how the instrument should be cradled in the arms – the posture being, it seemed, most important.

As I moved, he asked whether it would offend me if he removed his coat – and indeed it was extraordinarily warm even in my rooms, the sun blazing down upon the town outside and driving the hardiest visitors from their promenade upon the Steyne and on the Marine Parade, and even from beneath the Colonnade in North Street, that most fashionable of those places in which the fair of the town display their fashions and purchase new ones.

Needless to say, I happily gave my permission; and was not sorry that I had done so, for he wore a pristine white shirt which fell generously open to disclose a beautifully fluted, slightly brown neck, and which, though loosely cut about the body and arms, suggested that the frame which it concealed might well be sufficiently handsome to quicken the heartbeat of even so experienced a woman as myself.

Now, *Señor* Ganivet, having passed me the instrument, knelt behind me, taking my left hand in his in order to place it with the fingers on the strings to stop them, and curving my right hand in order to show how to pluck them. In doing so (whether with intent, I must leave the reader to determine) the inside of his right arm necessarily lay upon my breast, while my senses, already aroused (as they invariably are by the sight of a handsome member of the other sex) were further stimulated by the firm pressure of his breast against my back.

There is no way of disguising the fact that I was an easy target for his attentions. Even new readers (and I can scarcely believe that these words are being read by someone unacquainted with the numerous other volumes of my memoirs, which almost daily flood into the market-place from the admirably capacious store rooms of the publishing firm of Headline, in the city of London) – even new readers, I say, will be aware from the adventure I have already recorded that I am no blushing violet, and will not be surprised to hear that, though used to the heat of summer – and indeed rejoicing in it – I was now so overcome by the oppressive air of my rooms that I was forced, almost dropping the guitar, to relax quite into the arms of my teacher.

He seemed not in the least discomfited, but pausing only to take the guitar and place it upon the carpet, caught me without the least ado and supported me to the settee, where he laid me down and began without ceremony to unloose the ties at the bodice of my dress, laying it open positively to my breast and lowering his head to blow softly upon the exposed surfaces!

I will not claim that the action was unwelcome, the fascinating sensation of his breath passing over my heated skin raising my spirits even further, so that I could not but lay my hand upon the nape of his neck, passing it through the thick hair there and encouraging him to lower his head still further and, brushing the loose material of my clothing aside, to place a kiss upon one revealed and jutting nipple.

It was clear to me from this action that what I had suspected for some moments was the case – that the young gentleman possessed all the fervour of the Latin races, which (for a reason yet to be discovered) makes them more ready for amorous play than most of the sex in our cooler climes. I therefore did not hesitate to raise one hand, which I had laid negligently over the side of the settee, and drawing it up the length of his thigh placed it upon that object which I felt sure would now be readily discernible below his belly – and which, indeed, not only filled my palm, but in as far as was possible through its being constricted by his clothing, positively leapt beneath my palm's pressure.

Señor Ganivet stood no longer on ceremony, but busied himself about my buttons and in a very few moments had laid me bare from breast to ankles, at which he stood and for a moment regarded me with a very evident mixture of admiration and appetite. For my part, I was now eager to discover whether his vigour would match his admirable appearance, and sitting up without his objection released first his shirt, which on his holding back his arms fell to the ground behind him, then his trousers, which I drew down – to reveal, somewhat to my surprise, the first undergarment of its kind I had ever seen on a gentleman, though I had been aware that for some time it had been the habit of the more fashionable gentlemen on the Continent to place an additional garment below their breeches, for what purpose other than compliance with fashion I could not say.

Here, then, was a garment of white linen, caught about the waist by a draw-string, and falling to the knee, but slit from waistband to the top of the thighs – presumably in order to allow the wearer to release his prick to perform the office of nature; indeed, at this very moment, that limb had so far made itself free as to project from the aperture so conveniently provided, and was nodding and positively beckoning – a slightly ludicrous sight, for only a part of its length was revealed, and it looked (as I must acknowledge to myself with an inward laugh) like nothing so much as a bald-headed man dressed in his night-shirt!

I did not, however, venture to express my amusement openly, for nothing so injures the male in such circumstances (and in particular the Continental male) as humour at the expense of his appearance! Rather, I took it upon myself to undo the ties and release the obscure garment (called *mutande* in his language), which fell about the *Señor*'s feet.

There was now, I must admit, nothing whatever to laugh at, every prospect pleasing (in the words of the hymnist). Completely unveiled, here was a prick of completely classic proportions, resembling those shown upon certain Greek vases which are laid up in the private rooms of the new National Museum in London (though alas the Greeks so depicted are too often employed in pleasing members of their own sex, this being a custom, as it seems, in ancient times).

The instrument before me was of perhaps nine or nine and a half inches in length, and rose at a steep angle from a pleasant thicket of curly black hair (beneath which two pendant spheres were drawn up as though in support). It was handsomely regular in its dimensions until at the top the column thickened and rounded to a dome punctured by a tiny aperture, through which an appreciative tear already peeped, and now enlarged until it formed into a bead and rolled down to lie where the skin was gathered in a stretched band just below the head.

It was too handsome a sight not to require acknowledgement, and placing my fingers about the base of the column to steady it, I ran the tip of my tongue up its length, along that thick vein which pulsed at the underside, until at the tip I was able to part my lips and slip them over the pink cupola (now transferring my hands to a backside whose twin globes had – as far as could be felt – only the slightest downy fur upon the skin, and where I felt the gentleman's muscles tighten in delighted response to the motion of my lips as, bowing my head, I moved them up and down the length of a fine mark of masculinity.

That *Señor* Ganivet was pleased by my actions was evident from his vocal response, which comprised a string of expletives in his native language, the precise nature of which I could not understand but which were clearly expressive of pleasure if not of ecstasy. Indeed, for a few moments I wondered whether he would be content to permit me to bring him to extremity – but he was not so selfish, at length bending and placing his hands beneath my arms to raise me so that we stood for a moment breast to breast, my skin and his scarcely distinguishable, so smooth and white was his body, only a few springy black hairs – few enough almost to be counted – lying about his brown paps.

Lowering me to the settee and kneeling at my side, he now applied his lips to my most sensitive part, and in a manner which proved him a master, for not content with diving immediately to the centre and going at his task with the apparent intention of bringing me off as speedily as possible, he dealt most expressively with every area – with thighs, outer lips, inner lips, and finally the boy in the boat, who in a moment was forced to raise his head and stretch himself almost to pain at such pleasure as the Spaniard was able to confer with a tongue surely as delicate and practised as his fingers were upon the guitar.

After but a few moments, I felt ready to faint with pleasure, and reaching out once more grasped his essential part in my hand and drew him atop me, throwing my legs about him – at which, inserting his hands between my limbs, he raised my calves upon his shoulders and plunged so far within me that I thought I felt the head of his prick at the back of my throat!

Such a position, attainable perhaps only by the more athletic and healthful of us, is always a pleasure; and especially so when the unusual nature of it does not so stimulate a lover that it brings him off too quickly – a mistake not made by the *Señor*, who though he took pleasure in bending his head to observe our parts moving in union, did not permit himself to reach his apogee until the tightening of my calves about his neck signalled that I was ready. Whereupon, after two or three lunges he withdrew, and I felt upon my belly the scalding evidence of his pleasure.

We lay for a moment, panting almost in unison from our endeavours; after which, producing a clean handkerchief from his pocket he mopped me clean and pressed a chaste kiss upon my brow with some words of thanks, before rising – unlike some English lovers, as unashamed after the act as before, and not hesitating to display his person, his cock now somewhat crestfallen, but as charmingly handsome in its diminished state as it had been in its pride, nestling between his cods, the skin now gathered into a little puckered point.

Hoping the meeting had been to my satisfaction (and this

without the slightest expression of irony) he left – and on my offering the advertised fee for a lesson upon the guitar, expressed himself entirely unwilling to take it: there were sufficient ladies whose persons were suited better to music than to love (as he put it) to afford him a profit, and he was only too happy that I should have found him sufficiently a man to afford him the freedom of my person (in so many words).

Having dressed himself and taken up his instrument – I mean, his musical instrument – he then left, after placing his card upon the table and hoping that I would not hesitate to call upon him should I find a further meeting at any time desirable; and left me to the warmest memories of the past hour, and reflections upon the contrast between the two amorous experiences which had marked my first days in Brighton – and the contrast pointed between the honest British artisan and the sensitive Continental artist: neither necessarily the more inspiriting, neither to be in the least despised!

Chapter Three

The Adventures of Andy

I spent a pleasant three days at Mr Fennel's house while my ankle grew sufficiently strong to be trusted once more with my weight. The gentleman confessed to me quite readily the fact that my friend and nurse was a young lady employed by him, among other purposes, for that of offering just the licentious comfort she had been so kind as to offer me; and he surprised me by having no objection at all to our connection – indeed, he fostered it by permitting her to spend as much time with me as either of us desired.

It was the case, it seems, that she was the orphaned child of a former servant of his, who had on her deathbed implored Mr Fennel to care for her daughter. This, he assured me (and I have no reason to disbelieve him), he had done in the strictest conformity with morality until at the age of fifteen she had confessed a devotion to him which she expressed a wish to demonstrate in physical form – and on his demurring, presented herself in his bed one night in a state of undress, and was so innocently insistent upon his satisfying her natural desires that he had no option but to do so, any lingering doubts he had as to the propriety of his actions vanishing in the face of an appetite as forthright as it was free.

She had, in short, seduced her guardian with an enthusiasm which was now – some two years on – extended to me, as the first gentleman to stay at the house since she had learned the tricks of the bedchamber. That she had been well taught by Mr Fennel (who must have been in his time a lover of considerable experience) was clear from the first, and she continued to demonstrate the fact over the whole period of my stay. She never at any time suggested that I, though young and vigorous, was in any way preferable as a bedfellow to her master – though he must have been of more than three score years of age – and no one could have questioned her devotion to him, which was of the nature expressed by Lord Rochester in his touching set of verses addressed by *A Young Lady to her Ancient Lover:*

> 'Ancient person, for whom I
> All the flatt'ring youth defy,
> Long be it e'er thou grow old,
> Aching, shaking, crazy, cold –
> But still continue as thou art,
> Ancient person of my heart.

> 'Thy nobler part, which but to name
> In our sex would be counted shame,
> By age's frozen grasp possessed
> From its ice shall be released
> And soothed by my reviving hand
> In former warmth and vigour stand.

> 'All a lover's wish can reach
> For thy joy my love shall teach
> And for thy pleasure shall improve
> All that art can add to love.
> Yet still I love thee without art,
> Ancient person of my heart.'

I will not disguise my reluctance to leave the house; however, leave I must – and in conversation Mr Fennel had suggested I investigate the small town of Newhaven, on the grounds that it had recently become popular with a minority of those visitors from London who found Brighton too metropolitan in tone, and who had consequently made their home at the smaller place. I would (he opined) be able to collect valuable opinion there as to the necessary contrivances which such a place must, for success, offer the visitor. So, having bade Miss Margaret an affectionate farewell (who had been encouraged to spend the last night in my bed, where she certainly – as a form of protracted leave-taking – demonstrated with enthusiasm 'all that art can add to love') I once more set off to the eastward on horseback, having upon my host's advice purchased a beast from a neighbouring farm, and placed what goods I would need for my journey into a small pack which the animal could easily bear as well as myself. From Rottingdean to Newhaven no villages are met with; the road ascends and descends several steep eminences, but has nothing interesting except, in summer, a quiet and pastoral appearance, when the sun shines upon the dark green of the South Downs, diversified by extensive and widespread flocks of fine sheep.

The cliffs to my right were in some places bold, with many inequalities of height, but continuing upon the whole on the ascent. On approaching Newhaven, an interesting view opened into the interior of the country, following the course of the Ouse to Lewes; from the hill, about a mile west of the town, both sides of the river appeared absolutely spotted with little villages, not a mile distant from each other, each consisting of a small cluster of houses, some dark shading trees, and a church. Here, or hereabouts, are Piddinghoe, Telscombe, Southease, Rodmell, Iford, Tarring Neville, South Heighton, Denton . . .

It was by the river, a little to the south of Piddinghoe, that I tethered my horse and fetched out of my saddle-bag a package of bread, cheese and potted meat that had been pressed upon me by Fennel's housekeeper, and prepared to take luncheon. A pleasant bank of soft moss shelved down towards the slow running water of the river, and I soon settled there to my meal; and having consumed it and refreshed myself from my water bottle, I fell asleep (I may say that I do not believe in consuming alcohol in the full heat of the day and upon a journey: the drunken riding of a horse is a dangerous matter both for the rider and any pedestrian in the vicinity).

I know not how long I was unconscious; the next thing I was aware of was being waked by some noise or other – and as soon as I was in my senses, was aware that a protesting female voice was raised somewhere nearby. Getting to my feet, I made my way around a bunch of trees and found myself the spectator of a scene in which it was clearly my duty to intervene – viz., an assault upon the virtue of a young woman, whose voice it was that had roused me.

The lady in question was in the hands of a ruffian who, having apparently torn off all her clothing (which lay in a strangely orderly heap upon the grass), was now holding her from behind, her hands pinioned behind her back while one of his was upon a breast. Only a few feet away, another fellow leered upon the scene while undoing his belt – for a purpose easily surmised both by the female victim and by the onlooker!

Unseen, I returned behind the trees and from my saddle-bag removed the loaded weapon which it is always my habit to carry while abroad in the country; and retracing my steps was able (through the villains' preoccupation with their foul business) to get within a matter of two yards before hailing them in peremptory terms and bidding them submit to my will, and release the lady. Sadly, my temporary absence from the scene – though brief enough – had enabled the two assailants to make some progress in their assault: the first was now kneeling upon the ground, having forced the lady upon her back, and holding her firmly by the shoulders while the other – now divested of his lower clothing, and with a prick deployed at a readily acute angle – was also upon his knees, and about to force his way between the lady's thighs.

On hearing my voice, both men looked around with expressions such that any unarmed man must have been placed in fear of his life; but finding themselves looking down the barrel of a gun, they had little other recourse than to obey me, release their captive, and rise to their feet, where in obedience to my further instructions they placed their hands above their heads with an alacrity equalled only by the speed with which the second man's cock decreased from something considerable to something nugatory!

I feared the young lady had suffered so much that she might be devoid of her senses. But she was remarkably self-possessed, and far from the hysteria which might have been expected of her. In fact, she got to her feet with complete coolness, and without pausing to acknowledge my presence, immediately directed a kick at the one man's unprotected cods – which, although her feet were bare, connected with an effect which brought tears of sympathy to my eye, and produced a howl of agony louder than any of the cries which his attack had produced from her.

Turning from him (who now lay upon the ground in agony) she demanded that the second man remove his clothing – which he did after turning to me with an appeal that I felt bound to refuse. He stood clutching his private parts and evidently anticipating assault; and when she demanded that he place his hands above his head, was only persuaded to do so upon my waving my weapon – I mean, my gun. The lady, however, was merciful – partly I believe because of the pathetic figure the fellow cut, his manly parts so shrunken and fearful that he might have been a woman, for they were almost invisible to the eye.

Instead of assaulting him, she merely picked up the clothes of the two of them, and throwing them into the river, bade them depart – at which the second bent and assisted the other to his feet, and they both made off with what speed they could command.

With – as I considered – some tact, I watched them into the distance, allowing the lady time to resume her clothes; however, when I turned I found her standing with her hands upon her hips, smiling at the discomfiture of her assailants, and having made not the slightest attempt to clothe herself.

She was good enough to thank me for my intervention, and to hope that I had not been incommoded by the action I had been so kind as to take.

Not at all, was my reply; but I hoped that she herself had not been too disturbed by the incident.

'Sir,' she said, 'if nothing worse occurs to me during my life, I shall have no cause to complain – though I must confess that the matter does somewhat confirm the opinion expressed by my maternal uncle, the Dean of Chichester, that if I continue to lie unclothed in the sun in those parts of the country not entirely private, I should encounter some such interruption to my leisure. It is, however, a habit I took to while living on the coast of the Mediterranean, and I should find it difficult to give it up.'

Before I could reply, we were interrupted by a splash a little way downstream, and caught a glimpse of one of the men swimming valiantly out into the stream in an attempt to recover at least some of his and his companion's clothes. The young woman laughed, her pretty bosom heaving again, but this time with pleasure – and it was undeniably a delightful sight, and one which she must have observed my enjoyment of; however, she appeared not to repine at this, and I was forced to admit (if only to myself) that had I come across her lying naked upon the sward in the sunlight, I might have found it difficult not to contrive some sort of approach to such comeliness – though I trust not in so bold or rapacious a manner as her recent companions.

She confirmed my supposition that she saw my admiration, for she smiled.

'I wonder, sir,' she said, 'since you have come upon the scene, whether I might trespass upon your kindness? The presence of a gentleman with a weapon – and one so ready for action as your own – is always conducive to repelling unwanted attentions. Might I ask that while you are able to remain here I may resume my interrupted rest? Indeed, you may care to join me? You will find – if you are not familiar with the custom – that sunbathing, as the Continentals call it, is extremely pleasant, the play of the sunlight upon the body conferring not only an apprehension of health, but that very health itself; in particular, the fact that the sun is not so scorching in this country as in Italy or Greece makes it possible to remain in it for some little time without the skin becoming red and sore.'

I was able to assure her that having travelled much in the Mediterranean and further afield, to the East, I was entirely familiar with the beneficial effects of the sun – though I was more careful than herself in choosing the occasions upon which to exercise the habit of lying in it, for nothing is so agreeable to a thief or man of violence than coming upon either a lady or a gentleman in so entirely a defenceless state as being without clothing: the gentleman frequently losing his purse, the lady something more. However, on the present occasion there could be no danger, and placing my pistol upon the ground, I, without further ado, divested myself of my clothing, and lay down at the lady's side (who was once more reclining upon the grass).

I must confess to lying on my face, for to tell the truth her beauty had already had an effect upon me, and although the swelling of that part of my anatomy upon which my admiration had acted was nothing but complimentary to her, I could not be sure that a further contemplation of her person (which I certainly was not inclined to forbid myself) would not have such an effect as to make what was a mere tribute, an offence.

The sun was remarkably warm for England in the early days of summer; and I believe I felt it particularly, this being the first time of my exposing myself to it during that year. The lady, I believed, must have done so even during sunny days in winter – unless she had very recently returned from the tropics – for her skin was uniformly tinted an almost dark brown. She lay upon her back, her eyes closed, so there was no reason for me to refrain from a closer inspection of her person than I would have made had she been aware of it (though I suspected she knew what I was about, for it was already clear that she was no blushing violet). Her shoulders were slim and her arms beautifully turned, muscly without being in the slightest degree masculine. Her breasts, while perfectly full and luscious when she was standing, now fell into the lines of gently swelling hillocks, each tipped by a tiny, darker brown pinnacle or fort; her belly was flat – but then, when one looked at it closely, not perfectly so, but just slightly convex, with a gentle curve too assured and perfect to be in any way flaccid, and with a charming pit or dimple at its centre. I must confess to finding it difficult not to stretch out a hand and test the resilience of its surface, for it must surely be springy and firm – as indeed must her thighs, strong and without the slightest touch of looseness in the skin, although she must clearly have been of an age close to thirty years or even more.

The entire sight was a most beguiling one, and in no way was its beauty diminished by the loose cluster of golden hairs at the base of her belly, here and there a single one glittering like gold as the sun caught it. My heart was in my mouth in admiration; and I shifted uneasily upon the grass, my attitude needing some adjustment through the effect her beauty had had, inevitably, upon me. As I did so, she opened her eyes and raised her head; and, not to be impertinent, I closed my own, knowing from instinct that she was now following my example and inspecting the lineaments of my person.

I did not repine at this, for although I have no desire to sound too self-assured or proud, I had frequently been told that one of my best features is that often admired by the ladies – that is, my backside. Sooner or later, of course, like all our features, this must deteriorate, the muscles allowing a certain sagging and thus destroying the firm curve and buoyancy of youth. However, at the time of which I write there was no such problem, and I was inclined to believe that the lady would not find my person too unpleasant.

I lay for some time, the silence of our surroundings broken only by the gentle murmur of the river among the reeds and the twittering of some bird or other (I am not a naturalist, and thus cannot report which of the feathered denizens of the place saw fit to comment upon the sight below him). Whether through the heat of the sun alone, or of this combined with my apprehension of the closeness of an object of desire keen enough to raise my spirits, I felt at length a bead of perspiration trickle from my neck down my back towards the hollow at the base of my spine. Almost immediately, I also felt my companion's finger tracing its course – between my shoulder-blades, to the bottom of my spine, and . . . But what was this? At the same time, I now felt the feathery touch of hair, and realised that it was not her finger which now tickled the small, fine hairs, but her tongue! which agile and slippery member began to lick at my skin, and, in a moment, to move even further downwards, positively passing between the globes

46

of my arse with a sensation so delicious that I could not resist throwing my legs open in order to facilitate – even encourage – her going further, which to my delight she had no hesitation in doing, flicking daintily at the very portals of an aperture even the most familiar of mistresses too often hesitates to approach.

I cannot hope that my pen is sufficiently skilful to convey the delight which her action gave me; but perhaps my gentlemen readers will believe me when I say that by the time the insertion of her hand beneath my body seemed to suggest that I should turn upon my back, I was in two minds which would be the more transporting – the continuance of her attention to my backside, or the transference of that attention to . . .

Well, of course, in the end I turned, and must report (though again appearing to boast) a quick indrawn breath on the part of the lady which seemed to suggest admiration of what she now saw – and, to be honest, I was not entirely surprised, for the congestion of the blood brought to my essential part by the titillation to which I had been subjected, had resulted in my prick swelling and hardening so that it might have been made of warm, tinted marble!

Her attentions to it were no less complete and efficient than her previous actions had been. It was already clear to me that her knowledge of what was most pleasant in love-making was comprehensive; but the play of her tongue, the motions of her lips, the admirable way in which the sensations they provoked were echoed and heightened to exhilaration by her hands moving about and caressing my parts, convinced me that she was one of those young ladies who was not only an experienced but an enthusiastic practitioner of the amatory arts – and a combination of knowledge with a delight in using it is, in any profession, a *sine qua non*.

I must not, however, ignore my own responsibilities, and I was now aware that if I did not at once take the initiative and turn to pleasing my companion, there would in no long time occur a phenomenon that would remove, if only for a time, my ability to do so.

On my turning to her and fixing my lips first upon those enchanting breasts, I was immediately aware again of the pleasure she took in our present occupation – for the mere touch of my tongue's tip upon her nipples, together with my laying a hand, ever so lightly, upon that charming cluster of golden hairs below, resulted in a positive whine of pleasure.

I have, I may in parenthesis remark, found that those ladies who most charmingly provoke and satisfy lust in their lovers, are most keen in their own appreciation of the efforts of those lovers, and, indeed, are least shy in advising them how to pleasure them most keenly – should such advice be required. The lady in this case was entirely frank, and reaching for my prick, took it gently but firmly in her hand, and by means of it drew me atop her. When throwing her legs apart she opened herself to me the utmost freedom. So slippery were we with the grume of love that I almost failed to feel the usual friction as I entered her body – yet to such a pitch of sensitivity had she brought me that the unctuousness itself was delicious, and we slid together to a meridian so high-pitched that neither of us could resist expressing it in a shout of pleasure which sent the birds from the nearby trees into a state of wild alarm.

When two persons have shared such an agreeable

experience it is to be expected that they should be pleased with each other, and for a time we lay simply entwined in each other's arms (though turning upon our sides, in order that my weight should not distress my companion): her thigh pressed against my privities, still glowing with such recently expressed pleasure; my hand upon one springy breast; and our lips from time to time complimenting each other in an expression no less of satisfaction than of gratitude. Finally, we must shift, upon which the lady was moved to the comment that she had not for some time been so pleasantly occupied, and being so good as to compliment me upon my performance – which was supererogatory, for I knew perfectly well that it was she who had most ingeniously transformed emotion into action (though I trusted that before necessity made it my duty to leave Newhaven, where I assumed she dwelt, I might have an opportunity to show her that I was no less enthusiastic in the art of love than herself).

It was, indeed, the fact that her home was in the town to which I was proceeding, and we agreed to walk together, I leading my horse. On the way, she introduced herself under the name of Mrs Emily Twyce-Knightley – a title which I must confess seemed to me as verging upon the comic; but which she explained as the product of her husband's (a Captain Knightley) being obliged as a condition of their marriage to add the name of her father, Baron Twyce of Farthingdale, to his own. I could make no comment upon this other than privately regarding it as probable that his companions in the Army – for he was a serving officer – might make such a name a ready subject of ribaldry.

Hearing that I was to occupy myself for a day or two in Newhaven, Emily (as she invited me to call her) insisted that

I should be the guest of herself and the Captain, and when I demurred was only the more insistent. They shared a large house upon the outskirts of the town, she explained, with a Naval officer and his wife – the Marjoribanks – both the gentlemen being concerned with those arrangements made for guarding Newhaven harbour (esteemed one of the best tide harbours between Dover and the Isle of Wight) against the possible incursions of an enemy. Captain Twyce-Knightley was attached to the fort which stood at the harbour entrance; his friend Marjoribanks to the *Hyperion* frigate, moored just off the fort, and the headquarters of the coastal blockade of the district, from which supplies of men were occasionally drafted to various points, and whose three cutters were busy about the defence of the coast.

We reached the house after a pleasant walk, somewhat lethargic (no doubt through the effect of our recent activities); it was a fine building, erected, as I guessed, within the past ten years or so, and I was immediately shown to a handsome room which I was invited to make my own for as long as might be necessary. I must confess that the heat of the day, together with those exertions I have mentioned, contrived to make me weary; and I fell upon the bed and into a sleep from which I awoke only towards the end of the afternoon – when, somewhat ashamed, I refreshed myself and ventured downstairs, where I found Emily at tea with another lady, introduced to me as Mrs Penelope Marjoribanks – slimmer, but no less handsome, than my hostess.

We had taken a dish of tea and were engaged in the kind of idle conversation which usually accompanies such a ceremony, when the sound of horses' hooves upon the shingle announced the arrival of the two gentlemen of the house, who shortly entered – two brisk young officers, equally upright, equally handsome, equally vigorous. Indeed, so personable were they that it was something of a surprise to me that Emily should have so briskly welcomed my attentions, such a husband seeming likely to be as demanding and as satisfactory a companion as would satisfy any wife.

However, as the evening went on, I began to suspect the reason; for though they were entirely pleasant to their wives, and as polite as was to be expected, their attentions seemed to be much more to each other than to the ladies – and not only in discussions of military and naval matters, but in a more personal sense. I could not but help observing that those little signs of affection normally directed at female companions – a hand occasionally pressed upon a shoulder, a smile peculiarly inviting, a glance almost coquettish – seemed to pass between the gentlemen themselves; and although I will not say I was not somewhat surprised, I was not entirely astonished when Emily remarked to her friend (entirely without self-consciousness) that she hoped she was ready for a roust, for tonight they had a proper man about the house – smiling in my direction so that there could be no possibility of a mistake in identity.

Far from taking offence at such a statement, Captain Twyce-Knightley grinned extravagantly, and clapping his hand upon his friend's shoulder remarked that they were clearly relieved of duties; and on observing that I was somewhat embarrassed, begged that I should take the household as I found it, assuring me that while I might expect little repose, he supposed from my bearing that I would be equal to what was expected of me – at which he and his friend left the room, and the ladies rose, and, placing themselves one upon each side of me, marched me up the staircase and into a fine bedroom where they occupied themselves in undressing first me and then themselves.

It is never my habit to describe with too great a particularity the physical beauties of those ladies who choose to reveal their persons to me in private; nevertheless, I must on this occasion record that my two companions made a fine pair: my former acquaintance, as I have intimated, with fine fair hair; her friend dark, her body slim almost to boyishness, who, sitting upon the bed, loosened her gown and allowed it to fall to her waist, revealing a pair of apple-like breasts which were none the less feminine for being smaller and less pendant than those of Emily. She, meanwhile, moved behind me so that her own charming boobies pressed warmly against my back, and placing her hands upon my shoulders, directed me towards the bed.

If there was a drawback to what followed, it was the product of the eagerness of the ladies; for while I was attending to the desires of one, the other found it impossible not to intervene, stealing one of my hands away and placing it upon some portion of her body where it could give her pleasure by stroking or pinching. Even when I was invited by Penelope to pay her the ultimate tribute, as I lay between her thighs in the most intimate of connections, Emily placed herself so that she could nibble with her teeth at the skin of my shoulders and back and the cheeks of my arse – until the urgency of movement required to satisfy her friend made such an approach uncomfortable, when she contented herself by lying with her head upon the pillow at the side of her friend's, stealing occasionally a kiss which more properly should have been Penelope's, and at last embracing us both and, by throwing her leg across my back, enjoying through friction the same pleasure (if not as keen) as our own.

The reader will not be surprised to learn that after such a passage my senses were no longer equal to maintaining consciousness, and, indeed, we all three fell into a sleep; the consequence not only of pleasure and weariness but of that free expression of the senses which inevitably results in innocent slumber.

We were not, however, allowed to sleep the whole night through, for at some time in the morning I awoke to find a candle held over the bed, and saw the two gentlemen – the husbands whose wives lay upon each side of me, the hand of one adjacent to an area of my body which is not generally considered proper to be fondled by the wife of another – standing over us, their arms about each other's waists! I must confess that for a moment I wondered whether I had mistaken the household, and some kind of revenge was to be taken for what most husbands would regard as a liberty, if not a downright impropriety. However, the fact that I now observed both men to be as naked as the day they were born somewhat reassured me, and upon their climbing on the bed (which was a large one) I supposed that they had come to take proper possession of their property, and prepared to remove myself to my room. However, on my doing so, one of the gentlemen took me by the shoulders and pressed me back once more upon the pillow, while the other removed the hand of his wife from that part of me it had previously been embracing, and replaced it with his own – with the remark, 'Hey, George, here's a boy that needs reviving!' – and, without further ado bent to take my shrunken reed between his lips, within a moment (and despite myself, for I am not among those who normally embraces my own sex) enlarging it to his purpose. Then, lifting his head, he regarded it with some satisfaction, patted his friend's rump, now turned towards me, and enquired whether I would like to put it to use! I have at this time to explain what was only made clear to me the following morning: that the house was one in which there reigned what one critic upon the Continent has described as *la perversité polygame* – that the occupants lived in a state of entire freedom where sensual compliments were in question. It appears that Captain Twice-Knightley and Lieutenant Fenwick Marjoribanks had attended school at Eton College together, where they had been introduced at an early age to the form of entertainment much in vogue at that place, and which Marjoribanks had later found of advantage, as a young midshipman, in currying favour with his superiors.

On finding themselves stationed in the same town they had taken house together, where in the natural course of things, one evening when they and their wives were somewhat in liquor, they had exchanged partners, to their mutual satisfaction. This freedom continuing led, as such freedom too often does, to a desire for further experiment, and Marjoribanks – who in recent years had relinquished the position of catamite for that of assailant – persuaded his friend to try whether their old amusement still held; and in short the pair had found those pleasures so keen that their enjoyment became a matter of course.

Neither, however, was so selfish or unkind as to suppose that their wives could live happily deprived of sensual pleasure; and since, while on station in the Far East with her husband, Emily had not only observed with interest his engagements with the local youth, but had herself been introduced to the pleasures of an exclusively female bed, it was not long before she induced Mrs Marjoribanks to try them too.

In short, nothing in the way of sexual exchange and extravagance was lacking which four people could enjoy with each other – a situation which I found in a way admirable, but in another way strange – for I can never persuade myself that a night spent by one beautiful woman with another is not wasted; nor can I agree that those activities enjoyed by two men together can be superior to those enjoyed between more conventional lovers.

I therefore excused myself from a connection with Lieutenant Marjoribanks, to whose arse (not, I must admit, unshapely or without charm) his friend now turned his attention – preferring to hope for more enjoyment with one of the ladies. However, I was too late – for (I suppose believing that their husbands would be successful in seducing me) they had turned to each other, their heads were buried in each other's laps, and no attempt of mine in the way of caresses or even implorings could persuade them to turn towards me.

In consequence, I took myself off, my tail between my legs, to my own room, and there at last fell into a proper sleep.

Chapter Four

Sophie's Story

The weather continuing to be hot, I was not in Brighton longer than two days before sea bathing became not only desirable but almost necessary (cold baths being no substitute, either for freshness or that saltiness which is so inspiriting). The town had been famous as a bathing resort for as long as that operation had become a fashionable form of medical treatment and healthful entertainment.

I have read in a lady's journal, written in Brighton in 1732, the information that 'it is the custom not only for gentlemen but the ladies also to bathe in the open sea. The gentlemen go out a little way in boats called cobbles, and jump in direct from them. The ladies have the conveniency of dressing-gowns and guides, and there are little houses on the shore for them to retire and dress in', and it is said that Dr Peter Shaw in 1730 and Sir John Floyer in 1734 both praised the value of cold-water bathing.

But it was I believe one Dr Richard Russell who made the little village of Brighthelmstone popular for sea bathing: I have found in my friend Chichley's extensive library a learned dissertation concerning the 'Use of Sea-water in Diseases of the Glands' published by the doctor in 1750, who claimed to have discovered in sea-water the medicinal values traditionally associated with spa waters (which of course had been used for bathing since time immemorial, at such healthful places as Bath and Buxton).

Dr Russell went so far as to move to the coast to practise what he preached, and within a matter of years had made Brighton (as we now call it) popular, attracting invalids there from far afield – I am reliably informed that by 1785 there was a line of twenty-six bathing machines along the beach, from which 'two women attend each lady who bathes, as guides; and one man every gentleman who requires it.'

And was it the case (you will ask) that men and women always donned those amazingly inconvenient and voluminous costumes which society now ridiculously forces upon those who wish to immerse their bodies in the sea? Not at all – although there were always complaints by those prudes whose sense of moral outrage was aroused by the fact that others were less squeamish about the exposure of the lineaments of the body with which nature has clothed our spirits. As early as the year '07, for instance, Brighton Parish Vestry met in particular to prevent 'the indecent practice of indiscriminate bathing in front of the town'.

Their deliberations and admonitions did not, however, have any effect, the gentlemen of the town being fixed in their determination not to have a natural habit interfered with – though sometimes exposure was from natural reasons, Dr A. B. Granville of the town reporting that 'many lacking the courage after they have stripped to the skin will stand on the outer steps of the machine, shivering and hesitating, their persons in the meanwhile wholly exposed . . . The practice remains as a stain on the gentility of the Brighthelmstonians.'

Two years later an unfortunate tailor, Mr John Crunden, was fined for having 'daily exposed himself on the beach'. To encourage the timorous to take the plunge, here at Brighton, as at elsewhere, hardy females have been engaged to patrol the water's edge and hurry the reluctant bather beneath the waves, which they do with the utmost force and entirely without favour – his late Majesty King George IV having suffered at the hands of the best-known of those Amazons, Mrs Martha Gunn, during the period when he was Regent.

Though reluctant (as the reader will have gathered) to be forced to cloth myself in heavy flannel which, when immersed, becomes not only uncomfortable but (through its weight) positively dangerous, I had no desire to be harried from the town by the puritans among its denizens, and so took myself to a shop in St James's Street which advertised itself as providing at once the most tasteful and the most convenient bathing dresses or 'costumes for the elegant female swimmer', and on entering it I was greeted by a handsome woman of about my own age, though sturdy almost to the edge of masculinity, who politely asked whether she could show me a range of costumes, and on my acquiescing, did so.

From these I chose a garment which seemed to consist of as light a fabric as possible, so cut as to confine the limbs to the least degree; on which the lady invited me to accompany her into what she called the fitting room – this being a room behind the shop fitted with a dressing-table, two long mirrors and a *chaise-longue*.

There was a lock upon the door, which she turned – and on my expressing some surprise at this precaution, she suggested that security was of the essence during a fitting which necessitated the removal of clothing, and maintained that in the earliest days of the shop's being open the brother of a young lady (who had with some impropriety been permitted to accompany her into the shop) had wantonly, or otherwise, thrown open the door, revealing another young female just stepping from a costume, and therefore clad in nothing but a pair of short stockings – at which the young gentleman had shown an interest sufficiently venereal to startle the female customer, and while he had, after a pause somewhat too protracted, at last closed the door, the startled victim of his intrusion had fallen into a faint, and had only been recovered by the administration of strong salts.

I now understood; but was somewhat surprised that the attendant had locked herself in with me, and now stood holding the bathing costume and clearly expected me to unclothe myself – which, nevertheless, I did without embarrassment, the act of exposing myself before a lady being not in the least deleterious.

Upon my stepping out of my skirts, the assistant insisted upon helping me into the costume, smoothing it over my body with what seemed particular attentiveness, and going so far as to pass her hands over my thighs and breasts as she stood behind me at the mirror, in order (she asserted) to assure herself that the fitting was sufficiently snug to be unobtrusive when wet, yet loose enough to be unconstricting – in order to illustrate the latter quality, she was so good as to insert her hands beneath the material, showing how easily it lifted away from the skin; at the same time, no doubt inadvertently, brushing with her palms my nipples, which through the stimulation stood up as though under the caress of a lover (the body, in my experience, often shows an inability to distinguish between the caresses of a male or a female hand).

'Madame need have no fears through the thinness of the material revealing her form,' she remarked, 'for her figure is such that any onlooker will only rejoice at the privilege of observing it, while the prude can be enraged only with envy!'

I engaged to purchase the garment – at which the assistant lifted the material from my shoulders and drew it down, thus exposing my upper body – when she stopped (still standing behind me as she was) and enquired whether my body had been at all irritated by contact with the cotton – for, she said, it was sometimes the case that the skin of the breasts, being particularly sensitive, was affected . . . and as if to test it, once more passed her hands across my naked bosoms, with a peculiarly pleasant brushing motion which brought my titties into an even greater prominence – at which, as though she found it a compulsion, she drew the costume down from my waist, falling to her knees to do so, and on completing the action, turned me with her hands, and, to my astonishment (though 'twas less of a surprise than it would have been without her earlier clear interest in my person), fixed her lips to a part more used to that compliment from members of the stronger sex!

In my surprise I confess to recoiling somewhat; at which the lady looked up at me with an appeal so ingratiating that I was immediately impelled to smile, whereupon she begged my pardon if she had been too forward, but confessed that my personal beauty was such that she could not resist paying it a tribute and, rising to her feet, clasped me to her bosom with an ardour expressive of extreme desire.

Now desire in a would-be lover is the greatest of all

aphrodisiacs, and I confess myself ever subject to the thrill of it – as readers of our previously published memoirs will recall, I have from time to time been persuaded to give way to the force of admiration expressed even by the least desirable of partners – and on this occasion the unmistakable sensation of a glowing lust made it inappropriate to repine. On my making no objection to her embrace, then, my companion with the utmost alacrity stepped back, undid the tie of her coat-dress, and, undoing only a couple of buttons, was able to draw it down over the bosom and hips, and was instantly in the same state as I – then she stepped forward and drew me once more into a tight embrace, our bosoms pressed together and a thigh pressed between my own.

It was the first time for a considerable period that I had been clasped in the arms of a handsome woman. The experience could not be said to be a common one with me, but upon its occurring I was always surprised – but by no means repelled – by the difference between a man's embrace and that of my own sex. That may seem to those readers to whom Sapphic passion is unfamiliar to be a statement innocent in the extreme – yet those who have shared the experience will immediately recognise the meaning of my statement: while on embracing a male lover one is aware only of hardness and muscularity (however soft the skin, the muscles beneath it – both as to shoulders, arms, thighs and to breast and belly – are, at least in the young, pithy and firm), a female in the same close embrace is all softness (the breasts, the thighs, the belly all receptively pliable and yielding). The sensations, therefore, are remarkably different – and the difference makes the experience the more delightful, even taking into account the knowledge that the culmination of the embrace of a female cannot, in my opinion, ultimately have the same degree of satisfaction as that shared with a handsome male lover.

I, however, allowed my admirer to draw me to the *chaise-longue* and persuade me to lie upon it, whereupon she began the most minute examination of my body, over every plane, concavity and convexity of which she passed her hands and lips. Here too was a circumstance indigenous to the female. A gentleman engaged in the same voyage of discovery is all urgency, and too often throws aside all patience – indeed, is all impatience, so eager for the final embrace that his attentions are, at least in the first instance, too frequently cursory, his kisses wild and undirected, his haste and frenzy productive certainly of high spirits but lacking in refinement and the finer sensitivities.

My present partner, though I believe fully as eager as any gentleman in the same situation, was in the last degree patient; her lips lingered upon my own, descending to my body only after her tongue had explored the intricacies of the whorls of my ears and passed gently over the closed lids of my eyes. They then passed like velvet over my shoulders and the curves of my breasts, explored the scyphate hollows beneath my arms, and teased my raised nipples with such care that when, only after some minutes, she nipped gently at them with her teeth, the sensation was so keen as almost to make me lose my senses. On hearing my gasp, she raised her head and looked for a moment into my eyes; but on seeing that my exhalation was one of pleasure rather than pain, lowered her lips once more, and, after a final salute to my breasts, proceeded to my belly, which she covered thickly with kisses before . . . But I must break off again to distinguish between the approach a gentleman makes to those regions where the keenest sensations are seated, and those of a fellow member of the gentle sex. A moment's thought must lead the reader to conclude that oneself best knows what he or she finds most keenly pleasing between the sheets: for only he or she is cognizant of the receptivity to pleasure of the various parts of the body – though indeed the most frank lovers will exchange such information, letting the other know (even in plain speech) what gesture or action is most delicious, with relative strangers the proceeding must be through guess work.

A member of one's own sex, however, must be already half-way to a conclusion: a woman knows best what pleases a woman – and (if I am to rely on the information I have gleaned from those of my lovers who have been abed with members of their own sex – a more frequent occurrence than many of our moralists would care to believe) a man is most thoroughly aware of what best pleases his fellows. I was now reminded of the fact by the gentleness and meticulousness with which my companion proceeded: for far from a negligent and hurried salute, she approached the centre of my being with a proper attention to the surrounding countryside, and rather than dashing forward with the nicety of a charging cavalryman, rather crept in like a spying scout, her first intimacy being gently to draw aside my lower lips, merely nudging them apart with her fingers to salute their interior surface with her tongue, drawing first along one side and then the other, and drawing from the area every hint of pleasure which such an action could raise before thrusting that same member (which seemed to possess the strength almost of a gentleman's prick) as thoroughly within the portals as it could pass, while her chin, in what must be a conscious action, was pressed upon the upper part of my intimacies, and therefore bore upon the most tender of female attributes, so frequently unfairly neglected by the ignorant male lover.

My readers will know that I take no pleasure in describing such intimacies with a close particularity, and do so on this occasion only to inform the ignorant reader of the benefit to be looked for in partnership with one of the same sex – an experience which I do not hesitate to assert is profitable to every woman who has the opportunity to grasp it.

It will perhaps be no surprise to the reader that I was by now so exhausted that any idea of taking further exercise was set by the board; I merely returned to my rooms and spent the rest of the day in a state of lethargy, rousing myself only to take some refreshment. However, a good night's sleep revived me, and having spent the morning in the town, I determined upon a bathe (as it is called) in the afternoon, and at three, when the most extreme heat of the midday was waning somewhat, took myself to the western part of the town and that stretch of the beach where a row of bathing machines stood, from which ladies and gentlemen were immersing themselves.

The row of machines furthest from the town was set aside for the gentlemen, as I realised when I walked by them. I could not but notice that one or two men still took the opportunity to bathe without the encumbrance of clothing of any kind, though they did so with some attention to decency, and all that was to be seen (even, I suppose, by the lower sort of ladies who I discerned peering through telescopes which were available for hire at a vantage-point some little distance away) was an occasional glimpse of a bare arse as its owner leaped from the top step of the machine into the water, or occasionally disclosed when a dip in the waves caught a bather in a shallow place.

The ladies were more careful, and I saw only a display of bathing clothes of various kinds – as did those gentlemen in the vicinity, who seemed to linger somewhat in their strolling, perhaps in the hope of a display of feminine charms; they seemed, however, to be doomed to disappointment.

I walked along the line of machines, outside which signs showed that most were occupied. However, from one of them a nymph in voluminous skirts, sufficiently threatening in stature to compare even with Mrs Gunn, stepped out and invited me to take advantage of its being vacant, which I was pleased to do.

The machines, I must explain, were little more than large boxes with two entrances, one at the side facing the promenade, the other on that facing the sea; and they were set upon wheels, so that they could be propelled to and fro in accordance with the state of the tide, and while the landward side was usually upon dry sand or shingle, the seaward side went out into the sea itself, where, by the way of a little flight of steps, one could descend waist deep into the ocean.

These small huts or wooden cottages were guarded, as I have said, by attendants – my title of 'nymph' I must admit to being somewhat satirical, for they were all extremely muscular females (as was necessary for the propulsion of the machines, though they helped each other to accomplish this – and through the necessity of their being able to defend their charges against the frenzied attacks of gentlemen driven to an extremity of desire by the occasional sight of a bare arm or ankle, though this to my knowledge had never been necessary). They were, then, for the most part, females somewhat less than beautiful, and occasionally positively ugly, having in common broad shoulders and muscular thighs and arms, these rarely accompanied by a pretty face.

The female in charge of my machine, who now handed me into it, was not especially corpulent, but was certainly well built, and her face (what I could see of it beneath a large bonnet, as worn by most of them to keep the sun from their faces, since they spent most of their days in its full blaze) was lantern-jawed and lacking in charm.

She was kind enough to assist me in removing my dress, which she hung upon a knob inside the machine, and even in drawing on the costume for bathing, though happily without the familiarity shown by the saleswoman – for though that had been by no means an unpleasant experience, another connection with a lady was not what I desired, and in particular not with so lumpen and clumsy a one.

The sea was as warm as the waters of the Channel can ever be expected to be; and I found the experience of swimming in it – rather than in the still waters of the lake at Alcovary – interesting, inspiriting and refreshing, and was much enlivened by the experience by the time that I once more mounted the steps with the help of the brawny hand of the attendant, who was waiting with a large towel.

In her company I did not, of course, hesitate immediately to throw off my wet costume (which clung disagreeably to my body, and was the single undesirable part of the experience of sea bathing), whereupon, the woman threw the towel over my shoulders and began to dry me at first with a spirited action, and then more gently, turning me and mopping my breasts with what was almost a caressing motion, while from beneath her bonnet her eyes seemed to dwell upon my body with an unexpected attention. I must confess to fearing that I had once more fallen into Sapphic hands – a fear disagreeably confirmed when, as though finding it impossible to resist, the woman bent forward and planted a kiss upon my bosom.

I will confess that – not through aversion to my own sex, for as I trust I have made clear I have no such prejudice, but simply from the condition of being unwilling at that moment to be subject to the woman's attentions – I threw up my arms and pushed her away, whereupon, her bonnet was caught by my hands and thrown from her head, revealing a tousled mop of jet-black hair cut remarkably short, and a pair of equally black eyes in which was a spark of lively humour. A second glance was not needed to reveal the owner of the eyes – and the hair, and a pair of firm smiling lips – as belonging without question to the male sex.

I was too surprised to cover myself (for the towel, falling to the ground, had left me naked and slippery as a fish) or to cry out. The gentleman took the opportunity of my silence to place his finger to his lips, no doubt in case I felt inclined to raise the alarm – which might have been the case had he not (I must be frank) been quite so good-looking or quite so openly admiring of myself. However, I did pick up the towel and place it about me before inviting him to explain himself.

He was there, he said, as the result of a bet placed between him and another chap, who had thought it improbable that he could sufficiently disguise himself as to pass successfully for a female attendant at the machines; he had bribed one of the women to absent herself and loan him her clothes; and I was the first customer to pass through the machine.

'Sadly, ma'am,' he said, 'it was my fate to be faced with the unimaginable task of remaining in disguise in the presence of such beauty, and my ten guineas must be lost!'

Ten guineas seemed a large sum to be lost by a young man, I remarked, but said nothing; his tones revealed him as being, if I mistook not, a gentleman from the metropolis, and no local lad; and indeed he introduced himself as the Hon. Rupert Montjoy, of Belgrave Square, giving a bow which was so inappropriate – clad as he was in petticoats – that I could not resist laughing. My laughter comforted him somewhat, as being a sign that perhaps I was not to confound him by complaining to the peelers; and taking my hand, he raised it to his lips – following this action, when he found that I did not oppose it, by taking me in his arms and drawing me close. The embrace was an agreeable one, though somewhat obstructed by the voluminousness of his petticoats (the machine women are modest creatures); which he felt as well as I, for he began immediately to attempt to divest himself of them – unfamiliarity, however, making this so difficult and clumsy that once more I was forced to laugh, just as I was forced in pity to assist him!

From the carapace of skirts emerged a slim, wand-like body it was impossible not to admire, the narrow waist and hips and handsome limbs commanding both regard and respect, while his own admiration for my charms was signalled by the fact that even the necessity to struggle with female clothes failed to diminish the anticipatory ferocity of a prick which stood close up against his belly; and which as I laid my hand upon it – which I did from a wish to calm him from the impatience into which the coil of clothing had thrown him – gave a great leap beneath my palm.

The next moment I found myself upon my back on the floor of the machine – the pile of my acquaintance's petticoats happily somewhat protecting my rump from the hard boards! The contrast between this and my experience of the previous day could not have been more marked: here had been no preliminaries save a single short embrace – and now I was immediately pierced (though not in a disagreeable way) by a prick hard as iron, the young gentleman's cheek meanwhile pressed roughly against my own, my skin apprehending a roughness which the most masculine of ladies lacks; and his hands serving not to caress me but merely somewhat to hold his weight from my body (for which I was certainly grateful) while the muscles of his arse served to thrust home in an action which resembled nothing more nice or tender than the swiving of a bull or a stallion!

The one thing which saved the experience from being disagreeable was that, unlike many men of his age (for he could surely be barely twenty, if so many years), he had the quality of endurance, and while I half expected him to spill his seed within a few moments of the full connection, this was far from the case, for with a forceful but easy action he continued with neither pause nor hesitation until not once but twice my emotions were fully aroused.

That his self-control was not without effort was to be seen when on raising his head in order to look into my eyes, I found that he had so bitten his lower lip (in order to relieve his emotions) that he had broken the skin, and a bead of blood had sprung from the wound. It was the action of my taking this on the tip of my tongue that for some reason provoked his sentiments to a height, and with a cry he drew away just as there spouted from his energetic prick a fountain so forcefully expressed that the drops flew up over my shoulder to fall upon the boards behind!

Sitting back upon his heels, he enquired solicitously whether I was content, upon which I remarked that his attentions had satisfied me as much as I had been satisfied by any bathing machine attendant I had ever previously encountered; which for a moment dismayed him, until my expression revealed that I jested, whereupon, a grin passing over his own face, he resembled an imp of fully fifteen years of age!

The least I could do was to assure him that I had no intention of betraying him; and I now replaced my clothes, while he climbed with greater difficulty into his disguise. I took my leave of him outside the machine with a condescending nod and the ostentatious presentation of a gratuity (noticing a young gentleman nearby observing us with great care, presumably to ensure himself that the conditions of his wager were satisfied).

The experience of bathing had been somewhat different to what I had anticipated, but in no way a disappointment – except inasmuch that the young gentleman who had contributed to its interesting nature was to be pitied in lacking those niceties which truly please a lady, for while the capacity to continue a connection indefinitely is certainly to be envied, there are few ladies, I believe, who would not agree with me that fully three-quarters of the pleasure of an amorous connection must be in the preliminaries; those gentle and spirit-raising courtesies which are not only charming in themselves, but which prepare us, both body and soul, for the climacteric which is to come. It even occurred to me that it might have been considered my duty to instruct young Rupert in the art of pleasing the fair – for while with a title (and presumably, from his address, a good supply of the world's goods) he would presumably have no difficulty in winning a bride, the future happiness of the Hon. and Mrs Montjoy would depend on more than the simple, if admirable, steadfastness of which he was capable. In short, however sturdy the prick, there must be some tenderness and skill in the preliminary exercises if a single passage is not to be so simple that a lady is not likely to wish for a second!

As to the circumstance of my seduction (if that is the name for it), I had found it most interesting, and believe that others may find it equally so – indeed, given the gentleman's admirable qualities as to looks and manners, and supposing he was willing to learn, I could not but believe he would be more than successful with any female bather – which led me to wonder whether the kind of attentions which I had received might not, if properly organised, commend themselves in general to female visitors to a seaside resort, as a means of amusing themselves while their husbands were at the gaming tables, or elsewhere. Might this not be of interest to my friend Andy, as a possible concomitant of any resort he might succeed in setting up? I determined at least to mention it to him on our next meeting.

Chapter Five

The Adventures of Andy

Through the hospitality offered by Captain Twyce-Knightley and Lieutenant Marjoribanks and their wives was clearly to be remarkable for its generosity, not only as to accommodation and vittals but as to matters of the bed chamber, upon reflection I concluded that I might find a prolonged stay in the household somewhat embarrassing. I could not suppose that any of the four would find much that was remarkable in whatever part I might play in the licentious revels which clearly were as open to me as to them – and the two gentlemen showed no sign (as I broke my fast in their company) of being put out at my declining to take part in their exclusively masculine pleasures. However, it seemed to me that the situation was not likely to be a comfortable one – it being my experience that however free a gentleman may be in offering a friend or guest access to his wife, the matter frequently ends in tears. I must confess to having no basis for such a suspicion in the particular case of the establishment at Newhaven, and it may be that my upbringing (which had been such that, despite my pleasure in making free with any lady who offered, I tended to do so with one at a time) was chiefly responsible for my decision to express my thanks, and pass on towards Eastbourne.

However, it was to my purpose to discover a little more about Newhaven before doing so, since it seemed a pleasant enough place; and on my expressing my intention of walking through the town, Lieutenant Marjoribanks and Captain Twyce-Knightley (or, to be familiar, Fenwick and George) declared their intention of escorting me.

The experience was brief enough, the town not being extensive as to size – the inhabitants numbering just over nine hundred only. It was then a decently built little town, without either meanness or splendour. The traffic through it seemed to be small, but the appearance of the harbour, as seen at a little distance, and particularly from the church hill, was cheerful, and indicated some employment.

The connection with the Navy is clearly of a long standing, if only through calamity: in the churchyard, for instance, is a neat monumental obelisk erected in memory of the sloop *Brazen*, of eighteen guns, lost in 1800 (the year of my birth) off the Ave Rocks, near the town, when Captain Hanson, its commander, a distinguished seaman who had lately made some extensive voyages, and all his crew of 105 men – with one exception only – perished.

The cliffs of Newhaven are about two hundred feet high, of striking and picturesque formation (a full account of their structure may be found in Mantell's *Geology of Sussex* published in 4to – a work of erudition prefixed to which is an ingenious elucidatory dissertation on the mosaic history of the creation). The town's harbour, as I have remarked, is an excellent one, and in tempestuous weather has offered shelter to ships of 350 tons.

Fenwick proudly pointed out the fort which offered shelter

to two dozen members of the Twelfth Light Dragoons, whose duty it was to guard the harbour, and whom he commanded – while George with equal pride indicated the frigate *Hyperion*, moored just off the town, which was crewed by an equivalent number of men drawn from the Woolwich Division of the Royal Marines, commanded by himself.

Was it not the case, I enquired, that there must be rivalry between the two troops, leading to discord in the town?

Not at all, was the reply; indeed the greatest concord, even to direct friendliness, prevailed, and the companies often dined together – in particular upon the second Thursday in every month, when a special entertainment was devised for them by their commanders, their aim being specifically to contribute to the well-being of the men. Indeed, one of these parties was to take place that very evening, to which I would be welcome.

I could not but accept the invitation; it would have been discourteous to decline – though I did not particularly welcome the prospect of a rowdy drunken party, with perhaps fifty men crowded into what was clearly a small place, and with the consumption of alcohol the chief – if not the only – form of pleasure upon hand. On my mentioning the appointment to Emily, when I returned to the house for luncheon, she exchanged a glance with Penelope before opining (in what I took to be a slightly ironic tone) that she believed I would find the occasion of considerably greater interest than I supposed; and when I asked whether she and her friend would be present, Emily simply replied in the negative, without further exegesis.

The accommodation offered at the fort was small, but there was one central round room, upon the first floor, sufficiently large to take a set of tables laid for supper; and in time a party of a dozen men – six from the Marine corps, six from the Army – convened, which together with my friends and I made up some fifteen, who were all that could comfortably be seated.

The men attended these parties, it seems – and for all I know may yet continue to do so – in a carefully governed rotation of turns. They appeared much interested by the prospect of the evening, and to my surprise consumed only as much liquor as made them free in the presence of their superiors – by whom they were treated with an informality which encouraged pleasantry without provoking impertinence.

Our conversation over a very decent meal was perfunctory, and, in my case, chiefly concerned the town of Newhaven itself, which I soon learned could only inconveniently be enlarged to take any number of additional visitors or residents, through a lack of facilities which it would be difficult to provide. I made a few notes, but concluded that I must continue to look elsewhere for a place more suited to the enterprise on whose account I was engaged.

After dinner the health of His Majesty was drunk (the company sitting, as is the custom both with the Navy and the Marine). Then the tables were cleared and folded, and, somewhat to my confusion, a number of sheepskin rugs brought from some cupboard and spread upon the floor. After which George distributed among the company slips of paper upon which the men each wrote a cipher of some description – a letter or number, or simply a scribbled sign. Without understanding, I (since I had also been presented with a slip) wrote my initials upon it, and placed it with the others in a cap set down in the centre of the floor.

As to what was to follow, I had no notion; but Fenwick went to the wall, where a large bell hung, and rang it with a flourish. There was a pause, after which the door opened and into the room came some eight women, all of an age (as I took it) between twenty and thirty, of various characters, but each considerably attractive, and each clad (for the evening was a warm one) in flowing robes of some diaphanous material which concealed little from the eye of the beholder.

These ladies advanced upon the cap, and each drew from it a single slip, then encouraged the men to discover whether they had been fortunate enough to own one of those slips drawn. There being only eight ladies and some fifteen men, seven of us must be disappointed – and I did not know whether I should hope to be of that company or no, for while any opportunity for a satisfactory connection is always welcome, it is not my habit to take part in orgies involving a large number of ladies and gentlemen; three or four to a bed is sufficiently confusing, eight couples engaged in the view of a number of unoccupied gentlemen is not to my taste, it tending towards a public meeting, and being (as I find) more than a little inhibiting as to performance.

It is, of course, not an unknown matter for a party of ladies and gentlemen to occupy themselves all together in the way of lascivious activity. The entertainments arranged by the Greeks and Romans must be familiar to every classical scholar; the Aphrodisia of Greece was a ceremony famed for erotic pleasure, while in Rome the celebration of the rites of the god Liber was held freely and without shame before a multitude of witnesses, all of whom were free to take part in any manner which suggested itself.

Nearer our own time – in particular since the demise of the

Commonwealth – the liberality of entertainment offered in those classical times, but celebrated with less freedom since, has been revived. Those familiar with the interesting Diaries of Mr Samuel Pepys may recall his entry for 30 May, 1668, when by the talk of Harris Killigrew and others at supper at the New Exchange he understood 'the meaning of the company that lately was called 'Ballers'; Harris telling how it was by a meeting of some young blades, where he was among them, and my Lady Bennet and her ladies; and there dancing naked, and all the roguish things in the world.'

Later, and yet more openly, Mrs Charlotte Hayes, who kept a brothel in King's Place, Pall Mall, some thirty years since, issued invitations in the following form:

'Mrs Hayes commends herself respectfully to Lord —
— and takes the liberty of advising him that this evening at seven o'clock precisely, twelve beautiful nymphs, spotless virgins, will carry out the famous Feast of Venus as it is celebrated in Tahiti, under the instructions and leadership of Queen Oberea (which role will be taken by Mrs Hayes herself).'

Mrs Hayes had heard from Mr Hawksworth, a traveller, how in Tahiti 'young men and girls often copulate publicly before the people, receiving good advice from the bystanders, usually women (among them the most important inhabitants are to be found). Thus the girls (of fifteen years) receive their information at an early age,' and decided to replicate the ceremonies before her guests in King's Place.

Twenty-three people responded to the invitation, including five members of the House of Commons, and (it is reported) 'punctually at seven o'clock the feast began, for which, for the men's parts, Mrs Hayes had engaged twelve athletic youths. These youths, with the nymphs, now celebrated the Tahiti Venus Feast before the eyes of the entranced audience; after which a sumptuous meal was taken.'

It was, of course, that remarkable person Sir Francis Dashwood, of West Wycombe House (above the village of the same name) who did most to bring the conception of the well organised orgy into modern Britain. He laid out a part of the garden of his house in the shape of a woman, with much suggestive grouping of pillars and bushes, and with his friend Francis Duffield founded the Medmenham Brotherhood, which, at the house of that name, celebrated rites of a freedom previously unknown in the English provinces.

A chapel was constructed in the grounds, above which was a room with two or three drinking sofas covered with silk damask, constructed upon the plan of the Romans when at the height of their luxuriance. The room was decorated in a manner intended to convey and inspire sentiments of immorality and lewdness. There was not a vice for the practising which Dashwood did not make provision for. His cellars were stored with the choicest wines, the larders with the delicacies of every climate; and there were separate cells fitted up for all purposes of lasciviousness.

The organisation resembled that of a monastery which through some aberration had become over-closely associated with a nunnery; the company of 'monks' was formed from Sir Francis's extensive acquaintances; the 'nuns' were recruited from various London houses, and were conveyed in closed wagons to Medmenham: and the company was enlarged by an adequate number of local wantons, who having heard of the luxury and wealth of the monks as well as of their carnality, were not unnaturally ready to join with them in prayer. They wore small silver brooches engraved with the words 'Love and Friendship' – and by no means all of them were whores or local girls, for friars sometimes introduced ladies to the society, who were allowed to appear masked, at first, in order that they might scrutinise the company and avoid any unfortunate meeting with husband or betrothed!

The office of Abbot was taken in rotation, the Abbot of the day having certain privileges, such as first choice of women, and various corresponding duties, such as the inspection of the cellars to make sure that there was a more than adequate supply of wine, and of the cells to make sure that they were equipped with everything that the brethren might find necessary.

During the evenings when a meeting was held, the monks and nuns settled down to the enjoyment of all pleasures: toast followed toast throughout a long meal, until replete with wine, brother after brother seized a nun and at the table or in the cells, or on the lawn lit by the setting summer sun, worshipped the goddess Venus, to whom the company was devoted.

The example of Sir Francis was followed only at a distance, for scarcely anyone who might wish to emulate him commanded his wealth; but many of those who heard of his celebrations followed them to the extent of forming small companies for common coupling, and the reputation of these clubs was in no small degree responsible for a general loosening of the over-strong bonds of puritanism which still restricted amorous activities in our country – a reputation pioneered in Europe by that of the well-known amorist

Giacomo Giovanni Casanova de Seingalt, who though he died as early as 1798, is still regarded as the happiest example of freedom in sensual matters.

But I digress, and for too long; the reader will be eager to hear whether I was to be favoured by the attentions of one of the ladies introduced to that much more modest society of men at Newhaven. The answer was, that I was not: or at least, that my slip was one of those which still remained in the cap after the ladies had each taken one. I therefore settled with some relief (though perhaps a little regret) on to a sofa at one end of the room, while the other rejected or unchosen gentlemen sat about the edges of it, as the others were taken in hand.

The system appeared to be well known, for what followed had clearly been rehearsed on more than one occasion. The chosen men made no motion other than to acknowledge their partners, but merely stood at attention while the ladies unclothed them (not with difficulty, for they had previously removed their jackets and stood now only in breeches and shirts). I was interested to see that as yet they appeared largely unaroused, partly perhaps through the circumstance; yet upon the ladies removing their own clothing, which they now did, it required only a single embrace to set them ready for congress – a selection of eight pricks soon enough presenting themselves in various degrees of shape and size; but one unmistakable aspect of eager anticipation.

The gentlemen now laid themselves down upon the floor, on the rugs provided, while each lady in the first place went on all fours, and presenting to those unfortunates about the edge of the room a selection of handsome bottoms as pert and pretty as one could wish, bent to salute their partners with a kiss – and not upon the mouth. Then, satisfied that the readiness was complete, each lady mounted her steed: but then, rather than moving straightway into the trot and canter, held out their hands.

I looked about me, and discovered that in the short space of time while my eyes had been occupied by the goings on in the centre of the room, the gentlemen about the sides had removed their clothing – and now stepped forward to such a position where both the hands and lips of the mounted ladies could attend to those parts most flattered by such attention!

The lady opposite me, seeing my uncertainty, smiled and beckoned. She was mounted upon the recumbent body of Lieutenant Marjoribanks (who I had been glad to see happily accept the invitation of a lady; that is, he was not entirely devoted to his own sex, as I had feared, which would have been irreparably damaging to his marriage). Unwilling to show impoliteness, I threw off my clothing and stepped forward, whereupon the lady in question placed her hand upon my prick, then, drawing me on to such a position as was convenient (standing astride Fenwick's body, and facing his partner) was pleasant enough to apply her lips and tongue to my service, at the same time beginning her jog – which not only gave her lover pleasure, as I assumed, but certainly through the necessary motion contributed a certain inspiriting friction to my own lower parts; to the pleasure of which she added certain movements of her hands upon my arse and cods.

At least, that is what I supposed – for having my eyes closed, the better to concentrate upon the delightful sensations offered, I did not observe her. On opening them, however, I noted that her hands were in fact placed upon the floor at each side of her, the better to preserve her balance; the exploring hands belonged rather to Fenwick – whose adeptness in manipulating those portions of my anatomy open to his caresses was that of an expert.

To preserve my equanimity, the sensations aroused by my two companions being considerable, I raised my eyes and addressed them to the rest of the room. This, however, was of no assistance, and would have been none to any gentleman save he in whom there is no element of the *voyeur*, as the French call those of us who are not repelled by observing other ladies and gentlemen in *coitus*.

On every side were gentlemen and ladies engaged in pleasuring each other (and themselves) with the utmost vigour. Many of the couples fortunate enough (as I would put it) not to have to concern themselves with a third party, had taken the decision to lie head to tail, and were consuming each other with every sign of satisfaction; while those ladies who must satisfy two lovers were doing so in a variety of ways – some in the posture in which we were engaged, others in different manners. Without much surprise, for instance, I noticed that one lady was being taken from behind by a handsome young trooper formerly dressed in the uniform of the Twelfth Light, while my friend – or acquaintance – Captain Twyce-Knightley was performing the act of sodomy upon him, none of the three, it seemed, inclined to complain at the situation; indeed, the lady seemed to profit, for the trooper's energetic plunging was reinforced at every move by the equally energetic ramming of George's loins, each of the participants, from their expression, being in a heightened state of pleasure.

These sights, as the reader may imagine, did nothing to

lower my sensations; and now I felt the most delightful additional pleasure – the result of Fenwick raising his body, and parting the cheeks of my behind with his hands, playing with his tongue about my anus or arsehole. This did my business; my relief was, I fear, at the expense of the lady whose lips were still firmly closed about my prick; but as she continued to suck upon it with the most insistent, though gentle, pressure, I took it that she was not displeased at the occurrence, but was one of those who considered the liquid expelled by the satisfied male to be both pleasant and nourishing. In fact, the only consequence was her somewhat more violent jogging upon the body of Lieutenant Marjoribanks, which (as I gathered first from the excitement, then from the relaxation of both my companions) had the desired result in both of them.

The three of us now collapsed upon the rug, the lady upon my left hand and the gentleman upon my right – their hands joined upon that part of me no longer able to please either of them, in a gesture which (as I saw on looking about me) was taken to be a signal of satisfaction and even of thanks. On George once more ringing the bell, three troopers (somewhat grumpily in full dress) now came with jugs of beer and wine, with which we refreshed ourselves. I noticed that they took no liberties with the ladies, merely serving them as they served us; and Fenwick explained that they had had their liberty with the ladies on the last occasion of the Club's meeting – though from signs unmistakable to any gentlemen, I observed that they were not immune to the spectacle of the naked bosoms about the room, while one young man, bending to serve a lady who reclined face downward upon the rugs and displayed an immaculately formed bottom, plump as a ripe pear, walked from the room as though in considerable pain. After a short period, it was clear that those who had not enjoyed full congress could, if they were willing and able, take the places of their more fortunate fellows; George this time was quick to take advantage of his female friend, while the trooper who had been the subject of his earlier attentions gently rejected the lady's offer, and turned his attention to the gentleman's rear – something which, far from objecting, George appeared to welcome, going so far as to seize his companion's prick and anoint it generously with saliva before permitting him to direct it as they both fancied.

For myself, I was happy to relax while the lady next me threw a thigh across my belly and sank upon me. Fenwick in turn now bestrode me and permitted her to attend to his needs, which she did with what seemed an unalloyed pleasure. I must confess that it was not an entirely new experience for me to be pleasured by a female companion who at the same time was occupied by another gentleman – this being in my experience almost always attended by some inconvenience; in this case her face was entirely obscured (and I find it desirable to be able to see the expression of those ladies with whom I am engaged).

I must also confess that in a sort of jealousy (a wasted but sometimes inevitable emotion), I paid particular attention to her breasts, and realising that the position in which she was poised, though pleasurable to me, was probably less so to her – and on reaching my own apogee – endeavoured to provoke a similar climax in her by reaching down to find with my thumb that knub of flesh at the top of her cunny where experience had taught me the keenest female sensation was seated. The result would have been amusing had it not been somewhat alarming: for as though she had received some kind of injury to her lower parts, the lady gave a great squeal and a great leap; Lieutenant Marjoribanks lost his balance and fell to the floor; the lady sprang to her feet, clutched at her privities, and with another excited cry fell on top of me in a faint! A lady whose partner had, for whatever reason, deserted her, attempted to recover her, and in part succeeding, assisted her into her clothing and out into the air.

For all practical purposes my own part in the proceedings ended here, as did that of Fenwick, who sadly had fallen upon his extended prick and thus through injury rendered himself incapable of further participation. So exhausted was I that even the frenzied activities of the young people around me (for some of the men were mere boys) failed to arouse my feelings further; and I was indeed pleased to regain my clothing and walk outside into the cool evening air, where I found my former companion leaning upon the balustrade of the fort's terrace.

Enquiring as to her health, I received the assurance that she was recovered – and the additional averment that the inconvenience of her collapse was a small price to pay for what she was pleased to call the sky-y height of pleasure to which my attentions had raised her!

Not unnaturally I was delighted by the compliment, though I turned it aside with the assertion that it was only a man's duty to ensure a pleasure in a mistress equivalent to his own. I then introduced myself, and she returned the compliment. She went by the name of Mlle Desirée Beauregard, and was the granddaughter of an emigré Frenchman who had come to England during the troubles in his benighted country and had settled in the town of Eastbourne. Her father had died young, to be followed by her mother – and she had been left to make her way in the world as best she might. She had done so by setting up as a dressmaker in the town; but was doomed to a lonely existence through the men of the area having a prejudice against foreigners (one of the less pleasant constituents of the British race) and declining to pay her polite attentions.

'I could,' she said, with the very faintest trace of a French accent, 'have made many conquests had I been content to accept the offers of several young men; but these did not include marriage, or even a polite connection – the young gentlemen simply being eager to spend their coin rather than to invest it. I therefore rejected it.

'But,' she said, '– and I say this because I take you for a gentleman to whom a lady may make the confession without diminishing herself in his eyes – I have a body tuned to a high pitch of desire, and those manipulations with which it is possible to satisfy oneself without conversation with others being unsatisfactory to me, I was pleased to hear through a female friend of the excursions made by a number of young ladies to this town of Newhaven, on one day in every month, when it is possible to relieve those excessively warm emotions which, if not satisfied, provoke many ills, from bad breath and pustules of the skin to the green sickness and dropping of the bosom.'

She hesitated here, as though to ensure that I was not shocked; but taking her hand and carrying it to my lips, I assured her that that was not the case – and from politeness changed the subject, mentioning the fact that I was myself about to set out for the town of Eastbourne, and asking whether I might call upon her.

She was happy to give me permission (and I must here set

down the fact that it was not from a desire to renew the carnal connection – or not only that – that I made the suggestion, but out of admiration for a young woman so forward looking and decisive in her actions, and from the conviction that she could introduce me to those features of the town which I needed to know).

Giving me her card, she advised me to set up at the Lamb – for though there were several inns deserving of praise, that was the most comfortable and moderate in price.

Bidding her farewell, I made my way back to the Twyce-Knightleys' abode, and there, in the morning, took my leave of the ladies, who from their allusions to their husbands' lying late and myself appearing somewhat weary (which was the truth), seemed to know what sort of an evening I had spent the night before.

I passed from Newhaven over the small draw-bridge on to the road to Seaford. Approaching this ancient port, now at a little distance from the sea (and thus not to my purpose), the shore is bold and wild, diversified with lofty cliffs, and an irregular strand intersected by several winding creeks. The views of the rocks of Newhaven are also striking.

I paused only for some ale, bread and cheese, then passed on along a hilly road, the sea in general lost to sight by the rise of the lofty cliffs. To the left of the road is a long valley in which are placed at small distances several inconsiderable villages, very similar in appearance, with little grey churches and dark elm foliage. West Dean is the only one passed through, to which I descended by a steep hill, through a pleasantly wooded lane.

Soon afterwards, the cliffs of Beachy Head and the lighthouse appear. I passed Friston church, belonging to a village of ten houses, and consequently of the humblest description, yet from its elevated situation serving as a landmark to vessels. The country now opened on descending to the town of Eastbourne; the sea-houses were seen, and the commencement of the long line of Martello towers indicated the level ground which extended to Hastings, beyond which is Fairlight Down, one of the most commanding eminences on the southern coast.

Riding past a barracks for a troop of horses, at present unoccupied, I descended into the town itself, formerly the Roman settlement of Anderida and now a place of resort which I feel strongly inclined to recommend to all those who require a keen and animating air – for which it is almost unrivalled; and on putting up at the Lamb, became at least for a while (as a recent poll has confirmed) the town's 2,727th inhabitant.

Chapter Six

Sophie's Story

A couple of days after the incident which I related in my last chapter, I received a message from Mr Montjoy asking whether I would do him the honour of taking a glass with him at Chalybeate on the morning of the following day.

I was pleased at this: I had failed to take a note of his address in Brighton, and regretted the fact – for I felt I had a moral duty to instruct him in the matter of love-making. No young fellow as handsome and virile as himself should be allowed to barge into manhood with so mistaken an idea of how to go about pleasing a woman; and though it was strictly none of my business, I could not but feel sorry for the result should he do so, for the word soon gets around, and he would swiftly find himself short of amorous partners of his own class, while even those ladies available to gentlemen upon payment of fee would accept his custom out of kindness rather than enthusiasm – and kindness, while the prerogative of many whores, is no recipe for satisfaction in amatory encounters when knowledge is lacking.

Indeed, in my experience (which is by no means small) the keenest pleasure can only come where there is not only

91

consideration and, if possible, affection on both sides, but also a thorough understanding of what engineers describe as *technique*. A professional lady must certainly accept the client who bids for her; but should she be assured that he is open and free in his manner, and rather than using her as a convenience, is not only determined that she should enjoy the connection as thoroughly as himself but capable of ensuring that that is the case, she will receive him with that additional enthusiasm which is all in ensuring satisfaction.

With the best of these ladies, a gentleman may not discern much difference, for each is capable of convincing that she has been waiting all day for the sight of him (even should he be her fifth or sixth client of the evening); but some few are incapable of excited conviction in the matter, and disappointment must ensue if the gentleman is one of those whose satisfaction is merely (as I have said) in using rather than pleasing his companion. Any hint I could give Mr Montjoy which would educate and set him into the right frame of mind would, therefore, be of use whether he marry or simply put himself about the town.

I, therefore, set myself out to dress as pleasingly as possible, and on leaving the hotel presented (I believe) a very different picture to that which he had viewed upon my seeking out his bathing machine – for it is not much to the purpose to take a great deal of trouble about one's dress when one's chief purpose is to remove it (at least, not for the purpose merely of bathing).

The chalybeate spring is situated behind the western end of Brighton, and is a pleasant walk of less than half a mile from Brunswick or Regency Squares. It may also be approached from the Western Road, and by a very pleasant footway from above the Old Church, over an intervening hill which commands a magnificent view and has a very fine air.

The edifice to which the spring is directed, and where it is confined, has an Ionic colonnade and a very handsome and airy reading room – decidedly one of the best in Brighton. The small well or fountain is a few feet below the floor of the right wing, and has a very neat staircase descending to it. At the top of the staircase stood Mr Montjoy, a considerably more handsome figure than when I had last seen him, for he was dressed in the complete fashion of the time – yet entirely without that overblown insistence on superfluous detail which marks the ineffectual dandy. He escorted me down to the spring, and we took a glass of the water – upon whose good qualities I am not competent to offer an observation: the visitor will find one or two pamphlets on the subject, but will perhaps do best to seek for the opinion of its promulgator, Dr Relhan.

The component parts of the water have some affinity to those of the Tunbridge Wells chalybeate, but are more strongly impregnated with iron, as may easily be discovered by the slightest taste. In an extensive variety of cases, where a powerful tonic is required, it is said, in conjunction with sea air and bathing, to have almost worked miracles.

On my sipping the water and leaving the greater quantity in the glass, Mr Montjoy – or Rupert (for so he did me the honour to ask me to address him) smiled, and asked whether a dish of coffee would be more acceptable? On which we retired to a cottage at the side of a lawn before the main building, kept by a confectioner, who produced an admirable brew, which we drank while listening to the music of four musicians who daily play there for some hours, in a most respectable style.

Our talk led in several directions, and I discovered that Rupert was the son of that Lord Montjoy of Pebble Quay in Northants, who was known in the City as a profligate attender at events of a sporting nature (and I mean not only horse races and betting meetings, though these he certainly supported, but also occasions when the sport involved the female sex, whom he treated much in the manner on which I had cause to animadvert in the opening paragraphs of this chapter: that is, he used us as mere instruments of his pleasure.) That forwardness which had led his son to accept a bet which must place him in proximity to unclad ladies seemed to be inherited, though I made no comment upon it; it must also have led to his invitation to walk with him up the hill above the spring – for it could surely only be one object he had in view; and if I did not dissent from it, it was rather because I had fixed upon his reformation than through ignorance of his intention.

The walk is a fine one: on the hill is a little sprinkling of wild heath and wooded scenery – not very superior, to be sure, but still a gem in the borders of Brighton. The view of the ocean, the harbour of Shoreham, and Worthing Point is very pleasing, and the air so excellent that it alone is worth a walk to the spot. The casual stroller, however, will be stopped by a high wall in which is set an iron gate; and so would we have been, had not Rupert produced from his pocket a key which opened the gate and led us into grounds handsomely set out – with, in the distance, a small but elegant dwelling where (he now told me) he was at present domiciled, the house being the property of a hospitable friend.

We continued our stroll along the side of the wall, which soon gave way to a low parapet above a cliff, where there was a patch of grass in a clearing protected on all sides by shrubs and trees, and where Rupert suggested we might rest, handing me down to sit on what was certainly warm and comfortable green sward, and seating himself beside me.

In a shorter time than a more shy or tactful man would have thought appropriate, he enquired whether I would object to his removing his shirt, for he found the heat of the sun (now rising towards midday) somewhat oppressive. I could raise no objection, and was soon able to admire without restriction a well-proportioned breast, entirely adult in its musculature, though the few dark hairs sprouting about his paps spoke of a youth by no means greatly advanced towards manhood. Apart from these, an admirably soft and unmarked skin was devoid of thatch, except at the point where his belt hung loosely about his waist, another little show of hair being cut off there by the line of his breeches before it could resolve into any declaration of a more positive virility.

He lay for a while entirely conscious, I am sure, of my examination – and no doubt of my admiration, for it was indeed impossible not to admire a figure which resembled, as much as anything, that statue of Adonis by Maestro Cutarcci which may be seen, even by ladies, upon payment of a special fee at a museum in Rome; and which, though it is considered indecent through the gentleman being unmistakably ready to prove his manhood, is sufficiently admired to be a first-rate source of finance to the city fathers. But after a minute or two he began to puff and exhale, to insert his hands below his belt to examine them for signs of perspiration, and finally to ask whether ('in view,' as he put it 'of a certain familiarity between us on a recent occasion') I would be offended should he strip off the remainder of his clothing.

Those readers of my previous memoirs will anticipate my reply (though indeed few women, I believe, would have had the heart, on any grounds, to refuse the request) – my only proviso being that he should tolerate my also removing my clothing. He offered no objection (must I again suggest that the reader will be unsurprised?) and the next moment we were both as bare as needles – and a pretty resemblance we bore, I dare say, to Adam and Eve before the Fall!

It was clear that both of us were in the habit of lying unclothed in the sun, for the entire expanse of our skins was unmarked by those ugly white patches which insult the eye of the 'connoisseur', and were without exception brown (though not to an offensive degree – being perhaps more golden than anything stronger). I cannot speak as to my own beauty, though the fact that it has frequently been admired, and that on this occasion Rupert was all eyes, suggested that it was at the very least inoffensive to him. As to himself, however, my female readers deserve a further description.

He was, as I believe I have already said, dark (almost to a Mediterranean appearance) and slim; he lay now, half raised upon an elbow, his underleg drawn up, the other stretched, so that a line, effortlessly drawn, fell from the base of a fine throat over a shoulder, down an arm to where the hand lay negligently upon the upper thigh, then on to the pointed foot. His breast, narrow but by no means weak, was marked by two dark circlets at the centre of which were drawn-up two tiny points, surrounded by rings of rougher goose-skin; about these lay the few dark hairs of which I have spoken, and which were in marked contrast to the lighter skin.

Now that his lower parts were exposed, it was possible to see that indeed a trickle of hair lay in a vertical line down his belly, broadening at the point where a squab cock lay upon his thigh. This, initially perhaps no more than two inches long and drawn to a delightful point, seemed to thicken even as I looked at it – for he was regarding my person with just such a keen attention as I gave to him, and his admiration could only be expressed in the common way of mankind. Indeed, it took only perhaps half a minute for the appendage of which I speak, not only to thicken and lengthen, but to raise itself from the hollow in which it lay (that hollow which in the young lies on the inside of the thigh) and to stand up against his belly so that only its underside could be seen, a thick vein mounting to the point just beneath the dome where a circle of skin revealed the head (for the young gentleman had evidently undergone the ceremony of circumcision – whether through a religious conviction of his parents, or their devotion to fashion, I cannot say). It only remains to remark that he had either been careful to guard this organ from being burnt in the sun (a circumstance extremely uncomfortable) or that for some other reason its skin had remained uncoloured, for while many gentlemen's pricks darken through the suffusing blood which causes them to erect, this remained white as ivory, the head only being delightfully pink.

I might mention here for the benefit of those who have not closely observed the matter, that the time taken for an entirely relaxed male member to erect itself to the point at which it is of use, greatly varies from gentleman to gentleman. The elderly must reconcile themselves to a slower arousal than the young; while those who indulge too much in liquor share the problem that it may take some considerable time before their pricks stand to any effect. But in the young and vigorous, I have seen the organ sprout from a relaxed to a ready condition in as short a time as three seconds, though to be sure that is an unusual effect.

At all events, Rupert was clearly under no difficulty in that department – but although I showed, I believe, no sign of embarrassment or disapproval, he seemed by no means over-confident of my reaction, for placing one hand over his prick and discovering that it was by no means sufficient in dimension, he lay back and brought the other hand into use, in an attempt to conceal it. Not only did he fail, through the size and angle of the organ, but the sight was, I fear, sufficiently comic to bring me to a peal of laughter, when I had immediately to explain that this was not so much at the sight itself as at his supposition that a glimpse of the instrument could possibly be offensive to me.

He was, I think, much relieved, and at all events now got to his knees and, approaching me, bent to kiss me upon the lips, while his hand fell between my thighs and with his fingers he began to draw my lower lips apart – without doubt a preparation for immediate congress.

Gently taking that hand, I removed it, asking him whether the speed with which he wished to proceed was the result of a fear that we might be disturbed.

'By no means,' he answered, 'the servants have the day at their own pleasure, and there is no way in which access can be gained to the park without my knowledge.'

'In that case,' I said, 'we can be at leisure.'

He clearly found this a strange suggestion, confirming my supposition that he had grown up in the conviction that the moment he was sufficiently excited by the presence of a woman, he must express that excitement by the ultimate action. It would I believe have been by no means satisfactory merely to read him a lecture on the subject; the lesson must be taught, as all lessons should, by example – and persuading him (most reluctantly) to lie back upon the ground, I bent, and taking his prick in my right hand, ran my tongue first along its length, while at the same time, with the fingers of my left hand, gently brushing his breasts and those little nodules of flesh which are in the male as tender and susceptible of excitement as in women.

The indrawn breath and the shudder with which this action was greeted was sufficient to assure me that no female had ever performed such an action upon him in the past; and much less had any taken his prick between her lips, as I did now, first encircling with them the naked dome, then running down the length of the organ as far as was possible.

I must, incidentally, here comment upon the view – general with women – that circumcision, or the removal of the hood of skin which normally conceals the head of the male organ, makes the prick more sensitive to caresses, and is therefore responsible for gentlemen reaching the zenith of their pleasure sooner than their partner finds convenient. This is certainly in my experience not necessarily so – nor was it so in this case. Setting aside the religious reason for interfering with the organ as nature designed it – and the custom is found among the ancient Egyptians and in Asia and Oceana as well as in the Middle East – the operation seems to have no effect more advantageous than in its being easier for the organ to be kept in a desirable state of cleanliness, thus making those familiarities which give most pleasure entirely inoffensive to the lady offering them (and let me not claim that this is a facile point, lack of such cleanliness being a chief obstacle in the way of increasing the variety of love-making between man and woman – or for that matter, I dare say, between man and man!). As to sensitivity, I can only repeat that I have never come across any gentleman to whom the operation has made the slightest difference in that respect: the question of reserving the ultimate emotion being rather a matter of the mind than the body.

To return to my narrative, it was, I am convinced, because of his relative inexperience in leisurely love-making that I found I must be particularly sparing in my attentions to Rupert's prick, for the trembling and shaking which was thereby produced signalled the fact that he felt the effect of my sucking upon it so keenly that if I persevered, the result would be a premature end to our pleasures. I therefore now sat up, and enquired whether my action was not an excellent reason for somewhat delaying full congress? – to which a vigorous nodding of the head was his response, the gentleman being for the moment incapable of speech!

I next took the opportunity (through his silence) of enquiring whether he would be so good as to return the compliment? – something as unthought of, by him, as my own action; and indeed, recovering his voice, he asked how that could be possible, since I lacked the appendage which . . . I interrupted him by assuring him that any oral compliment he cared to pay in the area to which I invited him to turn his attention would be as pleasurable to me as my own action had been to him; and in order to assist him, I lay back and spread my limbs, offering him – on his approach – the clearest and most open view of things.

Only my emotions, which were soon enough aroused,

prevented me from laughing at his pleasurable interest in what he now found, which was as curious as that of a squirrel examining a nut! His unfamiliarity with the most interesting part of women was clearly almost comprehensive: that is, he knew what most men demanded of it, but only that, and the fact that a mistress could be pleased by compliments properly paid in that quarter had never occurred to him.

However, it must be said that (whatever his eagerness in other areas of education) he was the most adept and instant scholar of lecherous learning I have yet come across. On his taking my example and reaching with his tongue (by accident rather than design, in that first place, I have no doubt) the little thumb where women's emotions are most readily to be engaged, I could not resist a cry of pleasure – at which for a moment he raised his head, believing (I think) that my exclamation may have been an indication of pain. But on my smile reassuring him, he returned to his work with redoubled interest and attention.

I must admit to prompting him somewhat by renewed sighs and exclamations, each one of which encouraged him to a renewed application of tongue, lips and fingers; for having discovered these as engines of emotion – which I believe he had never previously thought of – he soon learned to use them with a sort of unconscious and instinctive skill; for instance quickly finding with the tip of a finger that sensitive place at the inner top of the female passage which, when stimulated (together with the caressing of the tongue elsewhere) can render the least sensitive of ladies almost unconscious with passion.

Rupert Montjoy was, in short, one of those men – though I believe he had not previously suspected it – whose satisfaction was to be as much in pleasing a mistress as in his own coming off. These make the best lovers; and in the case of the gentleman with whom I was now engaged, the instinct was joined to a natural predilection for love-making itself, driven by the springs of an erotic urge almost unparalleled in my experience. Upon his face, when it was raised from between my thighs, could be seen an expression of almost religious ecstasy, while not a gesture was made by him which was not now directed at contributing to my pleasure – and not only in the area whence his main interest at first directed him, but elsewhere, his discovery of the sensitivity of my breasts being only just secondary to it; while almost every indication of my satisfaction added to his interest – the pleasure given by running the tongue about the whorls of the ears, of sucking upon the lips or of a thumb, of gently licking the eyelids . . . all of these. However, time and again he returned to that area of my body which most closely interested him.

I began almost to feel guilt at merely remaining recumbent (apart from an occasional leap or wriggle of my body which could not be prevented, through an access of feeling); except that if I attempted a movement which might allow me to direct a gesture of love at him, he firmly held me to the ground with arms sufficiently strong to brook no argument. However, since there seemed no prospect of the encounter coming to an end unless I took a hand, I now firmly caught hold of his hair and began to haul his head upward towards my own.

Since he had lately parted my thighs and now lay with his shoulders beneath them, the better to pay tribute to my cunny, the result of my action was that as his body slid upwards along mine, my knees were hooked above his shoulders and my rump must rise, thus bringing his cock into such a position that it was inevitable (especially in that state of slipperiness to which our intimate parts were reduced by the intensity of our passion) that it should slide into just that socket where it was most welcome.

I believe my lover to have been astonished by the situation in which he now found himself – the position without doubt being one he had never contemplated – but that he was none the less interested and delighted was clear from his looking down with fascination at the point of our junction, where his black hairs and my own lighter ones met then parted, then met again as the result of that inevitable motion which his body (as though unbidden) now made. That he found the motion itself as delicious as I, could not be doubted, both from his expression and from the sounds which issued from both our throats. (It is fortunate that no machine has been invented which can reproduce the noises which we make during such moments of emotion, for I believe we should be ashamed at hearing sounds so redolent of animal copulation!)

It has long been a theory of mine that the more concerned one is to give pleasure to a partner, the more heightened are one's own emotions; and certainly upon this occasion it seems to have been the truth where Rupert was concerned – for a series of cries became positive shouts, and at the moment of his supreme pleasure a yell so loud that the rooks in the trees took to the air with corresponding noises of their own, a black cloud of them passing between us and the sun and casting a dark shadow across our recumbent bodies as we collapsed in a tangle of limbs (myself, I should not omit to record, having been brought to my own climacteric by the eagerness of the moment of his).

We lay still for a while – but only for a while: within a couple of minutes there was a sound as of some wild animal charging through the undergrowth nearby, and in a moment a young man emerged from amid the shrubs, brandishing a pistol. He came to a halt standing right above us (the clearing being a small one), and to my amusement a dark red flush spread instantly over his face, and even extended downward to the upper part of his chest (which was unclad), while a stuttering apology fell from his panting lips. He had, it seemed, heard the cries, recognised one voice at least, and believing some assault was being attempted on his friend, had run to the rescue from a nearby place where he had been engaged in tending some plants (being, it seemed, a gardener – though not by profession).

Rupert immediately got to his feet and laid his hand on the gentleman's arm.

'My dear Vane,' he said, 'please abate your confusion! We have too long been friends for me to feel the least embarrassment at your presence, while this lady is too much a sophisticate to repine at being presented to you in a state of nature, and will only feel complimented at any admiration which she may discern in your eyes. May I present Mrs Sophia Nelham? – Mrs Nelham, Sir Harry Vane.'

The young man somewhat, though not altogether, recovered his self-possession, and at least was able to take the hand I held out to him and assist me to my feet, where I acknowledged him by a nod rather than a curtsy (the latter form of greeting being more than a little ridiculous when one entirely lacks clothing).

Rupert made no allusion to the reason for the cries which had brought his friend upon us; nor indeed was any allusion I believe necessary, for as if our unclothed state were not sufficient to suggest the form of our recent recreation, the fact that both our bodies were aswim with perspiration (brought on by a combination of our exertions and the heat of the sun) could not but confirm it. My own hair was limp and sticking to my shoulders, while his breast was glistening with sweat, and beads trickled down across his belly and into the area where a squat and diminished prick – from which a little pearl-coloured drop of liquid now depended – could only surely convince his friend that our association had been a complete one. For without undue pride, I must assert that very few gentlemen finding themselves alone with me when we are both in a state of nature, fail to announce their admiration by a natural enlarging of their genital organs!

Sir Harry, on his friend's invitation, sat down with us, and on my asking his pardon for remaining unclad (for I wished not to sully my dress by donning it over a body so wet), he replied with a graceful compliment, and on Rupert's suggesting it, stripped off his breeches in order that neither of us should feel out of the way in lacking cover. (I could not but notice, in confirmation of the statement with which I ended my last paragraph, that while by no means entirely erect, Sir Harry's prick was equally by no means entirely flaccid, which seemed to indicate that he did not find me unattractive). It was now Rupert's turn to admit that Sir Harry had been the friend responsible for the wager which had resulted in our meeting; at which Harry blushed again, and asked my pardon, which I was happy to give. Our talk then turned to the subject of Brighton as a place of recreation, which Sir Harry was thoroughly informed upon, since the house in whose park we were, belonged to his family –

sprung from that earlier Sir Harry Vane who, returning to England from Massachusetts, where he was Governor, sat in the Long Parliament and was one of the leaders of the Puritan sect responsible for the death of the late King Charles of blessed memory.

'I hope, however, that you will believe me no puritan,' said Sir Harry; and indeed, lying between myself and his friend, he had found himself incapable of reacting to my presence in any other than the natural way, and was now in possession of a weapon fully extended, which I observed him to stroke (when he thought I was not looking) as though it were a dog in urgent need of placating. Catching my eye, he observed my attention to this action, and blushed again! How badly some men are betrayed by this rush of blood to the skin! – almost as instantly and as truthfully as the rush of blood which results in a yet more forthright betrayal of feeling elsewhere, readying them for amorous play; and I have observed, indeed, that a ready blusher often possesses the hardest prick. Sir Harry's, for instance, was not only almost a dark red in colour, but seemed so entirely suffused with blood that it might burst, standing firmly up against his belly, positively curved like a tightly drawn bow! This was an interesting phenomenon – indeed, unconsciously I made a motion with my own hand as though to . . .

'Ah – if only you could be persuaded!' said Sir Harry, to whom my action had evidently offered hope of a service which he would have hesitated to request without some such sign of my interest.

How could I leave the poor young man in a state of discomfort? After all, it had been his friend and I who had disturbed him at his innocent horticultural pleasure! Yet to be frank, so thorough a rogering as I had only recently experienced had left me somewhat sore, and the thought of a second congress following so immediately was not entirely pleasurable. So, making the best of the situation, I took Sir Harry's instrument between my fingers, and lowering my head and placing it between my lips, began an operation which I trusted would release him from any dis-ease which might be the result of his admiration. From the way the young gentleman instantly lay back, and the beatific smile which came to his lips upon my head beginning to bob, I was convinced that it would not be a wearisomely long task upon which I had embarked, and got upon all fours the more conveniently to continue it.

This was, I almost immediately realised, a mistake: for in doing so I had presented Rupert with such a view of my nether regions, elevated and even somewhat thrust upward, as he had not previously enjoyed; and that he admired it was immediately clear to me, for I straightway felt his hands upon the cheeks of my arse, and in a moment his tongue was once more probing the fruit which lay between.

The degree to which the human body is capable of responding to the tender admiration of a person of the opposite sex can never be underestimated. Rupert's lips and tongue dealt so tenderly with my lower parts that in a moment any soreness was replaced by a delighted apprehension of pleasure – and it was impossible for me not to bend my waist yet further so as to present him with an even clearer mark!

My theory that here was a young man in whom the talent for love-making was almost unparalleled was confirmed; for continuing the titillation he was practising, he instinctively knew the moment at which to substitute his prick for his tongue, and kneeling behind me and transferring his hands from hips to shoulders, he sheathed his sword once more, and began a motion which mirrored my own in pleasing his friend. This time there was only one cry to raise the rooks: that of Sir Harry – for Rupert was more gentle, raising my spirits by a slow and rocking movement, rather than the fierce battering which had previously been his *forte*. We achieved our apogee almost together (myself a moment before my friend) just as Harry kindly reached out to lift my head, and to spurt forth a flood upon his belly and lower breast, which, by its copiousness, indicated the degree of his pleasure. (Though some doctors disagree, I have always supposed the keenness of a man's pleasure in the act is in proportion to the copiousness of his spending.)

There was now little conversation for half an hour, after which we reluctantly collected ourselves, donned our clothing, and made our way to Vane's house, where he busied himself with a kettle and produced a dish of tea, some bread and cold meats – an infinitely refreshing luncheon after the delightful and unexpected interlude of the forenoon.

Chapter Seven

The Adventures of Andy

Eastbourne is a place of resort which I feel strongly inclined to recommend to all who require a keen and animating air, for which it is almost unrivalled – a genteel, yet small watering-place not only providing the polite recreations of town but bringing the beauty of country scenes and stately trees almost close to the sea. Indeed, it is just the sort of small town which the friends upon whose business I was travelling had thought of providing, and my first reaction was that it made their plans supererogatory.

Three townships contain somewhat over 2,700 inhabitants: Eastbourne town is a mile and a half from the beach, the sea-houses, and Southbourne, which lies between the two. The walk to the sea from the Lamb Inn passes by, or leads through, the grounds of Compton-place, the seat of the Earl of Burlington – a pretty and commodious, though unpretending, villa with neat grounds, conservatories and lodges, and some fine trees. Nearer the town is the seat of my colleague Davies Gilbert Esq, MP, which also has some noble old trees, and sequestered park scenery; I would doubtless have been welcome to reside there had Mr Gilbert not been abroad at the time.

The sea-houses which form the actual watering-place are irregularly ranged along the beach, with no great extent or beauty; but they are substantial in size, comprising lodging houses, baths and the usual requisites, and certainly any person planning a centre of recreation along this coast would do well to reproduce something of the sort. Amongst the places of amusement are a library, billiard rooms and a small theatre, in South Street.

All this I was able to take in within an hour or so of walking about the town on the first morning of my stay there; when returning to the Lamb I found a card from Mlle Beauregard, inviting me to accompany her to the theatre that very evening. I naturally sent a message accepting her kind offer, and on our meeting she informed me that we were to be the guests of one of the company's leading performers, Mrs Clara Carclase, who (Mlle Beauregard confided) had expressed the desire to meet me upon her (the Mademoiselle) describing me – which was an interesting statement, since our knowledge of each other (apart from the carnal encounter which could surely not have been the subject of an idle conversation with another lady?) had been confined to but a few moments talk.

The play to be performed was Shakespeare's *As You Like It* – not an especial favourite of mine, but reasonably entertaining given excellent playing, which on this occasion it seemed unlikely to achieve through the efforts of a company playing so far out of town. But, indeed, from the very opening scene it had a lustre through the presence upon the boards of Mrs Carclase, pretty enough as the banished Duke's daughter, but ravishing when she changed into her man's habit – the breeches she wore being cut close to her lower limbs, showing off long legs, elegantly slim, and a bottom small and tight as a boy's – yet possessing those delectable curves which made it unmistakably a woman's. Nor was it possible for her altogether to disguise her bosoms, which though not plump were sufficiently rounded and peaked (her shirt being cut almost as closely to her breast as her trousers were to her arse) to display a degree of femininity which made the actor playing Orlando a nit wit for not recognising his mistress through her sex alone!

I must, I believe, have shown my admiration of the delightful Mrs Carclase more openly than I supposed, for Mlle Beauregard, taking advantage of our having a box to ourselves to place her hand upon my thigh in a position which would have been over familiar in anyone who had not previously been a close acquaintance, remarked that indeed Clara had a manner almost as fetching as her appearance, and offered the information that the title of 'Mrs' was given her in the complimentary manner of the stage, for she was not married.

She was born, it seems, in 1816 in Queen Street, May Fair, the daughter of a Captain Hehl, and was sent at an early age to a convent in France, from which, however, she derived but an imperfect education (except, as later appeared, in one matter). Having determined upon the stage as a profession, she applied for occupation to the manager of a small East-end theatre, the Coburg, and there she made her first appearance in public under the pseudonym of Miss Clara Carclase. Her next appearance was at the Pavilion as Zephyrina in *The Lady and the Devil*, and she had subsequently played in a great number of pieces, chiefly in the provinces.

'It is my opinion,' Mlle Beauregard stated (all this whispered under cover of a scene which did not require our attention, since Mrs Carclase did not appear in it), 'that no living actress can approach her in certain roles – particularly those which require the wearing of breeches – and if we except that slimness of figure which disappoints some gentlemen. She combines every qualification to produce a matchless embodiment of the piquant, the high-bred, the witty heroine.'

All this I could agree to, seeing her – and our conversation was indeed at this moment interrupted by Mrs Carclase's entrance in the third act of the comedy, when in her conversation with Orlando the lady in question reached a point of coquetry which was astonishingly arousing – she made so pretty a youth indeed that one could only wonder that the hero of the play could resist loving her even being convinced of her masculinity!

The play having ended in a tumult of applause, which the lady received as her due, we made our way from our box towards the back of the stage. On the way, I enquired why, in view of her remarkable talents, Mrs Carclase was not known to us in London? – to which Mlle Beauregard replied that it was partly through the actress's dislike of society – but that surely she would not long be able to disregard the pressure she was now under to present some of her more celebrated roles upon the boards of our metropolitan theatres.

Behind the scenes all was in the usual state of chaos, with the theatre's workmen demolishing the woodland of the Forest of Arden and establishing the sitting room in which the comedy of *The School for Scandal* would be performed upon the following night. In one corner, imperfectly concealed by a screen, some of those ladies and gentlemen of the company employed only in the meaner parts were changing their clothes, and exhibiting to any passer-by tracts of flesh which those not used to the somewhat cavalier life of the theatre would hesitate to expose to strangers except in the most intimate circumstances.

Mrs Carclase was still upon the stage, and in conversation with the colleague who had taken the part of Orlando, her hand upon his arm; she seemed to be pleading with him, and as we approached I heard him utter the words, 'My exhaustion is such that I find it impossible to accede to your request.' At which he bowed and left her.

At this moment, Mlle Beauregard took her opportunity to introduce us, with the comment that the actress would find me most agreeable company. Mrs Carclase's eyes seemed positively to glitter as she greeted me, and I could not miss the fact that she appeared not to find me repugnant – indeed, as she repeated my name she laid upon my arm, with an insinuating pressure, that hand which had only a moment previously been upon that of her fellow player.

She acknowledged my congratulations upon her performance with a sort of perfunctory grace, then kindly invited me to converse further with her in her dressing room – 'But perhaps, sir, you would give me first a few moments to remove these appurtenances of masculinity?'

I bowed briefly, and the lady made off, first indicating the direction in which her room was to be found.

'"A hit, a palpable hit!"' said Mlle Beauregard (in a quotation from another play), and upon my raising my eyebrows remarked that she could see that Mrs Carclase had immediately taken a liking to me. But before I could enquire precisely what she meant by the statement, she had excused herself and made off, and I found myself alone and in the way of the bustling scene-changers. I walked to a corner of the stage – which happened to be that where the other members of the company were engaged in changing their clothes. Here I was somewhat less obstructive, nor did the ladies and gentlemen indifferently concealed by the screen repine at my presence, one young gentleman indeed walking up to me clad only in a shirt which came barely below his belly, and invited me to take a chair – but on his eyeing me up and down I inferred that his invitation was one which might be directed at more than my immediate comfort, and declined (whereupon a buxom lady nearby giggled in a slightly bitter way, and remarked that Jack had scored another disappointment, going on to whisper something in the young gentleman's ear which resulted in his look of admiration turning to something of a sneer).

I waited for a few moments and then crossed the back of the stage, and stepping over the tree upon which Orlando had earlier hung his verses (how speedily does the fantasy of the theatre vanish when its delights are seen strewn in confusion behind the scenes), enquired of a gentleman where I might find Mrs Carclase's room.

Following his directions I made my way up a narrow stair, and at the top knocked at the door I found there, which was almost immediately opened by the lady with a warm exclamation of greeting.

The promptness of her attendance did not surprise me, for she was after all expecting me; nor was I astonished at the relative bareness of the room – which contained only a single chair, a table and looking glass, and a sofa – for I had had previous experience of the lack of comfort to be experienced in the dressing rooms of all but the most luxurious theatres.

What did surprise me, however, was the fact that Mrs Carclase opened to me clad only in that apparel offered to each of us upon our birth – that is, in nothing but her skin. Nor did she appear in the least hesitant to display herself to me in so frank a manner, but far from apologising or reaching for a piece of clothing to cover herself, she merely gripped my arm and drew me in, slamming the door with one hand and turning a key with an adeptness which suggested some practice. She then threw her arms about my neck and immediately planted a kiss upon my lips.

That I was not reluctant to receive such a compliment will surprise no one; but the action was not one I had expected, having experienced so immediate an approach only from professional exponents of the art of love – and in such cases only from those with whom a certain familiarity had made such a form of greeting apposite.

However, it was impossible to reject Miss Carclase's advance – not only through common politeness but through the sweetness of those lips which now opened in order to allow the play of an equally honeyed tongue, and which were quite sufficiently entrancing to seduce any gentleman. Moreover, counting (and with reason) upon the ingratiating nature of the kiss to prevent my drawing away, she had now lowered her hands, and – again with such skill as to suggest considerable application – undone my belt, insinuating her hands sufficiently between it and my body to lower my breeches to a degree which enabled her to confirm that the contiguousness of her naked body had had its effect.

Even had I been averse to such treatment, I would have found it impossible to recoil from her advances: is there any emotion keener than that experienced by a gentleman upon feeling a cool and unfamiliar female's hand falling upon his prick? I know of none; the anticipation raised by the frankness of such a gesture, the promise of further emotion to come, conspire to throw down the strongest defences which may be offered by morality.

That I was happy to receive her approach clearly pleased her, for my thoroughly aroused staff had not been held for more than a moment in the palm of her hand before, rejecting my lips, she sank to her knees, and, without even that moment's hesitation with which the most lascivious lady usually prefaces such an action, drew back with her fingers that hood of skin which now barely covered the dome of my prick, took me between her lips, and began such an ingratiating motion as proved her to be no tyro in the matter of oral stimulation of the male member – for not content with the up and down action which, while satisfying, is merely the obvious one, she rolled my member between her lips, kissed its length as though 'twere a pipe upon which she was playing, allowed its head to lie upon her tongue while her upper lip trembled upon it; and in short displayed all the skills of the naturally accomplished mistress.

It was one of those moments in the biography of a man's carnal life which imprints itself for ever upon the senses: I had now, for the first time, the opportunity of viewing the lady's body, although from such an angle as made a real conception of it difficult: for below the head of dark hair, relatively closely cropped, I could see only her back – a slim plane, tapering but slightly from narrow, shapely shoulders to a waist below which there swelled those oval spheres which presented a backside dented like a peach, the firm femininity of which had been sufficiently attractive in breeches, and which now, in a state of nature, lost none of its delightfulness.

I lost no time in shrugging my coat to the floor, where it was swiftly followed by my shirt. Bending, I caught the lady beneath the arms and persuaded her reluctantly to forgo her feast and rise, then after a swift embrace I stepped back for that moment necessary to step out of my breeches, before once clasping her in my arms and half carrying her (she needed no persuasion) to the sofa, upon which we both fell – it happily proving sufficiently substantial (despite its obvious age) to bear our combined weight, and sufficiently broad to make it a bed which would not too thoroughly restrict our motions.

I now sat up and for a brief moment inspected the entire aspect of the prize which lay beside me: now that she was no longer disguised in male dress, her femininity could not be in question. Within the triangle of dark hair between her thighs, slightly protruding purple lips seemed to pout in anticipation of that attention which they were shortly to receive – while those breasts whose presence had been suggested by the swelling of her shirt were now presented as possessing contours peculiarly tender: small and firm to the touch (for I could not resist testing the malleability of one with a finger's tip), they were nevertheless completely feminine, and betrayed as unmistakably as the lady's whole demeanour the extent of her passionate desire for masculine company, for each tit was gathered into a shape the size and almost the obduracy of a hazelnut, and almost of the same degree of brownness, and on my brushing one with a finger her whole frame shook.

My eagerness was now great – and was not diminished either by the lady's evident enthusiasm or by her once more diving her hand between my thighs and gathering up what she found there, gently squeezing the parcel in a manner as suggestive as it seemed admiring. I therefore rose and – not needing to prompt any movement from her, for she threw them open with a willing gesture – knelt between her thighs in preparation for the assault which I believed both of us wished.

Her own fervour for the moment prevented it, however – for there are moments when a desire for a simple embrace is stronger even than that for a penetration; and she now lifted herself upon her hands until she sat astride my thighs, my distended organ pressed between our bellies, and, throwing her arms about my neck, once more pressed such a kiss upon my lips as might have been given by the angel Shekinah – so tender but at the same time so hot!

My palms now passed down her back, the fingers touching, as it seemed, each distinct knob of her spine (so particular and individual was each, and so devoid was her person of any undue fleshiness), until they fell each upon a globe of her delectable haunches, to draw her even further to me and lift her body slightly so that I could feel at the base of my cock those other willing lips which I trusted soon to test. As this action occurred, my fingers slipped so into the groove between her cheeks that they grazed the most intimate part – which had the result which (we are told) is that of a shock of electricity – for her entire body was galvanised by a spasm which shook us both; and rising only sufficiently to free completely that part of me necessary to the result she required, she sank upon it with an emotion compounded of relief and ecstasy.

So high had our senses been raised by our proximity –

even though it had largely lacked those preparatory caresses more usually employed on such an occasion – that those parts of our body where conjunction occurred were bathed in the liquid emoluments essential to a comfortable jointure. Even so I was conscious of the narrowness of the passage into which I was now welcomed; the head of my prick passing into it almost like a cork through the neck of a bottle before being released into the most comfortable and voluptuous conduit. Here, every motion was accompanied by an all embracing caress; yet the very action of penetration had been enough to bring us both, as I believe at the same moment, to the very edge of the abyss – and upon only a moment's hesitation I came with a violence which drew an involuntary cry of pleasure from my lips, while she threw her head back, and her teeth clenched upon her lower lip with such force that I saw a bead of blood stand there.

I must for a moment pause to remark that here was an example of the truth that the quality of the orgasm is not always to be judged by the nature of the preparatory pleasure. Both the preliminaries and the culmination are of course delicious, and neither should be denigrated or rejected; but just as I have known occasions when (as now) a wonderful culmination is the result merely of an immediate conjunction of willing and ready partners, without more rehearsal than is absolutely necessary – I have also known occasions when perhaps as much of an hour has been spent in the most entrancing play, but led only to an apogee satisfying but devoid of remarkable intensity. Indeed, upon occasion I have spent an hour at leisure with the most inventive whore, all of whose skills have been employed to give pleasure, and have given it – yet the inevitable result has altogether lacked bite;

only a few hours later to experience the most remarkable zenith, the result merely of a sudden and unprepared coupling.

But it is anomalies such as these that make the art of love such a continual and fascinating study for those of us who approach it in an enquiring, as well as a celebratory, state of mind.

To return to my narrative, Mrs Carclase and I remained for a long moment in that position in which our delight had overtaken us: her slim thighs astride my own more substantial ones, my prick beginning to slink from that orifice which had welcomed it so willingly. I lowered my head in order to take up with my tongue the single bead of perspiration which hung like a jewel from the tip of one breast, and then transferring my lips to the lady's own, assisted her to dismount; whereupon we half reclined side by side, but head to tail, and exchanged a smile which assured me that this lady – unlike some as eager for the fray as herself – was not one of those whose love turned to dislike the moment an encounter had reached its first conclusion. Our heads upon each other's thighs, for some time we remained in a state of lethargy, then:

'I should perhaps ask your pardon for my eagerness,' she presently exclaimed; and upon my opening my mouth to protest, held a finger to her lips, 'but your own fervour suggests that you understand that the occasion of recognising a readiness for congress as complete as one's own is ever the excuse for a lack of polite hesitation!'

I was happy to agree, and to recognise in Mrs Carclase that rare thing, a female as ready to admit the compulsory nature of her own appetite as some (though by no means all) men.

'Though,' she said, on my remarking upon the fact, 'it is

not all gentlemen to whom I am able to acknowledge the fact, for some are scandalised by it. Nor is it always the case that gentlemen are ready to respond to an immediate approach by an equally immediate acceptance. Which makes it all the more delightful when someone to whom I take an instant liking is happy to return the tribute I feel impelled to offer him.'

I nodded, and the lady went on to pay some compliments which I do not feel the need to repeat, since they were entirely personal, and had reference not only to the size and obduracy of my tool (which other ladies have indeed remarked upon) but to other characteristics, such as the show of hair upon my buttocks, which I have ever regarded as unattractive (to the point even of considering having my haunches shaved, when eager to impress some female target): nothing, this lady confessed, so raised her spirits as a hirsute gentleman (not, she went on to state, to the extent of his being so covered with hair as to resemble an animal; but a skirmishing of hair upon the haunches, thighs, belly, chest and arms was entirely desirable).

My own eagerness (I replied) was no more than the mirror of the lady's own eagerness – which she acknowledged. We were then, she said, two of a kind – for I was a ready lover, while she must admit to being what she called a 'nymphomaniac'.

This was the first occasion upon which I had heard that word used in polite conversation by a lay person; I knew it, indeed, only through conversation with a doctor – my friend Dr Pensworthy, of Cambridge, whose care it was to make a study of the human procreative instinct. Hearing him on one occasion remark that 'nymphomaniacal symptoms are invariably present when young females are insane', I had asked his meaning, and he had defined 'nymphomania' as 'a feminine disease characterised by morbid and excessive sexual desire'. Mrs Carclase now confirmed that she too had become aware of the term through a medical friend – and agreed with Pensworthy's definition, although she demurred at the word 'morbid', and was inclined to think that 'excessive' was a complimentary rather than a denigratory description. Nor, I need not perhaps add, did she consider herself a prey to insanity.

'The best-known of us all,' she said (speaking of the clan of nymphomaniacs as though members of an established club) 'was certainly Valeria Messaline of ancient Rome, who married the Emperor Claudius when she was only sixteen, and had even then already enjoyed at least two years of active sensual life.

'She was happy in being married to so complaisant a husband,' Mrs Carclase remarked, 'for, you know, if her eye fell upon a likely fellow, her husband would happily procure him for her and order him to submit to her every whim – while in return (the historian Dio Cassius remarks) she would keep her lustful husband well supplied with housemaids for his bedfellows, while she often enjoyed herself in the local brothel.'

I must admit that these were facts of which I was not aware, and I was as pleased as I was surprised to find Mrs Carclase so educated as to have a grounding in the classics; on my remarking of which, she explained that she had learned Latin at the French convent where she had been educated, and while the nun who had taught her had carefully restricted her reading to those classics which she regarded as 'harmless' (necessarily omitting many of the works, for instance, of Ovid) she had been fortunate enough to be befriended by another nun, whose interests were nearer those of a woman of the outside world.

This lady (Mrs Carclase revealed) had taken it upon herself to educate her pupil in more practical matters than Latin verbs; partly (it must be confessed) for her own pleasure, for she had conceived a strong attraction to the young Clara, whose first carnal encounter had been with her mistress; but unlike some ladies of her persuasion, her teacher had confessed that there was such a thing as a conjunction of male and female – and using what she called a *dildo* had even shown the girl what to expect of the male member, which the nun herself averred ignorance of, but which she nevertheless drew with such accuracy that Mrs Carclase now suspected that her life outside the nunnery must have been less innocent than she would have had it believed.

The young girl's experiences with the dildo (which I should explain to those readers who have not encountered the term, is a simulacrum – in polished wood, ivory or some other material – of the erect male member) was such as to convince her that full coition was likely to be more delightful even than the caresses of her teacher's fingers and lips – skilfully though these (she said) were deployed. An encounter with a gardener's boy had convinced her of it; and she had early made it her ambition to test the delightfulness of coition by experiencing it as fully as might be; an ambition which she had ever since pursued.

By this time it was clear that Mrs Carclase's mind was running once more upon less intellectual lines, for she had permitted a hand to stray first to my knee, and then to the inside of my thigh, whence it proceeded to lie upon my ductile prick, which although only ten minutes had elapsed since its last employment had been enjoyably terminated, now began to raise its head, or at least to thicken somewhat under the warm caress.

'Perhaps,' said Mrs Carclase, 'since my eagerness deprived us of that enjoyable period of play with which every civilised congress should ideally be prefaced, you would not be averse to a little preliminary sport now?'

That I had no objection goes without saying: whereupon Mrs Carclase rose, and from a corner of the room produced a large fur of some kind – which, she said, was one she had acquired to wear as a cloak upon her first entrance as Lady Macbeth, but which was more usually employed for the purpose for which she now intended it: spreading it out upon the floor to make a bed from which there would be no danger of our toppling should our passions be so far aroused as to dull our sense of balance. She then disposed herself upon it, and within a very few moments was demonstrating that her adeptness in the preliminaries to congress was a perfect complement to her eagerness for the act itself.

I would be supererogatory to describe in detail those manœuvres with which we celebrated the sensitivity of various areas of our bodies to the touch of an ingenious partner; but I cannot but record that I have rarely met a woman so eager and ready to respond to even the slightest hint of pleasure in my reaction to a caress – thus, when she discovered my anus (or to use the common parlance, arsehole) to be peculiarly receptive to the tentative probing of a finger, she did not for a moment hesitate to test how much more deliciously her tongue could titillate that area so often neglected by lovers of either sex (but which, provided cleanliness is meticulously observed, need be no more offensive than man's attention to the most obvious of female orifices). Indeed, by throwing my legs over her shoulders and raising my buttocks, she was able to devote herself to that latter portion of my body to such effect that I was reduced almost to a female hysteria of pleasure, something which amused as well as intrigued her – though she later admitted to me that most gentlemen reacted in the same manner, no doubt due to the extreme rarity with which their partners showed a willingness to please them in that way.

Mrs Carclase's readiness for all primed my own enthusiasm, and I was not slow to react by attempting to find the happiest way of pleasing *her*: but this was difficult, since almost every motion I made seemed to delight her equally – though she seemed particularly receptive to my teasing her nipples with the tip of that object most blatantly the advertisement of my admiration (which she then attempted to close between her breasts, these however – being small – proving inadequate to the task of entirely surrounding it; whereupon with a charming laugh, she merely passed it rapidly over the surface of those charming orbs before admonishing me to allow her another taste of it, which I was by no means reluctant to do, since her expertise in oral manipulation was as extraordinary as her other skills).

On the moment coming when it was necessary – through fatigue as much as through our exhausting (for the time) those means of pleasure suggested even by the widest imagination – to reach a culmination, she surprised me by turning and kneeling with her back to me, and on my presenting my prick at the proper entrance asking, with a shy smile, whether I would object to using another aperture? Nothing loath, I was happy (having first, for fear of injuring her, lubricated the opening with a generous application of saliva) to agree, whereupon her rapture (expressed by a peculiarly inspiring wriggling action) was considerable.

I must confess that my own was somewhat less so; for given the pleasure of the resistance offered upon the initial presentation of the weapon to the orifice in question, once past that narrow gap there is no sensation such as the warm embrace of every surface offered by even the slackest quim. It is one reason (apart from custom and the law) which has ever made such a connection with members of my own sex relatively undesirable to me. However, ladies are occasionally particularly gratified by the posture we now adopted, and Mrs Carclase was clearly one of them, for in no time (and with the added compliment of my applying my fingers to that area of her person where I had rather been sheathed) her shrieks had twice advertised a climax; whereupon she was kind enough to invite me to take my own pleasure, and I was happy to withdraw and apply, this time, to the conventional avenue – the doors opening freely and the hallway being so warm and welcoming that I was immediately completely delighted, and the two of us collapsed without apology into a sort of swoon.

I enquired, on our resuming our clothing (not without regret, despite our state of enervation) whether she would wish me to leave first, for the sake of her reputation. However, she confessed that her predilection for the company of gentlemen was well known among her fellow actors, and even – by now – in the town; indeed, upon her once remarking, at a party, that when she acted a breeches part half the audience *believed* her to be a *man*, one wag had replied that the other half *knew* her to be a *woman*! – an anecdote she repeated with good humour.

As we walked from the theatre into the town, we encountered Mlle Beauregard, who condescended to enquire whether our encounter had been enjoyable; I must confess to blushing – a rare phenomenon. Mrs Carclase, however, replied that as her friend had suggested, I was one of the most adept, witty and inventive of conversationalists – whereupon both ladies smiled, acknowledged each other, and decided to take tea. While I, within twenty minutes, was as soundly asleep as the reader might suppose was necessary after such exertions.

Chapter Eight

Sophie's Story

On hearing that I was to visit Brighton my friend General George Obliveon, who had a position on the staff of His Majesty, enquired whether I would be interested to visit that Pavilion which the late King had erected there while he was Prince of Wales; and on my expressing some enthusiasm, kindly gave me a letter of introduction to Sir Herbert Taylor, who had been placed in charge of the building on King William's behalf – His Majesty showing no interest in the place, his inclinations being upon a less grand and less eccentric scale than those of his elder brother.

On my sending a note round to Sir Herbert's lodging he kindly waited upon me at my hotel, and to my pleasure turned out to be a gentleman of younger rather than middle years, with a dashing pair of moustaches, a confident air, and a person quite sufficiently charming. He offered to show me around the Pavilion on the following afternoon, and on my acquiescing called for me at three o'clock and walked me to the Steyn and the garden-front of the magnificent palace, which consists of three pavilions connected by two ranges of buildings – the centre with that large, bulbous-shaped dome so much resembling those of the churches in the Kremlin at Moscow, and flanked by minarets consisting of open cupolas on tall pillars.

We entered the building through the kitchens, sadly lacking in that bustle which would have signified the place being occupied, but with all the furniture in the most brilliant state of polish. Passing through the stately and beautiful dining room, we then came to the Chinese gallery – of immense length, with walls throughout of a dark pink or lilac, termed peach blossom, with foliage and birds painted in a subdued style of pale blue, which produces a very good combination. At the north and south ends are double staircases of iron, the fronts of the steps of open work giving them a very airy appearance, and the railings painted in imitation of bamboo. These staircases lead to a gallery with bedrooms on each side.

The general furniture is either really, or an imitation of, oriental. The centre chimneypiece resembles bamboo, while the open cabinets on the opposite side are actually of that material, covered with fine yellow marble slabs. There are various painted lanterns and Chinese cabinets with rare vases and figures; and the carpet, of English manufacture, is handsome and appropriate.

The dining room is sixty foot long and forty-two wide, and is transcendently beautiful – not merely oriental, still less barbaric, but with a quiet and chaste beauty – the *coup d'œil* being that of walls of mother-of-pearl with historic groups in rich enamels, varied by candelabra of blue lapis lazuli, surmounted by glass lilies and immense chandeliers of numerous flowers in silvery glass. The ceiling has a spacious and lofty dome occupied by a painted plantain tree from which hangs the principal lustre, which is thirty feet from top to bottom!

It is the music room which is by general consent marked out as the most beautiful of the palace, and indeed merits the honour, for it is the most splendid apartment, again with a fine dome, and with walls covered with crimson and gold Japan representing Chinese scenery, said to be taken from actual examples in the neighbourhood of that far famed but little known metropolis, Pekin.

I must not delay too long in descriptions of this nature, but cannot forbear to mention the organ – built by Lincoln in 1818, and unquestionably one of the most powerful, yet sweet-toned ones in England, with a compass from C.C.C. with a double diapason throughout, three rows of keys, twenty-eight stops and twenty pedals. Nor should one neglect to note the very grand mirror over the chimneypiece, about twelve feet by eight, with a gilded canopy supported by columns, and, in front, a curious and elaborately patterned timepiece – all presenting a most noble effect.

Sir Herbert was an admirable guide, who did not flinch from repeating yet again those facts and descriptions which he must have uttered upon innumerable occasions – for, thanks to the graciousness and generosity of His present Majesty, visits to the palace are not difficult to procure (which were almost impossible in the late King's day). Sir Herbert's attentions were most civil, but gradually became warmer as he realised my genuine interest and the friendliness of my disposition – and I was even inclined to suspect that he admired me, for he seemed increasingly to take any excuse to place a hand on my arm, or in the small of my back, when directing me around a corner or through a door.

Having shown me the organ, he now asked if I was curious to see the private apartments of the late King George IV, and on my expressing an interest, conducted me once more into the Chinese Gallery, and thence into several smaller and more domestic apartments on the ground floor, characterised on the whole by neatness and consistency: among them the sleeping room of the late King, containing a plain and simple bed, a golden Jordon still placed beneath it, and near the room a set of baths supplied from the sea – a remarkable example of engineering, the shore being at some considerable distance from the Pavilion.

I could not but mention to Sir Herbert my surprise at the simple furnishings of the bedroom, for like everyone else in the Kingdom I had heard of His Majesty's predilection for the other sex – at least in his youth – and had expected a less chaste couch. But Sir Herbert explained that the King had frequently entertained guests here (members of the clergy, for instance, and some of his ministers) who would have regarded any outward sign of sensual excess with displeasure; it was therefore politic to give at least the impression of restraint through the simple furnishing to be seen here.

'However,' he said, 'you may be interested in a phenomenon I do not usually display to ladies, but which I think you would appreciate . . .' And passing along the side of the bed, he reached around behind its headboard and appeared to depress a handle, for immediately, and with a smooth action which argued the most careful work in the construction of the trick, the simple single bed revolved, and its place was taken by a much larger divan which issued from the wall behind it! This was much more the sort of couch I had imagined the builder of the palace to occupy, and could not resist sitting upon it to test its resilience, which was considerable. Sir Herbert smiled to see my pleasure, and enquired whether I thought it was sufficiently comfortable? It had been built (as he remarked, somewhat unnecessarily) for pleasure, and as he understood it had been well used.

I replied that it struck me as an admirable platform for those performances for which it had been intended, which I understood were many.

'Indeed,' responded Sir Herbert, 'and I may say that such performances still occasionally take place, for some ladies feel it a particular pleasure to test that field laid out by a prince for gladiatorial conquest.'

I smiled, and he took this for the kind of response which he expected, enquiring with a gentility which made his question entirely unobjectionable, whether I would care to join that somewhat restricted club of ladies who could say that they had occupied the bed?

'But to do that without the company of an amiable companion,' I remarked, 'would be against nature!'

I must confess to a mischief, for I was in no doubt that Sir Herbert saw himself in just such a role – nor did I repine when, with perfect courtesy, he made the fact clear, for he was an upright and stalwart fellow, not to be supposed incapable of playing his part in any scene he proposed. He took my hand, then, and raising it to his lips confessed to an admiration which would make it a pleasure for him, should I accede, to play the part of Prince to my Princess!

My reply was to unbuckle that ceremonial sword which he wore as part of his uniform, and after only a brief time found myself able, without the restriction of his dress uniform, to handle that other sword which had as much tone and resilience as the first.

His figure, when revealed in full, was somewhat more upright and solid than that which is my ideal; through (no doubt) many days of drilling, his legs and back had a straightness and stiffness which seemed perhaps insufficiently capable of that limber and easy motion which is best able to give pleasure in that posture in which we were shortly to place ourselves.

He proved, however, to be by no means a tyro at the game – indeed, I suspected him of as many seductions as there had been female visitors to whom he had revealed the bed upon which we now fell; and while his first addresses were more than a little perfunctory, upon thrusting his sword into its apposite sheath he showed every indication of being what the racing fraternity describe as 'a stayer', for the motion which he made was that of an easy, regular and steady canter, making up in relentlessness what his addresses lacked in subtlety.

Lying as I now did upon my back, I was interested to see that a series of ingeniously disposed mirrors, which at first sight had seemed innocently placed about the walls, now showed in miniature, and from a number of angles, a complete view of the bed and its occupants, so that wherever I looked I had a prospect of Sir Herbert's busy rump – powerful and bulky rather than shapely, and constructed, as one might say, for use rather than ornament. I am by no means insensitive to a beautiful backside; but must confess that in the situation in which I now found myself there was something to be said for simple power, and Sir Herbert certainly made up in staunchness what he lacked in beauty, showing no sign of readiness to leave off until I had twice been roused to my peak – when, for the second time letting him know by a cry of pleasure that I was pleased with him, he simply drew the sword from the scabbard and packed it away, apparently without relieving himself of those emotions which had roused him to the degree of interest necessary for the whetting of his weapon.

I expressed some surprise at this: whereupon he explained that he had learned during some time spent in India the practice of *carezza*, as it is called – the ability to perform and receive pleasure from the act of love without necessarily enjoying that zenith which most men consider its proper end.

'The point is,' he explained in a most frank manner, 'that in this way one may enjoy as many partners as one pleases without the necessity to disappoint a second or third friend through sensual exhaustion.'

I could not repine, for I had had my pleasure of the gentleman; though somehow even his protestations that he had enjoyed the act failed entirely to satisfy my female nature, which is one which demands a positive proof of the completion of a lover's pleasure. Would he not, I suggested, return to bed and permit me to . . .

Sir Herbert, I was interested to see, blushed at this; and when pressed remarked that he had a commitment to what he called The Fitz Club, which had a meeting that very day which would demand his attention – an attention he could not give if he did not for the moment reserve his powers.

The reader will suppose that I pressed him on the matter; and realising by now that my nature was not one to repine at an adventure, he offered to make me privy to the Club – though membership was by invitation, he was sure that I would be accepted since (he was sufficiently complimentary to remark) I had as to my figure, face and person all those qualities most agreeable to the ladies and gentlemen who comprised the association.

We now resumed our dress, and upon being once more respectable, Sir Herbert escorted me from the bedroom, along a passage, and into the baths. These consisted of two rooms the walls of which were constructed of panels of slate – the baths themselves being sunk into the floor, the water, when present (for at this time they were empty), being heated by channels beneath it, passing from a nearby furnace.

Walking to a pair of handsome taps fixed into the wall above the central bath, Sir Herbert turned first one, and then the other – I noticed that one turned to the right, and the other to the left, which was an unexpected and interesting phenomenon. He then took the spout which stood out from the wall below them (from which no water had issued) and tugged upon it, whereupon a whole panel of slate swung aside to reveal a staircase leading into the bowels of the earth.

Handing me down the stairs, Sir Herbert procured from a niche a torch, and having lighted it took my arm and led me along a tunnel which seemed to pass for a very considerable distance through the earth. On my enquiring as to its purpose, Sir Herbert referred to that illicit romance which the Prince Regent had conducted with the beautiful Mrs Fitzherbert. Denied by his position the possibility of marriage to his mistress (although it is rumoured that such a marriage indeed took place), the Prince, when building the Pavilion, had taken care to construct this underground passage communicating directly between his own quarters and Mrs

Fitzherbert's house, not too far distant to render such a feat of engineering impractical; the purpose being to facilitate meetings which could be kept entirely secret from the inquisitive eyes of his father's courtiers or the spies of the Government.

As he finished explaining this, we came to a set of upward steps which led steeply past what I believed to be the level of the street, and ended in a small room with, at one end, what appeared to be a spyglass.

'Were I not entirely sure that you are a woman of the world,' Sir Herbert said (it seemed in a last attempt to assure himself that he made no mistake in taking me into his confidence), 'I would neither suggest your introduction to the Fitz Club, nor invite you – as I now do – to make use of the spyglass which the Prince constructed in order to reassure himself that none of his father's spies had by any means gained entrance to his beloved's chamber ...' And he gestured me towards the glass.

On looking through it I found it to be constructed so as to provide a diminished prospect of the entire room – a room which appeared to me to be ablaze with light; this was doubtless partly because my eyes had become accustomed to the gloom of the passage, but also because through climbing so many stairs we were now at the top of the house in East Street to which the secret corridor led (a house which, with a touch of irony, now faces that fine bronze statue of George IV by Chauntrey which, on a pedestal nine feet in height, stands in a pose far more dignified than those in which he must so often have placed himself with his mistress after following the course we had followed, and entering the room into which I now looked).

The room, being as I have said at the very top of the house, was lit by a large skylight which could be (as it now was) entirely drawn back, with the result that to all effects the room had no ceiling – allowing the rays of the sun to pass directly into it, and thus facilitating for at least two hours of each day that sunbathing which (it seems) the late King favoured during those earlier years when the sight of his unclothed body was not such a trial to onlookers as it later (through increased avoirdupois) became. The room was in such use at the moment – or, at least, sunbathing was one of the purposes for which it was being used.

It was occupied by three couples, all unclad and lying in the sun upon the floor, which appeared to consist not of hard boards but of some kind of mattress, for (as I was soon to discover) while insufficiently soft to be displeasing to heated bodies, it was at the same time quite comfortable enough to lie upon without bruising.

No lasciviousness was in progress, unless one counts those pleasant informalities which naturally occur between familiars – such as one gentleman tracing with a finger the fine line of his companion's hip, or a lady permitting her hand to lie upon the inside of her lover's thigh (without, however, any toying likely to have an effect upon his prick, which if swollen to any notable degree might have been damaged by the rays of the sun, such burning being uncomfortable enough when affecting any surface of the body, but particularly so in that place). There seemed at the moment to be a greater interest in the wine which was being tasted than in any more carnal activity.

But my companion now without ceremony pressed a spring, and the door in which was set the glass through which I looked, opened, and encouraged by him we stepped through it. The interest of those gathered there in seeing me did not seem unusual, and it turned out that it had been suggested to them that an additional lady might be presented to the Club – of which these were six of the members. (Again, I could conjecture that Sir Herbert's powers of persuasion were often exercised upon amiable females viewing the Prince Regent's bedroom, and were successful with sufficient frequency to ensure that his fellow members would have been more surprised had he appeared alone, than should he appear accompanied.)

While we undressed (for this was clearly a desideratum, and one to which I readily acceded, since as a guest it was clearly my duty to do so) I was informed that the Club had been formed some years since at the behest of one of the gentlemen present, Sir Tunbridge Waller, who had become the owner of the house in question and who upon breaking through a sealed door at the top of it had come upon the present chamber, and finding by accident the secret door, and following the course of the passage, had emerged in his late Majesty's private baths, which Sir Herbert at that moment was showing to a lady – as it happened, one of the ladies to whom I was now introduced, and who had just been testing the Prince's bed in the manner I have described earlier in the present chapter.

It had seemed both to Sir Tunbridge and Sir Herbert that it behoved them to carry on the tradition established by the Prince – both being strong supporters of those customs to which this country owes its historical greatness, and among which the enjoyment by its heroes of the company of ingratiating females was certainly one. The Fitz Club was consequently formed – its name, of course, taken from the former owner of the house, that Mrs Fitzherbert who was the Prince's favourite and perhaps his wife. The Club was restricted to a dozen members, and met irregularly, each meeting being convened when no fewer than two and no more than four couples felt inclined to an hour's dalliance (the room not being sufficiently capacious conveniently to contain more than eight people at one time).

My membership of the Club appeared to be taken for granted, though in common politeness I demurred: would I not disturb the balance of the meeting? I asked, since surely ladies and gentlemen were matched upon a pre-ordained basis.

Not at all, was the reply; indeed the whole point of the Club was that while couples joined it who were accustomed to each other's company, and were in some cases actually married, its purpose was to combat that *ennui* which is necessarily the accompaniment of a regular liaison. It must be a recognised fact that a continual diet even of caviare (and most gentlemen provide something more akin to roast beef, or even a pudding, than anything so unusual and delicious) can become boring after a period of years, or even of months; and a relationship can only be enlivened by a change of diet, provided that both the lady and gentleman concerned are agreed upon enjoying one. It must be an acknowledged fact that excursions outside the bounds of a regular liaison only sharpen the appetite for the usual partner.

Sir Herbert explained the procedure which, should I agree to it, would now be followed; and on my naturally agreeing – I was, after all, the guest of the members of the Club and must agree with its customs – I was (having first relieved myself once more of my clothing, something which caused no embarrassment in a company, the members of which were already in a state of nature) in a very short time blindfolded by a long strip of silk, and turned and turned about before being released. The other members of the Club in the meantime disposed themselves in recumbent positions about the room; and I was left to feel my way among them until, for one reason or for another, I found a partner whose lineaments, explored only by means of touch, gratified me – it having been suggested that for the time Sir Herbert should absent himself from the group, since he had already (as he said with a flattering enthusiasm) made himself familiar with my talents.

Having lowered myself to my hands and knees (if only to allay that slight dizziness consequent upon my being turned about), my hand first fell upon a calf, clearly (from its hairyness) that of a gentleman, and I carefully drew my fingers up its length, past the knee, and . . . but here I met a clutch of hair which seemed remarkably thick, and upon examining further discovered that it was attached to the head of a lady who, doubtless over-eager for pleasure, had fixed her lips (as only a little further exploration revealed) firmly about a prick which, from the hardness of its base and the manner in which the cods were drawn up, was delighted to receive her attentions.

I removed my hand with a start, not wishing to embarrass – though from the manner in which the gentleman in question lifted the upper part of his body in order to plant a kiss on or around my cunny, this was not an emotion much regarded by the members of the Club, and I resolved not to allow my explorations to be restricted by it. Kneeling at the side of the couple I had first encountered, I found my thigh pressing against a pair of buttocks which at first I was unable to place, as to sex – though I suspected from their shape that they might be masculine, and upon passing my hand over a convex surface sufficiently devoid of hair to be female, discovered indeed that an unattended but standing prick stood adjacent.

The gentleman in question was clearly not unoccupied, and feeling upwards past his belly and breast, I found his head to be thrust between a pair of thighs sufficiently soft to be unmistakably female, and in order to show from the start my amenability to whatever stimulation was upon offer, I laid myself upon my back and passing my head between the thighs of the gentleman, took his instrument between my lips and began to give it an attentive sucking – the action bringing a moment's applause from the party (as well as a somewhat muffled cry of approval, presumably from the possessor of the organ in question).

I felt, meanwhile, my ankles being taken in hand and drawn apart so that my exposed lower body was entirely open to caresses, which then began by hands (and more than one pair!) the sex of which I was entirely unable to conjecture, their tenderness being equally kind; they restricted themselves first to the most gentle caresses, but I then felt them replaced by lips and even tongues, two of which approached my intimate parts and, my lower lips being ever so gently drawn apart, played about them with the most avaricious delight.

After only a few moments of such attentions, I was ready to cease my ministrations to that cock and balls most accessible to me, and wriggling out from between the thighs which supported them, sat up and throwing out my hands discovered that upon my left lay a gentleman, and on my right a lady, who were applying themselves to pleasing me with equal enthusiasm.

Will my readers blame me for turning to the left? I must assure them (should they need such assurance) that I am by no means antipathetic to the caresses of my own sex, and indeed upon many occasions have enjoyed them. But equally, all those ladies who are not by a natural disposition drawn exclusively to their own sex, will perhaps agree with me that given a free choice we must incline towards the gentlemen, the possessors of those instruments which must ever be regarded as the desirable arrows to our bows, swords to our sheaths, or whatever other similes come to mind.

My decision was this time partly confirmed by the fact that on reaching out I found my hand in possession of a machine of the most remarkable dimensions. I had, I confess, noted while I still had my sight, that one of the gentlemen, somewhat darker as to skin than the others, and perhaps the youngest of them, seemed to possess a prick of an unusual size, even lying as it did in a relatively squab state upon its owner's thigh. Now, I could be in no doubt as to its remarkable proportions, for I found that on moving my hand up its length it seemed to have no end (though I later discovered that it was no more than about eleven inches in length), and, attempting to close my hand around it, I for a moment almost fainted with horror, for my forefinger and thumb could not nearly meet about its circumference, which would surely be likely to split open any lady whose organ was of a usual size.

Despite such an irrational fear – what male organ can be dangerous to a female part constructed to admit the passage of a babe? – it may be that few readers will condemn me for immediately deciding that this was the man I must try; nor, I guess, did my companions regard him as an unusual choice – indeed, I discovered later that there had been a move for the possessor of this extraordinary instrument to be dismissed from the Club, for the reason that almost every lady whose hand fell upon it inevitably wished to try his cock, a cause of jealousy to the other male members. However, for a reason which will shortly become obvious, Xavier Tanoski (the unusual name of the gentleman in question) was permitted to remain a member.

At all events, having signified my choice, the other ladies and gentlemen moved away, one of them loosening my blindfold as she went. When my eyes had become accustomed to the light, I was able to confirm what my hand (still clasped upon the object mentioned) had already suggested – that the tool which it gripped was indeed of singular dimensions, both as to size and length; indeed, regarding it, though not seriously fearing for my safety, I immediately took the precaution of lowering my head in order to lubricate it well with saliva and thus render it kinder to my parts than it might otherwise be. This in itself was a difficult action, for so large was it that I found it impossible to do more than simply place the great bulb which surmounted it (resembling, it struck me, almost that dome which was the chief feature of the Prince's Pavilion) between my lips, and impossible to take more of it within them than that cap, for on my lips closing around the ridge, it seemed entirely to fill my mouth. I therefore removed it, and devoted myself to licking its length, and applying my tongue particularly to the dome itself and the ridge which ran about it, where the hood of skin was gathered.

I had not, however, completed the motion more than two or three times when a shudder ran through the body of the gentleman concerned, and, the column shuddering in my grasp, I felt the huge vein, which ran like a conduit up its length, swell beneath my fingers, and from the aperture at the centre of the dome a positive fountain of milky liquor rose, perhaps, twelve inches in the air, to fall back onto Tanoski's belly and breast with a distinct sound, as of rain pattering upon a roof!

Raising my head, I saw the young gentleman regarding me with an expression so combined of regret and humorous dismay that I could not but laugh. I later learned (and indeed on future attendance at the Club witnessed) that poor Xavier, perhaps through youth and inexperience, married to a frenetic excitement which seemed to possess him at the sight of any unclad female, suffered more completely from the curse of a premature discharge than any other man of whom I have had experience; and remains the only one I have been unable to help to surmount the problem.

Fortunately, his predicament was not fatal to him; for through so many women wishing to try his remarkable prick, he was continually afforded pleasure, and while this was brief it was (he assured me) sufficiently considerable to be a satisfaction; while the ladies inevitably dissatisfied by so premature an end to their love-making were so aroused by the prospect of his person, and so disappointed by the result of a closer acquaintance with it, that when they turned elsewhere for their pleasure they did so with such avidity that their partners profited by it, and were not slow to satisfy their ladies' demands.

Even now, indeed, I felt a pair of hands upon my hips and the pressure of another prick against my arse – it being the custom of the Club that the first choice should be the lady's, but the second a gentleman's, previously selected by lot. The gentleman who had, as it were, won me, I never learned the name of – but he was young, vigorous and willing, and entering me from the rear showed he knew his business by ensuring that the underside of his prick pressed both in its inward and its outward movement upon just that spot most sensitive in my inner anatomy.

Two other gentlemen were meanwhile sufficiently kind (in their hospitality to a visitor) to raise my spirits further, one by caressing my bubbies (while at the same time rogering a friend laid at my side), while the other stood before me and permitted me to suck upon a prick which, while not as large as the unfortunate Xavier's, was by no means as quick in firing, and therefore provided an object for that emotion I could not express through caressing that partner who was pleasuring me. (It is, by the way, in my experience one of the disadvantages of rearward congress that the female subject of such an action – often preferred by gentlemen – is unable to express her affection by caressing her lover; the advantage of supplying this lack through the presence of some other gentleman, as in the situation I describe, cannot be sufficiently strongly advocated). As, by a panting and gasping which I could not restrain (the gentleman plumbing me being extremely efficacious in his attentions), I signalled that I approached my apogee, the possessor of the morsel I was consuming withdrew his weapon and transferred it to the ready quim of a lady nearby, who had been toying with the much reduced instrument of Xavier, hoping – but failing – to recover it, but without doubt enjoying her attempt. Receiving the smaller but readier instrument I had prepared, she was delighted by its obduracy. And, eventually, we all, at more or less the same time, were ready to express the ultimate degree of pleasure by those contractions and expulsions typical of ladies and gentlemen in our situation.

I was delighted to accept an honorary membership of the Club, and indeed visited it on more than one occasion during my stay in the town; but in the interests of restraint, and because – as is well known – it is not my custom to regale my readers with unwonted lascivious detail simply for the sake of arousing lubricious emotions which they may be in no situation to satisfy, I will refrain from further descriptions of the goings-on there, contenting myself with saying that as a means of pleasant and innocent enjoyment I cannot but recommend such an institution. Even when a really well run stable of professional whores is available, considerations of finance must make such a voluntary arrangement highly desirable, while for the female members it has an advantage not to be otherwise equalled without the loss of reputation.

Chapter Nine

The Adventures of Andy

To the left of Eastbourne, as one faces the sea, the sweep of the Martello towers is seen in perspective, and when brightened by the sun has a lively effect. Nearer the Esplanade, but a short distance further inland, is a large circular fort, or redoubt, of considerable strength, bomb proof, and capable of containing about 350 men with provisions for several weeks; it mounts about twelve pieces of cannon. All this is interesting, but of the features in and around the town Beachy Head is the favourite, and most remarkable. It is possible from Eastbourne to see at a distance of two or three miles, on the right hand of the beach-houses, part of that remarkable feature of the south coast, which turns a softened face towards the town, its more tremendous heights being concealed by a winding of the shore. It is about three miles distant from the town, and of course a favourite ride or walk in summer; in winter, the storm gusts would be too repulsive.

The perpendicular height of Beachy Head from the sea, on the best estimate, is 575 feet – more than one hundred feet higher than the cliff at Dover immortalised in *King Lear*, fifty feet higher than the spires of Strasburg and Antwerp (the loftiest in the world), and one hundred feet higher than the great Pyramid of Egypt. It is doubtless one of the finest marine eminences in Europe, whether seen from above or below, and the view from the summit has an air of solitary and sublime grandeur; the keen and ethereal air of this exalted spot would seem almost capable of restoring vigour to the dying.

The height of the cliff is not so much perceived by the spectator from contemplating the straight or waving snowy wall as by listening to the distant and indistinct murmur of the waves and looking down upon the thread-like outline of their foaming edges as they break upon the shore – which, to use the only illustration I can find applicable, looks like the trifling froth of a puddle after the most moderate shower.

Aquatic excursions are often made to view the Head when the tide serves; and rather than join a common crew of tourists (the phrase which, once applied only to those genuine travellers whose peregrinations take them beyond the shores of their own country, is now indiscriminately used to denote anyone who steps more than six feet from their front door) I hired a rowing boat and, being not unaccustomed to the exercise, rowed myself to the base of the cliffs, which are indeed so severe and lofty as to inspire in the meanest spirit some degree of fear and pity (pronounced by Burke to be essential to the sublime) at the recollected calamities the place has been the scene of. However, today was calm and sunny, a blazing orb shining down from a clear sky, so that by the time I had rowed three miles I was in a bath of perspiration, my shirt sticking to my body.

I therefore beached my skiff in a small cove, and stripping off my clothing (there being no one to prevent me through any misguided feeling of modesty), plunged into the sea, the coolness of the water at first being a delightful shock, but then upon my skin cooling, becoming merely a charming sensation. A strong swimmer, I struck out of the cove around the base of the cliff, where rocks plunged straight into the clear water (through which, if I ducked my head, a fine display of molluscs could be seen, together with fish of all sizes and shades of colour – though none as brilliant as those I had been fortunate enough to see about the coasts of the Indian Ocean, in those parts of the world so admirably described (as critics have been pleased to signify) in an earlier memoir[1], put out in the year of '90 by the zealous and sedulous firm of Headline (Publishers) of Euston Road in London, whose editors are ever conscious of the profit (both moral and financial) to be gained by publishing memoirs descriptive both of natural and human phenomena, unrestricted by those girlish sensibilities which prevent some authors from retailing their adventures with a proper degree of frankness.

After an hour's rowing and a quarter-hour's swimming, I began somewhat to tire, and was on the lookout for a convenient rock upon which I could take my ease, when on an occasion when my eye was caught by a particularly fine example of *Solea vulgaris* swimming just three feet below me, I saw a large aperture in the rock, under the water line, which appeared to me to frame – unlikely though this seemed – a staircase!

Taking a deep breath, I dived to look: and found that my eyes had not deceived me. Swimming through the entrance

[1]*Eros in the Far East*

and somewhat upward, my head emerged from the water in a semi-darkness – the only light being that reflected through the opening from the sunlit water beyond; and I found my feet upon the first of a series of steep and (through the greasiness of continual submersion) somewhat treacherous steps. All, however, was not silence, for in the distance there seemed to be the sound of human voices, and even of laughter!

I may as well take the opportunity before I go further of remarking that what I had come across was the seaward entrance of what was called Parson Darby's Cave. This lies below the highest summit of Beachy Head, and consists of two apartments to which one may ascend from below, at low tide, without the necessity of getting even one's feet wet (the small beach revealed by the receding waters being itself accessible only by a steep path from above, or from the sea).

The apartments were said to be the work of a clergyman called Darby at East Dean, a mile and a half distant, who formed it from considerations of humanity, visiting it in heavy storms and hanging out lights as an indication of refuge to wrecked mariners; an employment which is said ultimately to have caused his death from damp and cold (his visiting being most usually in the cold of winter).

Tradition has stated that the poor man's home was made insupportable by a termagant wife, and some have added that she was too fond of her cups. If so, the parson hit on the very wisest, as well as most noble and generous, method of alleviating his own misfortunes by the pleasure derived from relieving the distresses of others.

The extent to which he would have been pleased at the purpose to which his apartments were at present being put, I cannot tell; but I must now reveal to the doubtless impatient reader the nature of those amusements whose sounds had greeted me. Mounting the stairs, I found the greenish light reflected from the waters at length giving way to a warmer light which seemed (and indeed proved) to emanate from a set of candles set in apertures in the walls. The staircase which I had ascended gave way into the larger of the two apartments through an archway which enabled me to conceal myself, should any of the half-dozen people in the cave have turned to look: not that they were in the least inclined to do so, being entirely preoccupied with the activity they had in hand.

The participants in what appeared (to my dismay) to be the torture of two of their number, seemed to me to be of remarkably tender years: certainly no more than twenty, and probably a great deal less. Yet could this be so? for would children at play string two of their number – one male, one female – up against the wall of the cave, suspended by ropes placed about their wrists, their hands extended above their heads, their ankles parted and spread wide, so that their bodies counterfeited a capital X? And would both the victims and their assailants, in the innocence of youth, be similarly clad – the boys merely in what appeared to be a sort of leather apron wrapped about their loins, the girls in a similar garment, but in their case with the addition of another band about their breasts?

The four who were free each held what seemed to be a whip – though the punishing part of each was made not of cord or hair, but of a kinder material, perhaps a sort of cotton, which when it struck evidently inflicted some slight discomfort, but raised only a faint welt upon the fair skin of the young prisoners, which soon faded. I am notoriously bad at guessing the age of young women, or for that matter young men; yet it was clear to my eyes that these were indeed scarcely past the age of puberty – though from their behaviour, this was clearly the case, for their actions betrayed an interest in the sensual – an instinct for provoking pleasure – which could certainly not be expected from persons below the age at which Eve tasted the apple before offering it to her innocent mate. The four who were free, in turn, struck out, each directing a blow at a different part of the body before them – the two boys concentrating on the girl, the two girls on her companion, the blows falling on her thighs, shoulders and midriff, and on the breast of the boy. It surprised me that while the whippers appeared to be happy at their work, giggling and laughing aloud, the two prisoners seemed almost as content, for far from wailing or weeping, their lips parted in what seemed almost a smile, while when a blow somewhat stronger than the others resulted in a momentary cry of pain, it was almost immediately replaced by a look almost of reassurance – and moreover a necessary one, for at any sign of discomfort from one of the victims, the inflictors of that discomfort appeared to be discomfited and even repentant. Indeed, it was soon clear to me that what I had come upon was some sort of charade – and in a moment that became even more evident, for a misdirected blow from the weapon of one of the young ladies entangled the end of the whip in her victim's loincloth – and on her pulling it away, the knot fastening this item of clothing came undone. It did not immediately fall to the ground, however, for it was prevented from doing so by a part of the boy's body which, by its dimensions and angle, betrayed the fact that what pain he had been suffering had been enjoyable rather than distressing!

154

The two girls giggled anew at this, and one, stepping forward, pulled the cloth away, revealing a prick which, while of no unusual size, was certainly not to be sneered at, especially taking into consideration the age of its possessor, which was now confirmed (by the sparseness of hair even about the most important part of his body) as being no more than I had suspected.

The two girls now dropping their whips strode forward, and, falling to their knees, began to toy with this promising piece of flesh, extracting from its owner (by their ingenuity and the teasing nature of their play) cries far more urgent than any which had been the result of their blows!

Their two companions meanwhile, seeing the state of play, took it as cue to relieve their victim of her coverings, which they did somewhat more kindly than any true victim of a torture could expect. The body then revealed was, while entirely womanly, that of no older a person than any others present, though as ready (it seemed) for pleasure. One boy devoted himself to kissing and toying with her breasts – small but beautifully formed – while the other, upon his knees, gave close attention to that other part of her body most interesting to a lover, parting what hairs decorated it in order to reveal and caress the tenderly pink folds of skin. The prisoners were now released, and any pretence at maintaining the pageant was from this moment rejected, the couples pairing off and enjoying each other with the greatest enthusiasm – one pair falling to it in the most convenient posture, while the others gave themselves over to a little more toying before preparing for a final ecstasy, and displaying, by the way, either the most extraordinary instinct for the means of provoking pleasure, or the fact that they had been better educated in the manners of the bed chamber than any young people of their age might have been supposed to be.

Having delighted each other sufficiently long to make the final gesture necessary, they adopted postures convenient for ultimate pleasure, but again most ingeniously, one boy playing at wheelbarrow with his girl (holding her not only with his hands upon her calves, but with the assistance of another part of his anatomy; while the third girl asserted her right to ride upon her companion, which she did with enthusiasm and skill, her steed raising no objection, but bucking and leaping – insofar as he could – with a vigour sufficient to add to their pleasure.

By now, the reader will not be surprised to hear me confess that I was myself in a state of considerable excitation; indeed, I must confess that – since it would have created too startling a surprise had I revealed myself, especially in view of the youth of the participants in the orgy, who might well have been embarrassed by the sudden appearance of a gentleman at least twice the age of the oldest of them – I took myself in hand, and bedewed the rock of the cave with evidence of the not especially satisfactory relief of my emotion before, on bare feet, making my way down the steps and plunging into the sea – which seemed a great deal cooler than it had previously been, due to the heat of my body, raised not by the sun but by emotion.

Swimming back to my boat, I found my clothes completely dry of the perspiration which had soaked them, and donning my trousers rowed back to Eastbourne, fascinated to have discovered that the youth of a town so eminently respectable should have formed themselves into a club devoted to such an interesting purpose as the exploration of a harmless form of some of the exercises beloved of the late Marquis de Sade!

I spent the next day examining the town – increasingly coming to the conclusion that any attempt to enlarge it would be superfluous, its arrangements for visitors being complete; but two days later, on my walking one morning from the town towards Pevensea and passing the fort at Anthony Hill, I came up with a young gentleman who politely doffed his cap to me – and was interested to recognise him as one of the participants in the orgy I had witnessed in Parson Darby's Cave. Needless to say, I took the opportunity of concealing myself in the hedge and watching where he went, and seeing him turn into the drive of a house nearby, on following his footsteps, I found a notice asserting the privacy of the house and grounds which lay beyond the gate, and advertising it as 'Henby's School for Young Gentlefolk'.

On walking up the drive, I found a pleasant house which showed signs of occupancy, there being perhaps a dozen young gentlemen and girls of ages somewhat about sixteen or seventeen playing at tennis and otherwise recreating themselves upon the lawn – all of them, however (even those whom I recognised from the event I have just described), being properly dressed and showing no sign of behaviour which might be considered indecent even by the most puritan of observers.

On my approaching the door, one of the girls came up to me and asked with every degree of amiability whether she could be of assistance, and on my asking whether it would be possible for me to speak to the proprietor of the school, kindly escorted me to the front door and into a spacious hallway, where she rung a bell and asked the maid-servant

who swiftly appeared, whether Mr Henby could see a visitor?
The maid-servant disappeared, shortly to reappear and escort
me into a drawing room where a pleasant gentleman of
perhaps fifty years of age was sitting at a desk, and introducing
himself as Henby, asked in what way he could be of service
to me.

I gave him my name and credentials, and explained my
mission, and we had a brief conversation on the topic of
seaside towns and the desirability, or otherwise, of increasing
the number of houses generally available along the south
coast. Mr Henby was doubtful of anything which might
detract from the impression of that wildness and naturalness
which was at present to be found along those coastal roadways
between the already established towns: 'for what,' he said,
'is grander, more noble or more everlastingly fresh in its
interest, than the seas? The medium of history, of arts, of
happiness, the source of all the most varied themes of tradition,
of romance and chivalry; of poetic aspirations and of heartfelt
affections; ever recent, still venerable, and flourishing in
immortal youth; the unfailing cause and support of industry
and domestic welfare; the most liberal and universal dispenser
of pleasure as well as health; which receives all into its arms
ungrudgingly, which

> sooths unpitied care
> And smooths the wrinkled forehead of despair.

Who could wish to diminish its effect by too great an intrusion
of humanity upon its natural boundary, the coast?'

I cannot deny that this speech had its effect upon me, for it
comprised many of the emotions I felt when I contemplated

this unspoiled coast, and even made me doubt the propriety of my mission.

Mr Henby now asked whether I would care to take tea with himself and his wife, and on my assenting, Mrs Henby was soon introduced – a still handsome dame some few years younger (if appearances were to be trusted) than her husband.

Over tea we continued our discussion; but I could not prevent myself from bringing up the topic of which I had been reminded by the sight of the youth whose appearance on the road had led me to the place, and turned the conversation that way by asking what sort of school it was in which I found myself, since all the pupils appeared to be around the ages of sixteen or seventeen?

It was (I was told) what was beginning to be called 'a finishing school', whose purpose was to ready young people for a place in civilised society.

My enquiry having led to a dead end, I next turned the conversation again to the coast, and remarked that I had been exploring the Head a day previously, and had been especially interested by the place called Parson Darby's Cave. Mr and Mrs Henby exchanged a glance, and, on looking back at me, clearly read in my face that my interest had been more than topographical.

'Ah,' said Henby, 'I suppose that you chanced upon some of our pupils there?'

To cut my report of the conversation short, I merely record that I admitted having done so, and remarked that their games appeared to be unusual for young people of that age, whose interest in corporeal matters was usually a great deal less sophisticated. Mr and Mrs Henby were then drawn to explain more fully the nature of their school, one of whose chiefest aims was, it appears, to inform pupils of the nature of physical desire and instruct them in the means of satisfying it as fully and exhaustively as possible.

'I have been a teacher for many years,' said the gentleman, 'and my wife has acted as a school mother; and we have for some time been concerned that the one subject neglected by even the most admired schools in the country is the one which can make both men and women most thoroughly unhappy through lack of knowledge.

'I must confess that the notion which led me to my present situation came through reading that admirable book Sir Thomas More's *Utopia*. You will remember, Mr Archer, that in the country of which Sir Thomas wrote, it is the custom upon a marriage being proposed, for the bride to be shown quite naked to the groom, and for him to be similarly exhibited to her – on grounds of complete honesty. It struck me immediately that, as Sir Thomas expostulates, we treat our offspring with far less consideration than animals, for we choose carefully how we breed *them*, are careful to match them, assist them with their copulation if there appear to be difficulties . . .

'Why should we not do the same with our children?

'On enquiry, I found that a number of parents felt the same as I, though they showed a considerable hesitation in expressing their agreement; however, I encouraged some few to entrust their boys to me in this matter, and on my pupils reaching a proper age, instructed them in the 'minutiae' of the subject in as far as I understood it, increasing my own knowledge by the study of books, from Ovid to Ariosto, from Suetonius to Pierre-François Hughes d'Hancarville . . .'

My interest in Henby's school was so clear that he kindly

invited me to stay for the night, and to observe more closely how it was conducted; and I must report that it seemed to me to be a model of such organisations, and one which might to advantage be copied – especially in the country, where any interest shown by young people in the venereal act, except from the viewpoint of procreation, is considered in general to be improper (and even among the farming classes the observation of the behaviour of the beasts, while it may result in an early understanding of the nature of the conjugal act, must necessarily be devoid of any conception of the more sophisticated pleasure which can and should accompany it).

Impropriety of any kind was entirely absent from the school. While there can be little doubt that Mr Henby himself, despite his considerable age, had still a keen appetite for sensual pleasure (shared, I have little doubt, by his wife, whose eye was bright and inviting), there was under no circumstance (they averred, and I have no hesitation in accepting their word) any conversation of that kind between him and his female pupils, any more than between his wife and the boys. On the contrary, the latter were taught entirely by their master, and the former by Mrs Henby. During the afternoon I was permitted to visit the classrooms, which consisted only of two large rooms, one containing a dozen girls, the other a similar number of boys; in one, Mrs Henby was instructing the girls – but in what subject I cannot say, since I was politely informed that the presence of a gentleman in the room at such a time would be embarrassing and improper.

I was, however, permitted to be an observer in the room where Henby was addressing his boys – on this occasion upon a subject not unknown in our public schools, but only slyly; that of those men who show a preference for erotic conversation with members of their own sex.

I must be careful in expressing any opinion here other than that sanctioned by the present law, which condemns completely any expression of such an emotion, though (if we are to believe the ancient authors) it was highly regarded in the great days of that most admirable of all civilisations, the ancient Greek. Mr Henby did not shrink from an exposition of the present law of the land – but neither did he deny that some men and women are, through the particular composition of their nature, unsuited for married life, and therefore (if they are not to live the life of eunuchs) must turn to their own sex.

'Moreover, we should ask ourselves if it is proper,' he said, 'that while two young women may live together in the same house, share the same bedroom – nay, occupy the same bed – and do within it as they wish without the condemnation of society or the law, two gentlemen must conduct themselves, in the same situation, with the utmost secrecy for fear of the law.'

He then added, to my shame and confusion, that a Member of Parliament was among them, and that if they had questions they should turn to me for an answer – but kindly added that while from his conversation with me he would guess that I shared his own view of the matter, it would be kind if they refrained from an expectation that I should support his view with passion, since he was sure I would find it improper through my membership of the Commons to take an attitude contrary to the law.

He then went on to speak, from a fount of knowledge which was clearly most thoroughly researched, of the history of relationships between young men – of David and Jonathan (in the Bible); of Socrates and Alcibiades; of Achilles and Patroclas, and many other faithful couples in the ancient world. While quoting from the sonnets of the great Michelangelo (which he had himself translated) he asked whether it could be supposed that such affection no longer existed in the world?

But, one of his pupils asked, was it not the case that men who took sensual pleasure with those of their own sex were effeminate and womanly in appearance and behaviour?

Why, replied his master, I have only to ask you to consider the life of Alexander the Great, as recorded by the historian Flavius Arrianus. Throughout his whole life his devotion was centred upon his friend Hephaestion; when he died, Alexander (it is written) was grief-stricken beyond all bounds of propriety, flung himself on the body of his friend and lay there nearly all day in tears, and refused to be parted from him until he was dragged away by force; in emulation of Achilles he cut his hair short in mourning, and personally drove for a short distance the funeral carriage with Hephaestion's body in it – something unheard of in the ancient world.

And yet could it be supposed that Alexander was effeminate, lacked manliness or courage? Indeed, could that be said of the hero Hephaestion, entrusted with the command of many legions and the victor of many battles? Does the friendship not confirm the opinion of the Greeks, that lovers make the finest soldiers? And is not this the strongest argument for the acceptance into our armed services of male lovers whose devotion to each other would withstand the utmost test that warfare could put out?

His arguments provoked from the young men (who had

followed him with the most sympathetic attention – far removed from that generally ill-natured prejudice most men show toward the subject) questions of various sorts, including an enquiry into how such men expressed their love in the physical sense. To which Mr Henby replied by a very frank exposition: in general, he remarked, two men abed together behaved much as a man behaved with a woman: that is, any caress that seemed natural was permissable – even that one which is most condemned by society, for it sometimes was preferred even by married couples: 'though again,' said Mr Henby, 'I must point out that such an action is against the law of the country, and that the most severe sanction would be exacted against any man discovered employing it, even with his wife, let alone with one of his own gender.'

This provoked a final question: whether the master's advice would be to follow one's instincts, but to be careful not to be found out? – to which he answered merely with a smile, and declared the lesson terminated.

I could not but congratulate him on his tact and thoroughness. He was complimented, and pointed out that a lesson on the same subject was at the same time being given by his wife to the girls – for, as far as possible, pupils of both sexes were taught 'in parallel', as he put it, using a geometric term which I took to mean that the same lessons were taught, where possible, at the same time.

And were young ladies offered information with the same freedom as the young gentlemen?

Naturally, replied the master; for could it be proper that one sex should be kept in ignorance of facts freely available to the other?

This was another revolutionary idea: for who among our

educationalists would argue that information should be as liberally provided to females as to males? Yet this seemed to me to be, at least as Mr Henby expressed it, a notion which must be accepted by anyone who believed at all in the notion of female education.

One question remained, which I put to the master and his wife over an excellent cold supper which they invited me to share.

Was it not impossible to prevent the pupils experimenting with each other? And was the scene at the Cave (which I described inasmuch as I could do so without offending Mrs Henby's sensitivities) one which was frequently counterfeited?

Of course, replied the master, such experiments did take place; how could it be that lessons taught in the schoolroom should not be practically expressed outside it? – if only through curiosity and that habit of experimentation common in all men and women, but especially in the young. The scene which I had overlooked had been consequent upon a lesson which dealt with the relationship between pain and pleasure, during which both teachers had been careful to point out that although some men and women took pleasure not only in inflicting but being in receipt of pain, it was in common decency necessary to assure oneself that this practice was only followed with the consent of both parties. I had not – he trusted – felt that the scene I had been a witness of had resulted even in slight discomfort as a result of this advice being ignored?

Not at all, I said. But was there not always the danger that unsupervised experimentation – the result even of a wonderfully careful explanation of the facts, accompanied with however accurate a description of what should and should not be done – might result, through that unbridled emotion too often experienced by the young, in their damaging each other's sensibilities, or even persons?

They believed not, said the master and his wife; indeed, they would give me a further insight into the matter that very evening – and most interesting it was; but I find that my space is exhausted, and that I must delay any further explication until my next chapter.

Chapter Ten

Sophie's Story

I would not care for the reader to believe that all my time in Brighton was spent in exercise with gentlemen of one condition or another: I took every opportunity to familiarise myself with the town and those cultural and rural pleasures it had to offer: not only the Pavilion (my visit to which certainly, as has been recorded, resulted in incidents of a fleshly sort – which for some reason often seem to be provoked by my very presence), but also the Royal Gardens, once a pleasure ground to be compared with the Dandelion at Margate – a mimic Vauxhall or Tivoli, though of a quieter character.

In past years these gardens comprised bowling greens, a fives court, cricket ground, tea-boxes, an aviary, a Merlin's swing, and so forth – but now all this has passed away, and has been superseded by zoological gardens established by the industrious Mr Ireland (who lost some thousands of pounds by the speculation, and is now – having certainly conferred some benefit on the town – in reduced circumstances).

The zoological establishment occupies beautifully disposed grounds (somewhat like those at Primrose Hill), with many improvements, at present only in their infancy. A neat but not very handsome gate has been erected, just inside which is to be found a large ballroom, eighty feet by thirty, where hitherto balls were held for the amusement of the middle classes, with coloured lamps, fireworks, etc., and which is to be *orientalised* to correspond with some other erections of a smaller character, for beasts and birds.

The collection of animals is at present small and kept in a temporary place, but is very well managed. It consists of two young tigers, a panther, hyaena, a lynx, two Russian bears, foreign goats, deer, lamas, monkeys, and two fine leopards (it is not generally known – but I have seen these creatures passing the night, in India – that several of this tribe, but especially the cheetah, when at ease in their own haunts, *purrs* like the domestic cat).

The collection is incomplete, for it wants a lion and an elephant; a boa constrictor is the only curiosity of that class. But there is in addition a beautiful assortment of birds, paroquets, cockatoos, macaws, *et cetera, et cetera, et cetera* – and the admission price of only one shilling for the day is a small price to pay for the amusement the place can provide, as I found upon the morning I visited it.

Having taken some refreshment, I decided to go in search of some shady place in which to recreate myself, being somewhat tired with walking. I found a beautiful avenue of small trees terminated by a narrow canal, or ditch, and a bridge leading to a Saxon tower, which, if it was a little higher, would have an admirable effect.

Terminating the gardens is a maze, a remnant of the original pleasure park, on each side of which are other walks and lawns, also a grotto, tent, basin of water, and so forth. I decided that the maze offered me the best opportunity of escape from the few other people who braved the early afternoon sun – for outside it was a notice announcing that entry was forbidden unless accompanied by a servant of the gardens, through the impossibility of a person being able, once in, to find the exit, the maze being so complicated in its construction.

The maze is indeed an excellent one, tall hedges making it impossible to be confident of direction or turning – but I had once been taught, by a maker of mazes, a perfect way of subduing the mystery of such places, and so was entirely confident that I would not be bemused by the problem of finding my way out again – and indeed on entering found it sufficiently easy to find the centre, emerging from the passageways to find myself in a circular clearing, the floor of which was perfectly soft and green, and which was overshadowed on one side by a handsome cherry tree.

I was not, however, the only person who had decided that this was a place for undisturbed relaxation, for a gentleman lay in the full sunlight before me, apparently asleep. The fact that he believed in the perfect inaccessibility of the place was advertised through his having removed every item of clothing, bundling his effects up to form a cushion which he had thrust beneath his head.

I was not deterred from myself reclining upon the grass – though at a reasonable distance, with my back against the trunk of the cherry; nor was I in the least put out by the sight before me, for quite apart from the fact that I had long since concluded that the human body was no matter for embarrassment, the gentleman in this case possessed a frame of handsome proportions, having the effect of a piece of living statuary, not only through his immobility, but from the contours of his limbs, which were extremely well shaped. He lay upon his face, his arms thrown up, for his hands were placed beneath his head; his broad shoulders tapered to a slender but by no means effete waist, his backside then swelling to take the eye with a brave assertion of youth through each cheek being rounded, plump and firm, the sunlight glinting upon a slight fuzz of amber which was all the hair to be seen there – or, indeed, upon those thighs which, again muscular but un-massive, lay slightly parted, one knee thrown a little out to one side, so that one ankle could lie upon the other.

That the gentleman was used to taking his rest in the sun was clear from there being no band of white skin about his loins to suggest that he was used to hiding any part of himself from the amorous embrace of its rays; indeed, so used was he to the sun's kiss that his skin appeared to me to be almost as brown as that of an inhabitant of some Mediterranean country.

With my eyes, half-closed, feasting upon so pleasant a sight, it was not long before warmth and my lethargy had their effect, and I swooned into a doze which in time became complete unconsciousness.

I cannot tell what woke me, but wake I did – not with a start, but with a pleasurable lethargy – to find the gentleman now himself awake, and, without otherwise moving, resting with his chin upon his hands and regarding me with the same frankness with which I had examined him – the difference being that I was aware of his gaze.

To show that I was not by any means dismayed by the situation, I smiled; whereupon he returned the salutation, and remarked in a voice heavily accented with the tones of the county that the sun was hot and the day a pleasant one for relaxation.

To my astonishment, having exchanged a few more courtesies, I heard the gentleman remark that he hoped that I enjoyed the opportunity of observing his person, and asked if I admired his body!

Although I had certainly as much experience of masculine pride and vanity as any other person, this was the first time that a compliment had positively been invited in such a manner. But I could not lie, and after only a brief pause confessed that I certainly found it admirable, at which the gentleman smiled, thanked me, and rose to his feet in order (he said) to give me a further opportunity of confirming that he was a man whose limbs were in perfect proportion – so much so that he had been, in the past, in demand by a number of artists who had produced portraits much admired by collectors of such works.

He slowly revolved before me, one hand placed upon his hip, the other behind his head – in just such a pose as might have been admired by the Italian master Michelangelo – though I cannot believe that my rustic friend could ever have seen a reproduction of such a work. There is no question, however, that the pose was flattering, the line from knee upwards over the hip and side to the elbow being particularly admirable.

While it would have given me no small pleasure to have been able to criticise the self-satisfied gentleman I saw before me, on the grounds of any disproportion of his body, I must confess that I could find none – and, indeed, being a woman perfectly incapable of not admiring perfection wherever I saw it, I was forced to admit (though without expressing the conclusion aloud!) that the body before me was one which it would be difficult to fault – and as I now saw, was as well proportioned before as behind; the broad platform of his chest being shaped like one of those breastpieces modelled by the great armourers of the past – and shining as it did with perspiration, bearing more than a slight resemblance to such a piece of armour.

Below his breast, his belly was, if not quite flat, at least only very slightly rounded, and dinted with a navel perfectly placed and formed; while the curls which lay yet further below, the locks being caught by the sun so that separate hairs could be seen to shine like spun gold, might have been formed by curling irons and shaped by the action of a scissors, so beautifully tight and rounded were they – while the appendage which nestled at the centre of the bush, its head only slightly raised, was of the most delightful proportions: I know not whether the effect of the sun had been to bring the blood down, but here was neither a shrunken prick nor one at too rude a stand – but it was a member sufficiently large to be notable, yet still only of such dimensions as to present the proper picture of a man.

Having permitted me to look my fill, this remarkable gentleman once again asked whether I liked him, and upon my replying to the affirmative, stepped forward and fell to his knees at my side. The reader will suppose that I now waited for some physical contact between us, the natural result of his approach and my failure to be offended by it; yet rather than placing a kiss upon my lips – or indeed any other portion of my anatomy – rather than making any corporeal attempt to arouse my feelings, the gentleman instead raised his arm and flexing it invited me to feel the muscle!

Any lady whose emotions were aroused by muscularity would no doubt have experienced a considerable *frisson*, for, indeed, beneath a silken skin the hardness, no less than the size of the tuberosity springing in the upper arm, was impressive. Again, 'You like it?' enquired the gentleman.

I must confess I was now somewhat impatient in my assurance that I was impressed – for to be frank, the heat of the day and his display of interest had more than a little roused my spirits. But I was still, it seemed, to wait for any compliment to my own person, for now, raising himself on his knees, the gentleman turned somewhat sideways, and placing his palm upon that cheek of his arse nearest me, exclaimed: 'And I have a fine, springy backside!'

I was too astonished to say anything – whereupon, he took my hand and placed it beneath his own on the warm skin of his arse, which indeed offered to my palm a sensation by no means unappealing, especially when once more he took care by flexing his muscles that I was made aware of the strength and virtuosity which might be expected to inhabit every part of his frame.

But now he was running his hands over his entire body, swaying as though displaying himself as a dancer might before an appreciative audience – offering, however, no virtuosity of movement, no skilful leaps or posturings, but simply a desire to be admired! He tweaked with his fingers the nipples of his chest, smoothed his waist (which indeed was devoid of any plumpness) and belly, and finally placing his hand beneath his cods, lifted and displayed his male accoutrements to their best advantage – though to my mind the effect was somewhat diminished through his being still less than fully aroused.

This was not, however, to remain long the case, for taking his prick in the fingers of his right hand, he placed it carefully upon the palm of his left as though to invite me to admire it – which was indeed the purpose of the exercise, for he repeated those very words: 'You like my cock?'

I was sorely tempted now, through sheer impatience, to dismiss him – which the simple statement that I had seen better would surely do, for his overweening pride would have sent him scampering (I was convinced) at the slightest sign of disapprobation. However, I could not tell a lie: the instrument so freely displayed to me was indeed of an admirable shape, and, in any event, my senses were now highly aroused, and even the strangeness of his approach must be forgiven if a connection was to be achieved. I therefore forced myself to utter some words of commendation: at which I expected at last some action, and to that end unlaced the ties of my dress the more readily to permit him access.

Alas, I need not have taken the trouble – for by now, having spat on to the palm of his right hand, he was manipulating his prick with considerable enthusiasm and dexterity – the immediate result being its swelling to a degree which made it even more admirable than previously, for its length became such that, when enclosed within his fist, both head and root were clearly visible, while the hood, drawn back, revealed a knob of luscious, shining pink flesh which positively invited one's lips to taste it.

I was still convinced that I must be the recipient of the attentions of this handsome instrument, and my spirits were roused even further by the sight presented to me. I lay back in readiness. To my astonishment the gentleman still made no approach, but simply continued those motions with which he had brought his prick to its present state – even accelerating them, while at the same time fumbling with his left hand at his bollocks in a manner which was rough and ready, but no doubt contributed to the (to me) disgusting result – for in a period of time so brief that, indeed, (when I later considered the matter) any connection with the gentleman could only have been unsatisfactory to a feeling woman – he suddenly paused in his work, and throwing back his head grunted as a forceful expulsion of liquid showed that his passion had been satisfied.

I must point out that I have no objection in the world to a young man, devoid of the opportunity for connection with a female (or indeed with another male, should that be his inclination), pleasuring himself; the fallacious and silly objection of some members of the medical profession to such a custom appears to me to be tendentious and tergiversate. But when a lady, not only willing but possessed (as I am assured) of certain charms, is before him – what gentleman would prefer to attend to himself in the manner of my companion?

He was, however, clearly entirely unashamed at a situation which would surely in any normal man have produced feelings of mortification, now smiled at me and, wiping his prick with a dock leaf, asked if I did not admire the velocity and vigour of his spending?

I offered him compliments as enthusiastic as they were false (though in truth I was in some difficulty, for my admiration of his person was still difficult to disguise). The irony of my felicitations was (I am convinced) entirely lost upon him, for his smiles became even more insistent as, standing, he resumed his clothes – being careful, as it seemed to me, still to display himself to me from the best possible angle, and even turning (as he bent over to resume his pantaloons) to afford me a full view of his posteriors – so handsome, in truth, that I could still not resist some feeling of regret at not having had the opportunity to lie with him.

My emotions were indeed, as he departed with a moderate expression of duty, extremely mixed. I was upon the one hand pleased to have had the opportunity of adding yet one more remarkable character to those I have observed; but on the other irritated by such an astonishing degree of self-congratulation – and (this latter emotion being the strongest) remarkably hot in my emotions, being unused to such a degree of arousal not being accompanied by the opportunity to assuage it.

Having somewhat tidied my clothes, I rose and left the maze without any further view of my companion – who I assume must be a workman in some way attached to them, his clothing marking him as an artisan. The reader may ask why I did not follow the fellow's example and pleasure myself; but this I reserve for those situations in which no other opportunity can possibly be available – and I was by no means clear that there was not, somewhere in Brighton, a gentleman who would be pleased to satisfy me during the course of the day.

Shortly, I found myself upon the western esplanade, which is between half and three-quarters of a mile in length, and very spacious and convenient. Some time ago, through an extraordinarily stupid management, the walks were paved with bruised chalk, which rendered them inaccessible in sunshiney weather, on pain of blindness; but on strong remonstrances being made in the newspapers, this was removed and gravel substituted.

The esplanade was now a very lively scene, with ladies, gentlemen and children, bathing machines, horses, donkeys, pleasure-boats *et cetera*, all of which would form a good subject for a landscape. A band, consisting of ten persons, plays here on three afternoons a week, and was at present rendering selections from the operas of M. Auber – and very delightful this was, especially in the solos being performed upon the cornet, which laid a skein of melody upon the still afternoon air which was both attractive and inspiriting.

I made a particular point of walking to the bandstand in order to place a contribution of a sixpence into the hand of the gentlemen collecting subscriptions – for only the previous year, I had been informed, the fact that the people of Brighton are contented to walk and listen but keep their purses closed, had resulted in a deficiency of subscriptions and the abandonment of the concerts – though the small town of St Leonard's, which has not one-thirtieth part of the population of Brighton, supports a parade band with ease.

As I reached the bandstand the music ceased with those several culminatory chords with which M. Auber usually concludes his operas, and the musicians, laying down their instruments, prepared to take a rest from their sonorous labours. I could not but congratulate the cornet-player upon his performance as he stepped down beside me – my admiration of his accomplishments being in no way diminished by the fact that he was an uncommonly good-looking young fellow, slim and dark, with lips perfectly formed and smiling, and eyes at once sparkling and soulful, with that depth and intensity so often the sign of an artistic being.

He replied to my compliment in an accent which suggested

that he was of foreign birth, and indeed proved to be a Frenchman. Our Gallic neighbours are very partial to Brighton, compared with which their Bains de Mer at Dieppe must hide their diminished heads. The promenades here are very well suited to their taste, and they delight to 'take a little turn of walking', either of an evening or 'of good morning', which enables them to 'carry themselves well'. Sometimes they undertake that feat, perilous in sound, which they, by a most ludicrous perversion of ideas, call 'walking on a horse', which, however, we have no wish to see them literally put in practice, as especially in the case of ladies it would be very hazardous.

I must not, however, mock the difficulty that these visitors have with the English language, which has many absurd idioms: our 'shall' and 'will', for instance, must ever be the torment of foreigners, as they were near proving fatal to the poor Frenchman who in falling from London Bridge exclaimed: 'I *will* be drowned – nobody *shall* save me!'

But I digress, and without good reason, for Mr Charles Tronc, as the young man now introduced himself, spoke extremely good English, and on my accepting with pleasure his suggestion that I should accompany him on a walk along the esplanade, revealed that having ended his musical studies at school in Paris, he was spending the summer in England in order to improve his knowledge of the language, to get to know the country and its people – and in the meantime meant to support himself by playing the cornet, which (as I have already remarked) he did with skill and artistry.

Since I have some knowledge of his native city, and he was eager to hear about London (where he hoped to spend some time at the end of the summer, but which he had not yet visited), we had plenty to talk about; and – perhaps because of the warmth of the afternoon and the fact that we found each other not unattractive – our talk soon turned to those idiosyncrasies which separate the French and the English: one of these, inevitably, being our attitude to *l'amour* (as the French call the art of love).

M. Tronc remarked that to his regret he had found English ladies more than a little cold – and those of the lower classes, as chambermaids, who were willing to welcome him to their arms, were devoid of those amorous skills which in his country came to women as naturally as the leaves to the tree. I could only agree with him that some ladies found an approach from an unknown gentleman difficult to accept without embarrassment – but remarked that I found it strange that in his particular case there should be any difficulty, and added my assurance that he would not find all ladies as devoid of skill in the bedroom as he feared.

He was cheered by this – for, he said, he had thought that perhaps his personal appearance was such that he was unappealing to the English female, who might prefer those portly young gentlemen who seemed to be somewhat more typical of young English manhood. I was happy to inform him that I had always found French gentlemen entirely pleasant in manner and indeed (I added, since we were being frank) in physique; for although the Gallic *paterfamilias* was as prone to plumpness and indeed somnambulance as his English counterpart, the youth of my friend's country was, in my view, brisker and more lively than, in general, was our youth.

By this time we had reached the end of the esplanade and were opposite Mohammed's baths. Was I aware – my companion enquired – that these were celebrated for the process of *shampooing*? I was not, and said so – but was able to forestall his explanation of what that comfort comprised by explaining that I had experienced it during my visit to Greece, some years ago – during a journey related, with full attention to detail, in the volume entitled *Eros on the Grand Tour*, written (as are all my works) in collaboration with my friend Andy, whose chapters here march with my own.

M. Tronc expressed the view that I was perhaps unaware of the true pleasure which could be given by a 'shampooer', since he could not believe that a female practitioner of that art would be as expert as a man – whereupon to his surprise I agreed with him, for it was from the hands of a man (I explained) that I had learned the art, which I had been known to practise on my own account. He was somewhat surprised at this, but still supposed that my experience must be limited – at which I continued to demur, for the Greek gentleman who had devoted his skills to my pleasure had not hesitated to . . . But here I paused, feeling that after all I was insufficiently acquainted with my companion to go further. However, from the look in his fine and humorous eyes, he perfectly understood the nature of the skills to which I alluded.

We now went on to remark upon the plethora of baths which were at the service of the population of Brighton, for in addition to Mohammed's – and of course the salt-water baths which could be taken in the sea, from the convenience of a bathing machine – there were Wood's, Williams's and Lamprell's establishments in the vicinity of the Steyn (the latter possesses a very large circular plunging bath); Hobden's, further west near the battery, has in the main an indifferent reputation, being attended chiefly by the lower classes – and M. Tronc confirmed this to me, for he had been (he said) surprised at the freedom with which the female bathers there comported themselves, some of them not hesitating to join in the most free and lascivious behaviour with any of the rougher sort of men at the place.

I had to confess to being by now somewhat footsore, and M. Tronc, becoming aware of the fact, asked if he could offer me a dish of tea. The frankness of our talk and the somewhat insinuating pressure of his hand upon my arm convinced me that while tea might certainly accompany any visit to his lodgings, I might also expect to find there the solution to the vacuum which had resulted from my earlier encounter – my only reservation being that I did not especially look forward to taking my pleasure in the doubtful comfort of an indifferent lodging house (which was all, I was convinced, my friend could afford upon the income to be derived from his instrument).

To my surprise, on my acquiescence M. Tronc signalled to a brougham which was just passing, and on our mounting it gave instructions to the man to drive to the western terrace off Brunswick Square, the largest square in the town, with gracious circular-fronted houses ornamented with columns. The houses of the terrace are no whit inferior – indeed, they are among the best erections in Brighton, ornamented in a very good style with bold and handsome Corinthian pillars. A room in one of them must surely of necessity be comfortable, though I was somewhat surprised to find any owner here letting one.

Indeed this proved not to be the case: for on our descending, and my companion paying off the driver with a half-guinea from which he required no change (even after so short a journey!), the door was opened by a footman who addressed

M. Tronc as '*votre Grandeur*' – my friend was a Lord! –
though on my apologising (but how could I have guessed?)
he begged me to forget the fact, and indeed to address him as
Charles, which I was pleased to do.

I later discovered that he was indeed of high birth, and
being committed to a career in the diplomatic service of his
country had been sent, partly on the advice of his father and
partly on his own initiative, to live among the ordinary people
of England for a while, in order the better to understand us! It
was to the same purpose that – having had an excellent
amateur education in music and being a proficient performer
upon the cornet – he masqueraded as a member of the
orchestra, which allowed him to make the acquaintance of
members of the public without offering them the slightest
opportunity of discovering his true rank.

Mounting the stairs, we found ourselves in a handsome
drawing room, and tea was ordered; before which, however,
Charles asked whether I would care to cool myself after the
heat of the afternoon – and on my gratefully assenting, escorted
me to a room on the ground floor, where he threw open a door
and revealed the finest bathroom it has ever been my pleasure
to see – a large circular bath in marble having been set up in
the centre of the room, supplied with water by pipes from
above, one of which dispensed water which, while not hot,
was certainly warm – although we now allowed an admixture
of cold to join with it, providing a bath which would be cool
without being chilling.

If Charles considered it natural that he should join me by
removing his own clothes as I removed mine, this was no
surprise to me – indeed, knowing the temperament of the
French, I would have been amazed if such had not been the

case. On his joining me in the bath I was able to admire a figure which, while no way as sturdy as that of the gentleman in the maze, was by no means featureless, being almost entirely hairless and enjoyably lithe, its lines unspoiled by any tendency to obesity.

It was a great pleasure merely to lie in the water, and my heated limbs were soon comfortably cool. Charles having asked after my comfort and being assured of it, now leaned over the edge of the bath, took up a phial of greenish liquid, and, asking my leave, poured some of it into the palm of one hand, rubbed both his palms together, and applied them to my shoulders – when it became clear that this was some kind of soap, rendered into a liquid form. It had, I later learned, been introduced but recently into the country from the Continent, and was catching on quickly through its avoiding the severe tax (of three pence in the pound) which a rapacious government had imposed on solid soap since the year 1712.

I can only recommend this liquid as delightful: easier to apply than other kinds of soap, and delightfully perfumed (in that respect having an advantage over soapwort or *Saponaria officinali* used by the poorer sort of person – sharp and refreshing though that is).

I will not say that my pleasure was not increased by the pleasant and even provocative manner in which the soap was applied by young Charles, who now knelt before me and invited me to raise myself somewhat in the water so that he could pass his slippery hands over my breasts. This attention soon roused my nipples to a handsome stand, whereupon, he could not resist the temptation to kiss them – at first having the misfortune to take some of the soap upon his tongue! Nor in the natural course of events could he resist requesting what

I felt obliged to agree to: my sitting upon the edge of the bath in order that, having paid my private person the compliment of thorough washing, he could lower his head between my thighs and . . .

But even in the quiet of my study and with pen in hand, I find that I can think of no words to describe what now occurred: and can only put the ecstasy I experienced down to that delay between my arousal by the fellow in the maze, and the moment when Charles's lips fell upon my lower ones; though in retrospect I am inclined to suppose that a lifetime playing the cornet had given to his tongue and lips a pliancy and strength which made them more remarkably insinuate and pleasing than any others I have known – that, and the usual Frenchman's pleasure in this particular kind of love-making. While the Englishman must frequently be invited and encouraged to it, the Frenchman naturally regards one pair of lips as quite as apposite as the other (an advantage the merits of which cannot be over-emphasised, especially when so many young men of our country suffer from the inability to contain their passion for more than a few moments).

I naturally could not allow myself to luxuriate for too long without being so polite as to offer a similar compliment.

Charles was somewhat reluctant to eschew his feast; but under my persuasion adopted a position similar to my own, when it was my turn to kneel before him – and to be (I must confess) somewhat disappointed by the dish I found before me; though beautifully shaped, his prick was without doubt below the average in size.

It was by no means outrageously so – and when he was polite enough to apologise for any disappointment (the size of his cock certainly being the reason for his reluctance to

offer me the opportunity to salute it) I was able to tell him
that one of the best lovers I ever had, a Siamese boy, had
possessed a prick a mere inch long!

Having cheered him thus, I fell to, and found that while he
was certainly modestly endowed (his masculine part being
perhaps three inches in length, and merely proportionate in
circumference) it felt almost as though made of ivory, so
smoothly hard did it become; while that it was sufficiently
sensitive could be believed from the pleasure I was able to
give Charles, whose sighs and moans became ever more
delighted under my ministrations.

I was by now more than ready – indeed, eager – for
congress; but he demurred at this taking place in the bath, for
comfort (he remarked) was in his view a prerequisite; therefore,
wrapping me in a large and very soft towel, he lifted me in his
arms and carried me upstairs and into a large bedroom, where
stood a bed quite as admirable in construction and comfort as
the bath.

Upon this, we disposed ourselves, and without further
preamble he lifted my ankles upon his shoulders and minus
that fumbling or difficulty sometimes experienced by
gentlemen with small parts, placed himself in the proper
position – when, lifting himself almost upright, so that the
undersides of my thighs were flat against his belly and chest,
he so disposed his prick that it was next to the most sensitive
part of my cunny; and then set up what I can only term a
vibration.

Unable to make the conventional motions, lest his too
small instrument should slip from its socket, he by some
alchemy *trembled* it (as it were), the pulsation being so quick
and insistent that in next to no time I was almost fainting

with the pleasure of it – and within as many minutes experienced three separate flushes of pleasure, and was forced to separate myself from him lest I should rise to a state of hysteria: though needless to say I did not do so before signalling to him that I was ready for a rest, for he had not himself, I believed, reached that point at which a gentleman finds it easy to relinquish a pleasure which has not been completed.

However, withdraw he did; and on my enquiring whether this was not painful to him, made no reply but gave a mute look of appeal which I properly interpreted – and without hesitation once more took that delightful, if diminutive, organ between my lips, and with a little dexterity and no small enjoyment (derived in the main from the wish to give him at least as much pleasure as he had afforded me) succeeded, by the play of lips and tongue and a little assistance from an explorative index finger placed between the charming spheres of his arse and in the proximity to the aperture to be found there, brought him off to his entire satisfaction.

We then took our tea, which was none the less refreshing from being almost cold; after which I took my leave, entirely contented that a morning which had started so unsatisfactorily had been so amiably concluded.

Chapter Eleven

The Adventures of Andy

The regime which Mr and Mrs Henby upheld at their admirable school represented the most perfect application of my own opinions of the manner in which the young should be prepared for life – those relationships we carry on with members of the other sex being among the most important experiences we are ever likely to have upon this earth, and preparation for them being almost entirely lacking at our conventional educational establishments.

The scene which I had witnessed in the cave below Beachy Head had been, it was explained to me, an extra-mural activity devised by the children themselves after a lecture upon the subject of the connection between pain and love – the schoolmaster and his wife having been careful to explain to their charges that such an impulse is relatively rare, having been most freely expressed by the late Donatien Alphonse, Comte de Sade, a former cavalry officer the manuscript of one of whose filthily violent books – *Justine, ou les malheurs de la vertu* – I was once shown in France. That gentleman could find satisfaction, it seemed, only in the infliction of pain; others only in feeling it. Mr Henby was right to explain this – but was equally right to advance the proposition that when used in play (rather than in that seriousness, which could result in physical danger) the infliction of some slight degree of physical discomfort could be inspiriting and amusing – which the boys and girls had been endeavouring to prove by the scene which I had inadvertently stumbled upon.

But, I enquired, was it not the case that such teaching as took place here resulted in the natural susceptibility to physical pleasure which may be observed in every young person being fanned to an unconscionable degree, and might not the result be dangerous at least to the female part of the population of the area?

Not at all, replied Mr Henby; for it was a condition of any young person's being accepted at the school – of one sex or the other – that there should be no objection to their cohabitation, for the very reason I had put forward: it was (he said) ridiculous to suppose that a young man of seventeen years of age should be expected to contain himself after some hours of education in and reflections upon the sensual pleasures without an outlet being allowed for that degree of heat which would necessarily result.

Moreover (Mrs Henby put in), the same was true of the female students, for it was entirely wrong to suppose that a young woman was not subject to the same urge for pleasure as the young man.

'We do, however,' her husband explained, 'make it a condition that unsupervised connections should not occur before the age of sixteen, it being our experience that that age is the lowest at which young people can be made aware of the consequences of their actions and the effect which they may have upon others. Past that age, however, they are permitted to couple as they wish – though to avoid one or the other for some reason finding himself or herself unpartnered, we have a system which results in a sharing of pleasure and experience; this comes into operation at bedtime, and as I see that time of the evening has now come when I must ring the bell, you might care to accompany us on our rounds – for we make it a point of honour to ensure that careful supervision continues, lest intervention should, for any purpose, become necessary.'

Mr Henby now led his wife and myself into the hallway, where he rang the school bell – and from the sitting rooms came the pupils, perhaps twenty in all, who formed two orderly lines, one before Mr Henby and one before his wife. These two now produced a bag in which, I was told, were slips, each bearing the name of a male pupil. On a signal, the girls began to move forward – and as each passed Mrs Henby to proceed up the stairs, she dipped her hand into the bag and picked out a slip, reading out the name written upon it. The boy thus named then stepped forward and took the hand of the girl who had picked him, the couple proceeding together with every sign of willingness and even affection.

When the pattern was completed, and no pupils were left, I asked Mr Henby whether the consequence of this proceeding was what I supposed it to be – and learned that indeed it was.

'It would clearly be inadvisable at so early an age,' he said, 'for any one of our female pupils to form a strong bond with one of her male fellows – or *vice versa* – though in the natural course of things this cannot be entirely precluded, and indeed more than one marriage has been solemnised between former attenders here. However, it is our practice to discourage a premature union of an emotional nature; and the easiest way to ensure that that does not occur is to make it improbable that any couple should spend more than an occasional night in intimate cohabitation.'

But was it absolutely necessary, I asked, for pupils to be positively encouraged to cohabit?

Mr Henby looked at me as though my mental faculties had been damaged at birth. Naturally, it was, he said; for how could these young people be prepared for married life – or indeed even for the kind of casual love-making which very often now obtains among the upper class – without being allowed leisure in which to put into practice, and experiment in, the lessons they had learned?

I had nothing more to say – partly because Mr and Mrs Henby were my hosts, partly because what he said seemed to me to be good sense, and partly because I was too interested in his theories to risk his discontinuing the explanation of them as a result of my expressing any doubt.

After a decent interval, Mr and Mrs Henby invited me to accompany them on what they called their 'rounds'. With some diffidence, I enquired whether they thought it right to spy upon their pupils? – to be answered by the argument that it was necessary for the sake of safety to keep an eye on what went on during, at least, the early hours of the night – 'though after midnight,' said Mr Henby, 'these young people are usually too exhausted by their lessons to do anything but indulge themselves in sound sleep!'

The pupils occupied two dormitories, one for the girls and one for the boys – for several nights of the week were spent apart, and it was at all events necessary from a sanitary, no less than any other, point of view for the sexes to be separated one from the other. Now, however, each bed – and there were ten in a room – was occupied by a pair. For privacy, curtains were drawn about the beds, providing the lovers with what amounted to a little room of their own – though the privacy did not extend of course to sound, and indeed shouts of encouragement and sometimes peals of laughter were heard as the young ladies and gentlemen expressed their pleasure or amusement at the experiments they conducted – indeed, I was told that from time to time some problem encountered was shared with others through the medium of the voice, when instruction and advice was passed from one cubicle to the other.

Between the rows of beds was left a slim corridor along which the master and mistress of the establishment now led me. Each little compartment had a candle burning in it, but the corridor was left dark – and so there could be no question of the embedded couples knowing when they were observed through the small gaps left in the curtains for the purpose. They knew perfectly well that from time to time they *were* observed (Mr Henby explained) – for master and mistress believed in entire honesty (indeed, I have never come across an establishment of any kind – least of all at Westminster – where so perfect a standard of truthfulness was observed!). The purpose of such observation having been explained to them, they took it in good part – and from their behaviour had no notion of allowing even the fact that a stranger such as myself might overlook their most intimate moments to have the least effect upon them.

For half an hour after the striking of the first bell, Mr Henby now explained, complete union was denied to the pupils: for, he said, the emotions of the male were different in intensity from those of the female, and if no inhibition were placed upon them, a number of the boys would certainly not be able to contain themselves in patience, but would leap to an immediate conclusion – thus not only disappointing their partners through an insufficient consideration in rousing reciprocal feelings, but failing to learn the art of pleasing a female friend.

I was amused and delighted to observe that the manner in which the couples behaved was as varied almost as the number of them: here a couple remained completely clothed, the lad perhaps only going so far as to place his hand within the lass's clothing to cup a breast, while she might permit her palm to lie upon his thigh, but otherwise kisses alone (though certainly with some enthusiasm) being exchanged. In the next cubicle, however, the pair might not have hesitated to remove every vestige of clothing before retiring, and now lay head to tail, lapping with considerable enjoyment at each other's privates.

Again, here was a couple equally unclad, but who simply lay within each other's arms, the boy's thigh certainly pressed between the girl's, while his lips were fixed to her bosom, but tenderness predominating over passion – as it seemed to do, somewhat to my surprise (and certainly approbation) with most couples, though in two cases where kindred spirits had been matched the heat was considerably raised, in one case the girl, upon all fours, crouched above her lover's body, her hands beneath his arse, lifting him so that she could lick and nip at his cods while his attention and the abilities of his tongue were employed upon her cunny, and at the same time his fingers played about her breasts.

I have no means of knowing how my companions, the master and mistress of this extraordinary school, dealt with the matter of their emotions – but that my own spirits were very considerably raised by these sights may be imagined by the sympathetic reader, and I rapidly became extremely uncomfortable through my prick attempting to burst from my trousers, positively weeping with frustration, not only at its confinement, but at the sight of those pleasures in which through consideration for the age of the participants no less than my own position as a guest, I could by no means hope to participate.

Having passed through both dormitories, and half an hour having elapsed, my hosts now rang a second bell and began a second perambulation. This second signal was by no means (I was told) a command to begin copulation, but simply a signal that if that was desired by both parties, it could now take place. At all events it led to the most remarkable demonstration of how properly educated young people could be brought to an understanding of what complete love-making should be – for a good third of them indeed refrained from immediate fucking, rather choosing to continue a leisurely exploration of each other's bodies, a lethargic pleasuring one of the other which no doubt would in not too brief a time lead to a complete embrace, but which showed at present only such a slow progress towards that desirable result as would please any female and cause any male to be applauded.

Other couples indeed progressed a little more quickly towards their goal: here, a girl was busily lubricating her companion's prick with her lips, less to ensure an easier entry (for in most cases the love-making so completely taught them had resulted in the desired mucosity) as to practise the means by which this could be achieved with a less enthusiastic partner. Elsewhere the young gentleman would be taking care of that necessary procedure by applying his saliva generously to the socket to which he meant shortly to offer his tool.

The couple who had been most closely and tenderly embraced had made the least complicated manœuvre, for the boy had merely shifted himself so that his whole body, rather than one leg, lay between his friend's thighs – when, by throwing them open, she made it easy for him to slip into the most convenient and indeed common of postures, the slow rise and fall of his posteriors together with the look of ineffable pleasure on the face of his companion revealing that such simplicity need by no means be pitied. On my commenting upon the fact that they seemed to have been less inclined to amorous experiment than their friends, Henby explained that they were much preoccupied with each other, and so preoccupied that on their being paired, they could slip immediately into a complete embrace and reach the apogee of pleasure without any necessity for what he termed 'fore play' – a phrase new to me, but usefully encapsulating those lascivious practices which must more usually be encouraged.

Several couples were plainly intent upon experiment, some of them even consulting a paper – upon which, Henby informed me, he had made a copy of a number of the postures of Aretine, which they were attempting to emulate. I was particularly pleased to notice that humour attended these attempts almost as strongly as passion, for laughter and giggling, rather then disappointment or anger, were the result of a failure to duplicate some of the more complicated positions – though here and there the litheness of young bodies had resulted in a perfect reproduction of the postures (as far as I remembered them): as where one boy stood his ground steadily while his companion hung about neck to clasp his waist with her legs, requiring only the assistance of his palms beneath her arse to maintain one of the most difficult of postures for a couple perhaps heavier and less athletic.

In only two cases did passion clearly hold the most lascivious sway – and these were clearly identifiable as being the couples whose previous love-making had been most frenzied: later it was explained to me that all four children had been sick for some two weeks and had been withheld from the exercises which they were now performing with such enthusiasm, the girls being no less enthusiastic than the boys – and by no means afraid to instigate actions, for as we watched one such lass who had been receiving the attentions of her lover from behind, drew away, turned, seized him and throwing him to the bed mounted him with such a bound that I winced in sympathy, lest his parts should be crushed beneath her; but her aim had clearly been excellent, for he certainly showed no hesitation in continuing to participate by what means he might – including sucking at and biting her small, tight breasts – while she rode him as the most eager of jockeys rides a winner at the course at Newmarket, and though he clearly came and afterwards (from his change of expression) felt somewhat tender, continued to ride him for another twenty or thirty seconds, until, with a cry so delighted that a little ripple of applause was the response from other beds nearby (where couples were less thoroughly engaged), she was satisfied.

'You will notice, Mr Archer,' said Mr Henby, 'that young Richard, though it was certainly the case that he reached a climax before Jane, showed no hesitation in permitting her to remain in the saddle until she had past the post – uncomfortable though it may have been for him. An excellent, attentive and considerate pupil!' – and he actually popped his head through the curtain to congratulate the boy, who showed no sign of embarrassment, but clearly took pleasure in the compliment – though this may have had less to do with the approval of his schoolmaster than the fact that Miss Jane, either by way of thanks or by way of hoping for a rebirth, was now attentively kissing the fallen pole upon which she had recently been riding.

Our rounds completed, we left the dormitories – where activity, though by no means ceased, continued in a manner sufficiently leisurely – after the first frenzies – to afford no necessity of supervision, though Mr and Mrs Henby said that they always looked through once more before finally retiring.

'However,' Mrs Henby said, 'you will forgive us, Mr Archer, if we leave you for a while? We usually find it necessary to seek privacy for a while after . . .'

I understood perfectly, and said so, and when Henby was kind enough to hope that I was not myself in too much discomfort – and to explain that he hesitated to offer the services of his wife, for the sake of honour – I assured him that I was capable of control. (In fact I was in a considerable state of heat, though even had I had the opportunity of entertaining Mrs Henby I would have hesitated, not least because she was twice my age, but also to a degree because she was – to be honest – a woman unattractive to me, though happily not so to her husband, with whom she now happily retired.)

I, meanwhile, made for the open air, thinking that a breath or two might somewhat recover me. This was not, as it happened, the case – for the evening was sultry and warm. It was not yet past ten o'clock, and still light, and from over the hedge next to the garden came the sound of lowing, which, when I looked, I found to emanate from a shed where milking was no doubt in progress.

There being a way through the hedge near where I walked, I made my way through it, and found myself in a small, neat farmyard, a cottage upon one side of it and on the other – a couple of geese and some chickens scurrying between – a little shed from which to the sound of lowing was added the unmistakable sound of milk squirting into a bucket. This took me back immediately to my childhood, for among the very few possessions of my father and mother was a single cow, which from time to time I was allowed – nay, enjoined – to milk. Suddenly, the idea came to me that I would like to see whether my expertise in that matter had yet entirely left me, and stepped into the shed.

When my eyes had become accustomed to the gloom I saw before me the most delightful sight that rural England can afford – a pretty milkmaid applying herself to her duty. Clad in the simple smock which was the badge of her calling, she sat on a three-legged stool, bending over the task so that it was impossible for the eye not to be taken by two of the most delightful, full and pendant breasts – positively inviting the lips of an infant, or some other lips, to be fixed to their nut-brown teats, which were in plain view beneath the low neck of her loose dress. Though no doubt aware of my entrance, her eyes were fixed upon the cow's udders, which she milked with that slow, careful, tender touch which can coax the last drop of milk from the most refractory animal.

I stepped forward, and, laying my hand on the animal's hindquarter, enquired of the maid whether I might watch her at work – to which she answered with a merry laugh and the reply that she could think of no reason to deny me, and continued her milking – though I could swear with an eye to my presence, for her hands seemed to move with a more perfectly tender and even lascivious motion, the fortunate animal's teats being not only squeezed, but caressed with her fingers, even with finger and thumb, in a motion which I am sure was not in the least efficacious in milking, but would have been charmingly sensuous had they been applied to . . .

Will the reader be surprised to hear that I felt my emotions once more rising, the close air of the shed, the rank warm smell of it, and the proximity of a pretty young woman with an inviting eye doing nothing to lower them. At last, releasing the teats and exclaiming, "Tis done!', she turned and stooped to lift the pail out of the way – as she did so contriving (I am sure purposely) to allow her smock to fall off one shoulder, so that an entire breast, round and full, came into view. Turning, she bent to place the pail upon the ground, and the smock being pulled tightly about her rump by the exercise, displayed a backside so inviting that it would have taken a stronger man than I to refrain from stepping forward and caressing it.

It immediately became clear that – like so many country maids who, brought up next to a farmyard, knew the ways of a cock with a hen, a bull with a cow, a stallion with a mare – she was far from averse to toying, for unlike a city girl she did not immediately spring to her feet upon feeling my palms about her buttocks, but on the contrary remained in her present position, even giving a delightful wriggle to her loins (no doubt to make me fully aware of her pleasure) and allowing me to feel all the voluptuous rotundity of her arse, the flesh so springy and firm to the touch that she was clearly at that time of life when youth, giving way to womanliness, clings delightfully to its first flowering, reluctant to give way to the years.

But I was now impatient, and pausing only to loose the tie of my trousers, threw up the skirts of her smock – revealing, as I expected, that no covering else concealed her figure – a triangular space now framing a dark fig which I would have tasted with my lips had not my prick been the hungrier.

I am ashamed to say that so raised were my emotions by the events of the evening that three or four lunges were all the enjoyment I could stand before coming off; so the poor girl – who had patiently remained in her stooping position while I fumbled with my clothing to release the instrument which served her so ill – was poorly rewarded for her pains. However, she showed no resentment – and on my pressing half a crown into her hand (picked from my pocket as I reassembled my pantaloons) seemed delighted – though her expression changed somewhat as she glanced up after biting it to test its worth; indeed, it almost seemed that she saw someone behind her – and now that I turned, I too saw that another female figure stood in the doorway of the shed.

'Good evening, sir,' said a cool and assured female voice; 'I trust my Mally gave you every satisfaction.'

A younger and more inexperienced man would doubtless have been covered with embarrassment at the words; but I had been in the world too long to allow myself to be put down, certainly by someone as cool as Madam, and simply replied: 'Indeed, ma'am, she has been most hospitable – as you no doubt observed; but I fear that the speed with which my sudden need provoked me to complete my action denied her the satisfaction which every man should offer even a companion so suddenly taken.'

A delightful laugh greeted my doubtless somewhat impertinent observation.

'I dare say that there was a reason for such celerity,' said the lady; 'and no doubt your next exercise will be the more protracted, by way of compensation, for it. I trust that you are not too exhausted to take a glass of claret with me?'

Though the evening was now drawing in, I could see by the reflected light of the setting sun that the lady was of perhaps forty years of age, but without any sign of advanced age other than a certain maturity of look; for she wore a dress carried upon the very edge of the shoulder and quite sufficiently low cut to show that although she was certainly twenty years older than her milkmaid, her breasts took the eye with a firm jutting which suggested that her body had none of the slackness which the years must eventually impose on that of even the finest female.

On our entering the farmhouse, the lady introduced herself as Mrs Winthrop, and bringing me into a small but elegantly furnished sitting room poured me an excellent glass of wine, and enquired whether I had not been staying with the Henbys and looking over their establishment?

How could she know this? I enquired.

Why, she said, when gentlemen came to visit that establishment her Mally was always richer for a crown or two.

'I have no means of knowing what goes on at that school,' she said, 'but gentlemen visiting it invariably leave in a state of spirits so high that they must necessarily be satisfied – and the hour almost always coinciding with milking time, Mally finds them a profitable line of business. Though all too often their actions are so swift as to be nugatory where physical enjoyment is concerned.'

I sipped my wine and contemplated my hostess. Mrs Winthrop was an extremely charming woman, and I could not but regard her with admiration – which in time, the wine descending to my stomach, and my spirits (not having been entirely dowsed by that quick passage of arms in the cowshed) reviving, turned to a warmth which began to insist upon a further adventure if I was not to spend a sleepless night in an empty bed.

In retrospect, I cannot believe that Mrs Winthrop had not from the first anticipated such a situation – nor can I believe that it had not occurred before, with other gentlemen whose contemplation of the events at the school had similarly inspirited them to a degree that they were in need of some toying in order to satisfy the high degree of lasciviousness provoked by the sight of the young persons at play. It goes without saying, however, that I would not have insulted a lady with whom I had been acquainted for only a matter of minutes by an invitation which, for all I knew, she might have regarded as a serious affront. I therefore contented myself with sipping my wine and regarding her with a look which I trusted might convey in the first place respect, in the second admiration, and in the third a desire to roger her as enthusiastically and as soon as might be convenient to her.

That she took my message seemed to me at the time to be surprising; and her response still seems somewhat astonishing in a woman who, to all appearances, was perfectly respectable – for rising to her feet she stepped towards me, held out her hand, and suggested that since it was clear that Mally had been simply a tasty soppet before a hoped-for banquet, she was entirely happy to act as the main course – and without further ado led me to her bedroom, removed her clothing in even less time than it took me to remove mine, and inviting me to sit upon the bed produced, as it were from nowhere, a bowl of warm water and a cloth and thoroughly washed my prick and bollocks, which no doubt still had about them something of that rankness which is necessarily the accompaniment of congress with a person in such a low state of life as Mally the milkmaid – who, nice enough child though she doubtless was, was unlikely to be given to a regular *toilette*, and would in any case be unlikely to possess the means to accomplish it.

Having dried my parts with a linen cloth, the lady failed to rise from her knees (a posture which she had adopted the better to prepare me for her company), but instead tested her work, as it were, by making sure that my prick was fully recovered from its recent endeavours. This was a needless task, for had it been any more swollen with blood than it already was, I would have been in pain; however, it appeared to give the lady pleasure to taste it, which she did with as much skill as her maid had used in milking, for not only did her tongue run up and down its surface upon every side, but her lips closed about its dome with a soft slipperiness which was exceedingly enjoyable – nor were her fingers quiet, for at the same time they fluttered upon my thighs, belly and chest, tweaking at my nipples. Then throwing me backwards upon the bed, rather than climbing atop me (as I must confess I had expected, and even looked forward to), she remained where she knelt, and enticing me (not with difficulty) to throw my thighs wide, began the most exquisite exploration of those parts which she found most interesting, and which even seemed to present themselves to her as some sort of food – for I felt her tongue licking at every surface, every nook, every concavity and convexity.

That this was by no means unpleasant will be obvious to any gentleman reading this paragraph – nor would any such gentleman have recoiled from the experience, any more than it occurred to me to do so; I even found myself gently taking the lady by the hair, the better to direct her to those areas which her attentions seemed most enjoyably to stimulate – not that the expert knowledge which she clearly had in the matter allowed much lenity, for, whether through instinct or experience, it was as complete as the knowledge of the most adept professional lady.

It was now the position with me that another half-minute would have brought on that paroxysm which would have made a continuation of our pleasure impossible; and though I had positively to pull upon her hair to do so, I managed to persuade her to relinquish (not without a final kiss) her hold upon my prick, and drew her up between my legs (her handsome breasts brushing my belly and breast as I did so) until I was able to take possession with my lips of her adventurous tongue, which proved as anxious to explore my mouth as it had been to pry about that other part of me!

I was now inclined to show that I was by no means one of those lazy fellows who allows the lady to do her work unrewarded, and rolling about contrived to place her beneath me, then, lowering myself to a task no less pleasant for me than (I trusted) it was enjoyable to her, set about pleasuring her.

There is little doubt, I believe, that I succeeded – unless it was the case that the moaning, whimpering, sighing and yelling which took place were all pretence; and even had that been the case, I must have been convinced simply from the liquidity which overcame her cunny, drenching my face, and on my mounting her making our parts so slippery that I was in some doubt whether or not I had entered her – as eventually, of course, I must – except that on my beginning to move, her response was so vigorous that I could no longer be uncertain: for to make the event even more ravishing than might otherwise have been the case, she opened wide her legs and throwing them first about my waist, soon transferred them to my shoulders, crossing her ankles behind my neck in order that with the muscles of her thighs, no less than with those hands which now clutched at the cheeks of my arse, she could add her strength to my own, encouraging me to plumb her with a violence that would surely have shattered a city woman.

We reached our apogee at almost the same moment (always a gratifying effect, though necessarily a rare one), and our shouts of delight were such that I feared it would wake Mr Henby's pupils from what was doubtless by now a sound and satisfied slumber – just such a one as we at present fell into, at least for a time; for I was awakened at some dark hour of the night from a dream in which my lower parts were being covered with icing by some diligent pastry-cook, to feel once more the unmistakable exploration of my hostess's insatiable tongue and lips. (I must aver now that I have never since found, nor did I before experience, so fervid an attention of this sort from a lady. I by no means found this either unfortunate or – much less – unpleasant, and have often wished that I had thought to advise Mr Henby to commission his neighbour to instruct and examine his pupils in the effect, so neglected often by the Britannic race.)

Waking again next morning, with the dawn, I found the lady in a sleep so sound that I was able to rise without waking her; and left my card upon the bedside table – any reward of a financial nature being of course out of the question – before leaving the house. The school, I found locked; but was fortunate to discover in a bothy a gardener's boy who showed me a broken window through which I was able to gain ingress, when finding my way to my room I took to my bed just in time to be awakened with morning tea, brought to me by a female pupil whose sly looks and interest in my unclad state (for I had simply thrown off my clothes and fallen upon the bed) might have led to an incident of a lecherous kind, had I not been (I do believe to her disappointment) exhausted by the night's adventures.

I made my departure later that morning, somewhat tired I must confess, having thanked the Henbys for their hospitality and assured them of my admiration for the excellent regime in which they educated their pupils, promising to recommend their establishment to any of my friends whose children would profit by it – which in some cases I did, receiving afterwards the thanks not only of the parents but of their children, both male and female, the success of whose relationships with the other sex they put down to the education they received there.

Chapter Twelve

Sophie's Story

Naturally, being interested in every aspect of any place in which I was to spend some time, I took in the local newspaper while in Brighton. This contained, as might be expected, reports of every exciting event in the neighbourhood from the birth of a son to the Mayor, to the arrival of the latest fashions from town; and as usual the pages of advertisements were not the least interesting of the contents.

Indeed, I was astonished to discover in the advertisement columns a notice the like of which I had never previously seen: it occupied considerable space on a prominent page of the journal, and was headed **OPPORTUNITIES FOR FRIENDSHIP** – but a cursory glance at the text taught one that more than friendship was the subject. The advertisement was divided into two columns, one headed 'Ladies', the other 'Gentlemen' – and the entries were graded, each preceded by the words 'First class', 'Second class', and so on.

The reader may find it interesting if I reproduce a few paragraphs: first with regard to the ladies:

'*First class*: I am twenty years of age, heiress to an

estate in the county of Sussex of the value of £30,000, well educated, and of domestic habits; of an agreeable, lively disposition, and genteel figure.'

'*Second class*: I am thirty years of age, a widow, in the grocery line in Brighton – have children. Of middle stature, full made, fair complexion and hair, temper agreeable, worth £3,000.'

And so down to an unfortunate female of only the *fifth class*: 'I am sixty years of age; income limited; active, and rather agreeable.'

The gentlemen were no less forthcoming:

'*First class*: A young gentleman with dark eyes and hair, stout made, well educated; have an estate of £500 per annum in the county of Sussex, besides £10,000 in three per cent consolidated annuities; am of an affable disposition, and very affectionate.'

'*Second class*: I am forty years of age, tall and slender, fair complexion and hair, well tempered and of sober habits, have a situation in the excise of £300 per annum, and a small estate in Wales of the annual value of £150.'

And in the case of the male advertisers, the gentleman of the *fifth class* set himself out as 'twenty-five years of age, a mechanic of sober habits, industrious, and of respectable connections.'

These paragraphs interested me strangely, and I determined

to look further into them (being at leisure, and ever curious as to the habits of society, even in the provinces). At the foot of the advertisement appeared the following words:

> 'It is presumed that the public will not find any difficulty in describing themselves; if they should, they will have the assistance of the managers, who will be in attendance at the office, No. 5, Old North Street, on Mondays, Wednesdays and Fridays, between the hours of eleven and three o'clock. Please to enquire for Mr Jameson, up one pair of stairs. The subscribers are to be furnished with a list of descriptions, and when one occurs likely to suit, the parties may correspond; and if mutually approved, the interview may be afterwards arranged.'

I had no hesitation in making my way to Old North Street at midday upon the following day. Attentive readers of our previous volumes will remember my experiences of establishing a house not far from London where interested ladies could arrange to meet gentlemen for the indulgence of the pleasures of conversation (both of a verbal and corporeal nature) – those who do not may consult our volume detailing the matter,[1] where the entire history of Riverside Lodge is set out in a detail almost superfluously full. It was these activities that first aroused my interest in the problems of those ladies and gentlemen who find it difficult to arrange meetings for mutual pleasure – and there are more of them than one might think. The advertisement in the Brighton newspaper seemed

[1]*Eros in the Country*

to me to be directed at just such a readership, and perhaps unsurprisingly aroused my curiosity to a remarkable degree. I determined to assuage it.

I found Mr Jameson in his office, on the first floor of the house whose address he had advertised. I say, his office; in point of fact this was more like a drawing room than anything else, for although there was a table upon which writing materials were to be seen, the room was, as to the rest of its furniture, comfortable and welcoming, Mr Jameson conducting me to a *chaise-longue* and taking his seat upon an easy chair placed a little way off.

He was a pleasant gentleman of middle years, and showed a certain sensitivity by asking immediately whether I had objection to discussing the matter on which I had called with a member of the opposite sex – for if I had, he would be glad to retire in favour of his assistant, Miss Tremble, whom I would find both sympathetic and tactful.

On my replying that on the contrary, I had hoped to hold a conversation with him, he bowed his head politely and waited for me to speak – whereupon I first handed him my card. Having perused it, he raised his eyes with an expression of surprise and pleasure.

'Why, Mrs Nelham,' he said, 'it is a pleasure to meet a lady of your reputation! I have long heard of your establishment at Hammersmith, and considered whether I might attempt to discover your whereabouts in order to discuss it with you, for I understand that you ceased to have that interest after the destruction by fire of your establishment, and it seems a thousand pities that ladies should be deprived of the service you offered.

'Moreover, my interest in the entire subject of the

relationship between the sexes is keen, and what I have heard has convinced me that you are one of the great modern thinkers of our time where that subject is concerned!'

Complimented, I was not especially surprised; for it had seemed to me upon reading the advertisements that Mr Jameson's activities were perhaps not so far from those in which both I and Andy had in the past been concerned; Mr Jameson now confirming this, I was immediately able to be frank with him and to inform him of my curiosity as to the organisation and real intention of his own business.

He now rose and going to the door turned the key in the lock – for, he said, it was the case that some members of the governing body of the town had recently shown an interest in terminating his activities, and he could not be too careful who might overhear a frank conversation.

He then informed me that while, as the advertisements suggested, a part of his business was certainly that of what he called a 'marital agency' (that is, its purpose was to introduce ladies and gentlemen to each other with the object of matrimony), another part, which was becoming by the day the larger part, was concerned with what he termed, 'introductions': the arrangement of meetings between ladies and gentlemen, for whatever purpose a couple might require.

And was it his experience (I asked) that those who requested such an arrangement invariably had the same end in view?

'To an astonishing extent,' he replied. 'On my first opening the establishment I determined merely to act as the moment and the attitude of the applicants seemed to suggest: I had no wish to force any set of circumstances upon my clientele – and, indeed, for the first two or three weeks the ladies and

211

gentlemen who called upon me were concerned only to publicise their circumstances in the form of newspaper advertisements in the hope of receiving the kind of polite addresses they wanted. Then, fortuitously upon the same day, a lady and a gentleman called upon me whose minds were working in another vein.

'The first was the lady: a Miss X – for I must respect her confidence, though I can perhaps go so far as to say that her Christian name was Emma. She was a spirited and vivacious young person of perhaps eighteen or nineteen years of age, and upon enquiring I discovered her to be the daughter of a prominent greengrocer of the town, a regular attender at the Nonconformist Church here, and extremely strict as to morals, permitting no young man to pay attentions to his daughter, who, having reached the age where the demands of the flesh begin to make themselves felt, was sorely in need of male companionship.

'My first supposition was that so innocent a creature must merely wish for polite conversation; however, in a very short time (and I find that ladies are usually not slow to see that I am someone in whom they can confide without the risk of discovery from my blabbing to anyone else) she admitted that her desire was somewhat different.

'Her mother had died some years previously, before Emma had arrived at years which required – nay, demanded – such a parent's assistance in understanding those changes in her emotions which were about to occur. She had, however, as it turned out, a brother some two years older than herself, with whom she was upon excellent terms, and who had not recoiled from describing to her – when she invited him to do so – his own adventures with the ladies, which seemed to have been very considerable and of a nature which one might expect of a young blade.

'His frank descriptions of the activities which he had enjoyed with a number of young persons whose respectability was considerably less established than her own, had whetted her appetite to such an extent that she had (she confessed to me) even invited a practical demonstration from brother Bob – which he had, however, declined to perform, not on the particular grounds of religion or of morals, but that he "could not fancy her", as he put it; and she now came to me in the hope that I could introduce her to a young gentleman of experience and practice who could show her what it meant to be a woman.

'Of course, I was inclined to help her. She was indeed so captivating and promising that in a moment of madness I considered offering her my own services; but as you see, I am almost twice her age, and although in general I see no objection in such a separation of years between lovers, I felt it politic, through concern for the reputation of my business, not to make any such move, and rather assuring her that I would do my best to attend to her request, declined to take the payment she offered until I was sure I could fulfil the conditions of the contract, and invited her to call upon me at the same time on the following day.

'She thanked me prettily, and left.

'I was now in a quandary: her circumstances touched me – quite apart from which it seemed to me that could I satisfy her request, the door might be opened to a remunerative business. I would doubtless not have found it difficult to engage the interest of any young ruffian in introducing Emma to the pleasures of love; a hundred such may be found on the promenade any weekday evening. But it seemed to me that I had a responsibility to find a lover who was at least as well bred as herself, and who would regard the circumstances of their conjunction with a more sensitive eye than could be expected of a mere artisan who, while no doubt willing and able, might frighten her by the violence of his advances.

'I had been considering the problem for perhaps twenty minutes when footsteps were heard upon the stairs and another knock came upon the door. On opening it, I discovered a youth of perhaps twenty and one or two, extremely neatly dressed, carrying a cane, and with an air at once polite and somewhat diffident.

'On his sitting down and being invited to state his business, Mr Y – for I must be at least as diffident in naming him as with the young lady of whom I have just spoken, though again perhaps I might take the liberty of recalling that his first name was Jack – needed some coaxing, for he was considerably more shy than she. However, at last he revealed that he was the only son of a gentleman whose name I knew, and who, although a tradesman, was much respected in the town. His father was (he said – although I already knew it) a member of the same Nonconformist Church as Emma's, and clearly took an extremely puritanical view of his son's becoming a man, for the information and advice he had given young Jack was, to say the least, questionably helpful.

'Discovering his son, on entering his bedroom suddenly, indulging in pleasuring himself by the application of Mrs Palm and her five daughters, his male parent had informed him that such an activity was not only unnecessary, but vile and sinful. He had (he said) for some months suspected Jack of this sin, for he had noticed that his common expression

214

had become lascivious and amorous, that he had a continual wanton smile, looked downwards when addressed, and never into his father's eye; he now walked, moreover (his father told him) with a masturbator's gait – "posteriorly, as though stiffened" – whatever that may have meant. He had also observed that Jack lost no opportunity to look at the other sex, especially at the bust. "More," said the father, whose very words had seemed so terrible to the poor boy that he was able accurately to recall every phrase, "you have that pallid, bloodless countenance, hollow, sunken and with half-ghastly eyes with red rims around the eyelids and black and blue semi-circles which mark out the self-polluter! The mirror will have shown you those red pimples on your face, with a black spot at their centre, which are a sure sign of self-pollution!

"'My boy, mark and remember your father's words! Self-abuse poisons your whole body, breaks down your nerves, paralyses your whole system. It will dwarf and enfeeble your sexual organs, corrupt your morals and endanger your very soul's salvation! You may almost as well die as to thus pollute yourself!"

'By this time, poor Jack told me – and his voice trembled as he remembered the conversation – he was in tears; yet his father continued:

"'This very excess causes more insanity than anything else except intemperance! Hundreds are brought to the lunatic asylum by this single form of self-indulgence, and some must be tied down to prevent further destruction. When you are tempted by this vice, remember the case of the splendid young man rendered a wreck by masturbation! Distracted with delirium tremens horrors, he exclaims from his asylum bed fifty times in an hour, 'O my God, what shall I do? I am going mad!!'"

'Jack's father advised him to think pure thoughts, take a cold bath daily, and study mathematics, which requires (he opined) such fixity of thought that the passions remain almost wholly at rest. He proscribed the reading of any fiction, and particularly damned the notion of the work of modern and especially French writers, which contained erotic pictures seductive to the impressionable mind of boyhood.

'It will be no surprise to you, Mrs Nelham, that the poor boy had been severely affected in his mind by such a lecture. For a time he found himself entirely unable to pursue that delightful and (as we know) entirely harmless pleasure to which he had introduced himself. Happily, however, a friend, seeing how miserable he had become, drew from him the reason for his depression – and did him the inestimable service of introducing him to his own father, a sympathetic and intelligent, modern medical man who was able to persuade Jack of the reality – that any young man unable through youth, or for any other reason, to satisfy himself with a woman should not hesitate to comfort his virility by the means of what is wickedly called "self-abuse"; not to do so, he said, would be exceedingly silly, such an activity being not only pleasurable in itself, but a great reliever of unnecessary irritation and nervousness.

'On Jack (a dutiful son) repeating some of the warnings uttered by his father, his friend's sire merely remarked that a moment's observation could negate all such argument – "for," he said, "I assure you that I have known no young man in my experience who has not at some time, to a greater or lesser degree, practised the art – some indeed continuing well into middle-age – and were your father's allegation correct, the streets of every town in the world would be entirely populated by idiots, which, even taking the most pessimistic possible view of mankind, is far from being the case."

'Comforted by this, Jack had returned to his nightly practice, though with care to be undiscovered, and had found it a comfort; but recently, hearing from his friends tales of their real conquests, now longed to experience in fact what he had only so far experienced in fantasy – that is, to clasp within his arms the body of a willing female companion, and, reading my advertisement, had come to discover whether I could be of assistance to him in attaining his goal.

'My mind naturally and immediately turned to Miss Emma; but before arranging a meeting between them, I must in all caution discover whether Jack was ready to entertain her in a manner proper to the occasion; and on questioning him found that he had only the most vague idea of the sensual connection, admitting that when he had done his best to discover from his friends the actions required of a lover, they had simply laughed at him for his innocence, and restricted their comments to the most crude description of the act.

'Fortunately, I have in my possession a number of manuals, chiefly published abroad, which are devoted to the education of the young in these matters – one indeed being a translation into English, made by myself, of the recent and admirable work of Dr Martino Schurigio, in which he discusses every aspect of the sensual life of women, and which he published in Latin (as being thus safe from the censors) under the title *Muliebria Historico-Medica, hoc est Partium Genitalium Muliebrium Consideratio Physico-Medico-Forensis, qua Pudendi Muliebris Partes tam externae, quam internae,*

*scilicet Uterus com Ipsi Annexis Ovariis et Tubis Fallopianis,
nex non Varia de Clitoride et Tribadismo de Hymen et
Nymphotomania seu Feminarum Circumsisione et
Castratione selectis et curiosis observationibus traduntur.*

'It is,' said Mr Jameson, 'a title peculiarly full in its
description of what the book contains; but I called it, more
simply, *The Parts of a Woman*, and was sure that it would
give young Jack some insight into the nature of the sex; I also
pressed upon him a number of well illustrated manuals,
including translations of the *Su Nu Ching* and the *Su Fang
Mi Chueg*, or *Secret Code of the Jade Room* (from China)
and of the *Kama Sutra of Natsyayana* (from India).'

'Your library must be an extensive one,' I remarked, 'and
I should be pleased at some time to have the opportunity of
studying it. But please proceed with your narrative, for I am
all eagerness to hear the outcome.'

'Urging Jack to peruse the books with all the diligence at
his command,' Mr Jameson continued, 'I invited him to
attend me here on the following day promptly at midday, also
advising him to wash very perfectly before doing so, and
even to perfume himself with some pleasantly smelling scent.
This latter advice I believe gave rise to some feelings of
excitation, and he certainly left these rooms in high spirits.

'When he returned, next day, he was neatly dressed, had
clearly had his hair cut, and was extremely excitable and
nervous. I did my best to put him at his ease, and found that a
nip of whisky helped more than a little – after which I
persuaded him to remove his topcoat, and, after some argument,
even his jacket (for the day was pleasantly warm) and to
loosen his cravat; he was – I should perhaps have remarked –
a handsome young fellow, and in his dishabille, though this

was far from suggestive, presented a picture such as might have been admired by any young lady.

'Upon Emma entering the room, which she did some fifteen minutes later, it was clear from the sparkle that leaped to her eye on his being introduced that she was certainly not immune to his charms. I introduced them as a young woman and a young gentleman who I felt sure would find pleasure in the meeting, and almost immediately made an excuse, and left.

'I wonder, Mrs Nelham, whether you will condemn me for what I must now admit – which is that I had during the earlier part of the morning taken the liberty of boring a small hole in the wainscot which divides this room from another next to it, usually occupied by my female assistant? And that, retiring, I lost no opportunity of placing my eye to it?

'You would not be deceived if I told you that I did not find it pleasurable to observe two pretty people making love; but you will perhaps credit me when I say that in this case I was particularly anxious that things should go well, and believed that I should be ready to intervene if they did not – for my future prosperity was certainly in these two pairs of hands.

'During the moments which had elapsed while I made my way from the room, the couple had seated themselves on the very *chaise-longue* upon which you are at the moment reposed; Jack at one end, Emma at the other, and a distance of certainly as much as two feet between them. Though I could see their lips move, I could not hear what they said; but guessed that they were merely exchanging those normal courtesies which may comprise a comment upon the weather, the season or the circumstances – the latter however being a minefield of danger, for in a moment I saw Emma blush and look down – whereupon Jack blushed, too, and stretching out his hand laid it upon hers by way of comfort.

'That the movement was welcomed by her was seen by the fact that she immediately turned her hand so that it was palm to palm with his own, the fingers interlaced – which so invigorated him that he instantly moved towards her, the gap between them shrinking considerably.

'His father had evidently been accurate (if in nothing else) in his observation that Jack showed some interest in the female bosom; and he now found himself in just such a position as it was impossible for his eye not to fall upon two delightfully rounded examples of that portion of his companion's anatomy (for her gown was sufficiently loose at the breast to show most of her bosom, and even I believe from where he was sitting may have disclosed a pert, pink nipple).

'At all events, the young man was entirely unable to contain himself, and, falling to his knees, pressed his face to that bosom, even going so far as to displace her gown with his hands in order (again, I say perhaps, for I could not see clearly) to press his lips to the very nipples themselves.

'Had his companion not been a lady who had been (I believe) looking forward eagerly to just such an encounter, this might have been a disastrous move; as it was, it simply released the tide of her own emotion, and placing her hands on the back of his head, she first pressed it voraciously to her breast, and then, lifting it, placed her lips upon his own, at the same time positively tearing at his shirt so that the buttons were rent and the material fell away.

'Her hands now began to explore his torso with the most interesting movements, particularly dwelling upon his own nipples, which, by erecting themselves into tiny nodules, delighted and amused her; the small show of hair which lay between them also interested her, and she could not resist drawing a few of them between her lips. But her hands fell most eagerly to his waist, where their progress was, however, disappointingly arrested by his belt.

'Jack at this jumped to his feet and in a moment had unloosed a buckle and stepped out of his lower clothing, revealing what I am sure Miss Emma had not previously seen – unless her brother had been bolder than she had admitted: that is a fine prick in full extension, not so much horizontal as almost vertical in its display, the column round and white, the pink dome shining with the liquescence of desire.

'The girl for a moment stared in wonder, and then threw up her hands in admiration and remarked so loudly that I clearly heard the words: "Oh, but how beautiful! I must kiss him – pray allow me!" – and leaning forward began to kiss and play with the engine, whose starts and leaps, instigated by the pleasantness of the sensation, were so excited that she was forced to take it in her hand in order to steady it as she finally drew it between her lips.

'That this delighted Jack goes without saying – but delicious though the caresses were, his curiosity was stronger, and soon he persuaded her (with the greatest difficulty) to stand, and, unhindered, began to unbutton her blouse, revealing in all their glory those globes which he had earlier too briefly saluted. His admiration of them was evidently great; yet his curiosity was still the stronger, and falling to his knees he drew her skirts down below her knees, revealing to him for the first time her chief glory – which I must confess was handsome, the golden flax only half concealing two pink lips which teased his eyes with what seemed a positive pouting!

'Now was his turn to salute her with a kiss – which so delighted her that to give him better access, she placed one foot upon the couch, opening herself more fully not only to his excited gaze, but to his exploring fingers and lips.

'Both of the youngsters were now in a state of positive frenzy; they did not know what to do next, so confused were they between the delights of sight and sense. Young Jack had clearly profited from his study of the books I had loaned him, and may even have had little sleep, so thoroughly did he seem to have studied them – for, unlike most boys of his age, he did not tumble her to the couch and ravish her at once, but kissed every part of her with peculiar tenderness and attention, even neglecting her tenderest parts to salute her fingers and toes, her shoulders and neck, her breasts – I need hardly say – but also her thighs and belly.

'She lay, not merely untroubled, but rejoicing at this; and did her best to allow him some pleasure also, by catching from time to time at his hands and smothering them with kisses, finally – discovering by instinct what more practised lovers have learned – reclining upon the bench with her head towards his feet, so that while (his head resting upon her thigh) he could caress with his tongue those fleshy lips which he now parted to reveal a plump simulacrum of his own cock, she could take the larger model between her fingers and lick every inch of it with her own perhaps more tender tongue.

'I believe that Emma was by now somewhat confused: she had not had the benefit of learning of the subtleties of love-making as described by the lovers of the ancient courts of China and India, and feeling obscurely that something more was to be expected of a lover even than this tender and pleasing attention, whispered something into her lover's ear – perhaps enquiring whether there was no more substantial play to follow this preamble?

'I am glad to say that although he must have given his attention to those many positions suggested for intercourse by the writers and artists who had prepared the books he had studied the previous night, Jack made no attempt at ambition, but kneeling between her knees gently parted them, and lowering himself slid easily and without obstruction into the most familiar of all loving embraces.

'The young lady appeared to suffer no pain at the rupture of her hymen. I am sure that she was a virgin, and the absence of discomfort seemed at the time surprising; I had feared indeed that it was at that point that she might have found the experience I had arranged less than pleasant – but whether the discomfort was so outweighed by the pleasure as to be entirely nugatory, or whether by their play the rupture had already taken place, I have no means of saying; all I can report is that Jack immediately fell into a vigorous swiving which was received by his partner with every sign of pleasure, and indeed soon enough with cries of enthusiasm so loudly expressed that I feared that the pedestrians in the street below might be alarmed by them.

'It was, I confess, a surprise to me that Jack was able to contain his excitement for a very considerable period, and was thus able to bring his partner to the full extent of her pleasure before completing his own. It may be that his nightly experiments in self-pleasuring had made him conscious of the additional enjoyment to be found in delay: and I have noticed that some gentlemen indeed find that to bring themselves by that means to the very edge of completion, then to retire, only to begin the action again when their excitation has somewhat diminished, results often in a more perfect control of emotion than in those who believe the practice to be supererogatory and damaging.

'However that may be, the completion of the bout was entirely satisfactory to both; and they lay for a while in their perspiration – which shone upon the boy's shoulders and arse in great beads, noticing which (not only by sight but by passing her hands over his body) the young lady persuaded him to move, and taking her petticoat (for she was wearing one of those new garments) wiped him down carefully from head to feet as she might have done an exhausted stallion – but on coming to that part of him which had given her such joy, could not resist trying to revive it in its glory. This proved to be entirely possible; and on his sitting up, in her eagerness to repeat their pleasure she crouched above him and to his joy sank upon him in a position he must have seen reproduced in the form of art, but would I believe have thought it too ambitious to try upon a first encounter.

'I will not delay you by further describing their experiments, which went on until about seven in the evening – during which time I was forced several times to leave my vantage point in order to take some refreshment, while they continued without any greater stimulant than their own enjoyment. They left with many expressions of gratitude, even more pleasant to me than the fee which they happily paid. I was able to gratify them by providing them, through a mutual friend, with a bedroom to which they still retire, I believe, upon a regular almost daily basis. Two young people are, therefore, a great deal happier for my intervention in their lives than would otherwise have been the case – and they have not been slow to inform those friends who might profit from calling upon me, of their satisfaction, which has resulted in a remarkable increase in this side of my business.'

It was a story which keenly interested me, and I took my leave of Mr Jameson with many thanks for his freedom in relating it; and returned to my hotel reflecting that some such business as his would be something desirable even in the smallest town, were our youth ever to be brought up with a more accurate conception of what was possible, in adult life, in the way of pleasant communion between the sexes.

Chapter Thirteen

The Adventures of Andy

Though most interested by my recent adventures, I was by now almost certain that my study of the coast must near completion, for so built-up is it by pleasant townships that it is impossible to think of establishing another centre in the area – it would not only be superfluous, but naughtily damaging to the amenities of the area, which must surely to some extent rely on supplying not only small centres of population, but also the stretches of unspoiled coast where one may take one's ease without the interruption of numerous holiday-makers.

I therefore took myself back to Brighton; but after a couple of days' relaxation there (not even concerning myself to discover where my friend Sophie was staying, for my experience is that reunions between us are productive less of rest than of additional activity of one kind or another) felt sufficiently restored to convince myself that I must make at least one excursion to the west of the town, in order to ensure that the situation there is much as it is to the eastward.

I travelled first through Worthing, a pleasant and sociable little watering place twelve miles distant from Brighton (two of these shortly to be curtailed by a road to be taken over a suspension bridge across the River Adur, at Shoreham). Worthing is a place which I will not flatter, though it certainly possesses strong inducements of comfort and pleasure not always found in larger places of resort. The resident population being united and friendly and the lower classes decent and orderly, I scarcely know a drawback to a visit here during its summer season.

Of Littlehampton and Bognor I intend also to say but little: the former contains some 1,600 inhabitants, having become a resort for sea bathing, and has a library, amateur band, baths and other accommodations. The latter has some 1,500 inhabitants, many residing in neat villas which excite rather high expectations; but the town itself is scattered and irregularly built, and though there are three or four good inns and some respectable ranges of building, also baths *et cetera*, and may have advantages to those who prefer quiet, its promenade has not been kept up, and it has an air of genteel decay.

The ancient town of Arundel, however, certainly when approached from Worthing, has a much more commanding presence, the stately front of the castle giving a strong impression of feudal and ancestral grandeur, the old central keep towering above the terrace and the whole being enveloped in ancient trees and contrasted in front by a river of scanty breadth but impetuous flow.

Arundel itself is a tolerably neat town, of no great extent, enlivened by its river and with an assembly room, a small theatre, a library, and one excellent inn – the Norfolk Arms – where I took a room. It is, however, the castle which is the town's chief glory: the late munificent Duke of Norfolk expended not less than £600,000 on the new buildings, which appeared to be very tactfully joined to the adjacent almost ruined part – and I was extremely eager to visit the place in order to inspect it. On my enquiring as to that possibility, I was delighted to hear that visits were possible.

Application, however, should be made (I was told) not as I expected to the Duke's housekeeper, but to a Mrs Emmeline Possett, a friend of that lady, who relied implicitly (it seemed) on her recommendation as to the credentials and respectability of those asking to be admitted to the castle. This I found, on reflection, to be entirely credible, for it is natural for those who recognise themselves to be indifferent judges of human nature to rely upon those whose superior judgement cannot result in errors of taste.

I called on Mrs Possett upon the following day, whose house was a handsome and relatively modern one – built, I would say, no earlier than 1800, in the main street of the town. Knocking on the door, I was admitted by a pretty young maid and shown into a pleasant parlour where, after a while I was joined by a lady of about my own years, by no means unattractive, and from the first, receptive to my compliments (which were perfectly honest, for she had that natural charm which made conversation pleasant and easy).

It seemed to me that she regarded me with an eye to my appearance as much as to my character (my card, disclosing me as a member of the Mother of Parliaments, presumably having convinced her immediately of my respectability). She appeared to look me up and down almost with the air of a horse dealer inspecting a beast – her close regard being inoffensive through clearly being admiring; and after a few minutes she proved perfectly willing to write a note of recommendation to her friend the housekeeper – her only request being that I would call upon her that evening to take supper and let her know my impressions of the castle.

Needless to say, this was a condition to which I did not find it difficult to assent – if not without some conjecture as to its purpose, for surely the lady must already have heard every possible shade of opinion as to the Duke's additions to the place – and no doubt frequently from those better equipped to pass a professional judgement than myself, a mere amateur of architecture and landscape.

Presenting myself an hour later at the main court of the castle, I found the housekeeper amiable and compliant, who herself escorted me through the building. The great court was immediately imposing, being built on three sides, the fourth rising on an ascent to the keep, a beautiful flower and fruit garden enclosed within the walls beyond it. The east and south sides of the court are very handsome, the former exhibiting a large and bold relief in artificial stone of 'Alfred instituting the Trial by Jury' and, in addition, being decorated with carved windows, an oriel, machicolations, open parapet, curiously wrought corbels and round turrets.

Of the interior I will speak only briefly: the gallery, 195 feet long, has magnificent polished mahogany furnishings in lavish profusion; the Baron's Hall was opened in the year 1815 (with a magnificent entertainment of ancient splendour to upward of three hundred persons); drawing room, dining room, breakfast room, library, are all equally splendid. The housekeeper even took it upon herself to allow me to view the

Earl Marshal's bedroom – which has splendid furniture and a bedstead of great beauty, with curtains of crimson damask silk – and that used by the Prince Regent when he visited the castle, a room hung with magnificent cut velvet, flowers and red and green velvet raised on a ground of white satin, with gold mouldings and other ornaments, and a bed with fine reeded pillars and a rich Gothic canopy.

Having finished my tour, I thanked the housekeeper, handed her a present and took the liberty of enquiring about her friend in the town, by whose offices I had applied to her.

'Ah,' she said, 'Emmeline is a lady of considerable taste as to those she commends to me.'

'Indeed,' I remarked, 'but upon what criteria does she recommend them? My reputation as a gentleman did not seem to impress her – it was almost as though she based her recommendation upon some other factor.'

'I do not think I can take it upon myself to answer that question,' replied the housekeeper. 'No doubt you have been asked to call upon her this evening?'

Indeed I had, I replied; but to what purpose? – for I could not believe that Mrs Possett desired to have the contents of the castle described to her.

'That, again, I must allow her to explain,' said the housekeeper. 'However, I will say to you that I have never known her to send a plain man to me, nor an old man, nor one too young, but only those in the prime of life and with (if you will allow me to say so) a carriage and appearance as handsome and manly as your own.'

I acknowledged her flattery with a bow, but failed to persuade her to say anything more on the matter, except that Mrs Possett had been for some ten years a widow, and might be described as of an active nature. A sneaking suspicion of what I had perhaps let myself in for now occurred to me, and I later made my toilet with special care.

The lady answered the door to me herself, and brought me into the parlour – her servants having, she explained, requested the liberty of absence during the evening, due to a servants' supper being given at the local assembly rooms – an annual event of great importance to the domestic classes. She immediately invited me to take a glass of claret, which I was naturally happy to do. She took care to sit opposite to me, and a very handsome figure she made, clad in a simple white dress the nature and design of which I am alas unable, as a man, to describe with any particularity, but which was cut sufficiently low at the neck to show the swelling of what, as far as I could see without the impertinence of staring, was a truly magnificent bosom, and which was pinched to show a narrow and appealing waist. She held her glass with a decorous and elegant poise, and having raised it to her lips passed her tongue slowly over the lower lip, no doubt to remove any surplus liquid which might remain there – but in a gesture which was quite remarkably stirring, for that lip swelled to such an effect as positively to invite the pressure of other lips upon it. Indeed, the instinct even to sink one's teeth into it in an amorous bite was so lascivious, powerful and immediate a temptation as to cause my fingers to close around the stem of my claret glass almost sufficiently hard to break it.

I did not, however, allow myself to be carried away sufficiently to make a gesture which, while natural, might have been construed as forward; and for some minutes we made polite conversation, exchanging comments upon the

Duke's improvements which, being to no great extent illuminating, made it clear to me that whatever had encouraged Mrs Possett to summon me to supper, it was not the idea of discussing the domestic architecture of Arundel Castle.

After a while, once more apologising for the absence of servants, Mrs Possett invited me to take her arm and escort her to a small, pleasant dining room, where the table was set for two persons. Upon a side table was a feast of cold meats and salads.

'I am sure that you will not object, Mr Archer, to serving yourself,' remarked my hostess.

Indeed I did not, and assisted us both to a helping of a cold white soup, flavoured with almonds and thickened with cream. This was delicious, and I will not disguise from the reader the fact that my enjoyment of it was by no means depreciated by the spectacle of my companion's pleasure in the dish – for she brought each spoonful to her lips with a deliberate relish: indeed, with an eagerness which resulted in a few drops oozing from the corner of her lips and standing upon the delightfully pink flesh; when abjuring the use of the napkin, she once more extruded a charmingly sinuous tongue and took up the drops upon it – an act which seemed to me to be so deliberately and sensually provocative that I began to believe that my hopes of an evening's entertainment, not entirely restricted to the gustatory, would be fulfilled.

My hostess had provided a couple of dozen oysters (these are not unknown in the area, there being an oyster farm not far from the town). They lay still in their shells, and it was with a delightfully robust enjoyment that Mrs Possett took them – her lips parting only to close over the body of the mollusc, positively embracing it as it slid between them and into the dark cavern of her mouth. I must confess to the doubtless somewhat provoking gesture of taking my own share of the oysters in a pantomime of her own style – which seemed to have the result of bringing us in emotion somewhat together, for her eyes took mine with a glancing spirit of excitement – but with a result unexpected and unplanned in that – whether from her hand shaking or from her eye being too closely engaged with my own, I would not be so impertinent as to guess – the shell she was lifting tilted, and the oyster fell from it into the neck of her dress, just between those charming snow-white hills which I had so admired!

I naturally leaped immediately to my feet and took the single stride which placed me at her side. Unhorrified by the accident, she remained seated – but whether from surprise or some other emotion, made no attempt to remove the offending item, which could be seen nestling in a cleft which I must confess I was now glad enough to have the opportunity to explore. With a gesture which I hope was as deferential and appropriate as could have been contrived in the circumstances – and with a whispered invitation to pardon any familiarity, I bent, and with my fingers regained the oyster, raising it to my lips and swallowing it immediately!

The gesture was of course meant for a compliment, and happily was taken as such – for the lady immediately smiled – but then in merry protest she accused me of depriving her of a share of the feast. My next action might seem daring – but nothing ventured, nothing gained; and taking an oyster from my own plate, I slid it into my mouth, and bending over the lady invited her to accept it from my lips.

She took my meaning immediately, and bending her head upwards held her mouth towards me, so that by approximating my lips to her own I could allow the oyster to slip from my mouth into hers, its passage bringing our lips – and even the inside curves of them – into the closest possible juxtaposition.

This familiarity was accepted with such grace that as the action was occurring I could not resist the temptation to slip my hand within the neck of her dress and place my palm upon one of those breasts so temptingly displayed below me, the nipple of which seemed almost to scratch my skin, so keenly erectile was it. Although we were but half-way through the meal, I could no longer contain my lust, which had been much aroused; and, grasping the lady, forced her to her feet and was soon tasting those oyster juices which remained clinging to the surface of her tongue; an action which she by no means rejected.

I need not describe the stages in which, within a very few moments, we had divested ourselves of our clothing and were embraced, skin to skin (only perhaps in parenthesis insisting that the lady was no more reluctant than I to strip herself of those encumbrances which concealed her figure).

I naturally now expected a more intimate connection than had previously been offered; but far from leading me from the dining room to her chamber, my friend, in a moment, lifted her lips from mine to suggest that we should proceed to the next course – which was a cold veal fricassee, swimming in cream!

It is always my habit to fall in with the desires of any lady companion who shows a strong predilection for any particular form of behaviour, in a situation such as the one in which I now found myself; it is the short cut to happiness, frequently revealing a taste which, if complied with, can immediately raise senses which otherwise might lie dormant for too long. I therefore permitted her to lead me to the side table – not allowing myself to be embarrassed by the fact that a certain feature of my person was swollen to such an extent that there was no disguising it (indeed, embarrassment would have served no purpose, for I noticed that Mrs Possett frankly permitted her eyes to rest upon it in what seemed an admiring vein, evidently not in the least dismayed by the sight).

We made rather a poor hand at the veal fricassee, however, our appetites being directed to another end; and even though I brought my chair to the end of the table and now sat next to my hostess, in order to tempt her with choice pieces from my plate, our consumption of the dish was more than a little faint-hearted – a situation which changed only as the result of an accident, when a piece of veal, thickly coated in cream sauce, fell from my fork into my lap.

As I reached to recover it, Mrs Possett stayed my hand, and pushing back her chair fell to her knees and with her lips removed the piece of meat from the place where it had come to rest upon the platform of a thigh. Nor did she stop there – but proceeded to lap up the sauce which lay there, even parting my legs with her hands in order to pursue a trickle which had made its way down the inside of my thigh.

That I found her action charming goes without saying; that she herself found it pleasurable soon became clear, for reaching to the table she dipped her hand into my plate, and smeared a mess of cream all over my belly and thighs and even that instrument of which I spoke some paragraphs ago, and which was no whit less upright than it had been before! Fearful lest the mess should damage the upholstery of the chair upon which I sat, I slipped – not without the lady's consent and even assistance – to the thick carpet, and lay there as with an attentive enjoyment she lapped at my body, licking the sauce from my skin, inserting her tongue into the channels between my thighs and bollocks, and taking up with it every trickle and drop that stood upon my distended staff – even going so far as to draw back the skin from the head in order to run her tongue around the groove beneath the dome (where no one could suppose any sauce to have found its way). Time and again she returned to the fricassee in order to apply a new coating of sauce to my body, which she then licked and sucked away with the enthusiasm of a *gourmand* and the exquisite taste of a *gourmet*! It was not as though her ambition was merely to enjoy the last drop of sauce, or even to cleanse my prick, for she might have stopped long since had that been the case; far from that – she continued to lick and suck for the sake, it seemed, of pure enjoyment. (I have found in my experience that a considerable proportion of ladies do take more pleasure in this act than they might in modesty care to admit to; and it is certainly the case that a little sweetening of the dish assists them, as though providing an excuse for starting the action, even if they do not need to be provided – by having removed every vestige of the sauce – with an excuse for ending it.)

I could not permit her, however, to continue to pleasure me indefinitely without returning the compliment, and intent on continuing the pleasant fantasy which she had begun, enquired whether she did not feel that a little dessert would be pleasant? – and without waiting for her to reply, rose only for a sufficient period as was necessary to take from the side table a dish of *blanc mange* and place it at our sides, now reclining in such a position as was convenient for me to apply some portion of it to her breasts, from which I took it with my tongue in a gesture which may certainly have appeared over-eager to an onlooker, but which brought forth no protests from the lady, who indeed reclined with an expression of contentment, varied by an occasional grimace of keener enjoyment (when, for instance, I pretended to mistake her nipples for cherries, giving each a gentle nip with my teeth).

The platform of her belly made an equally – in fact perhaps more – convenient table, her navel collecting a little lake of delightful liquid; while she assisted me, a moment later, by thrusting with her feet at the floor and elevating her middle parts – an attitude which I assisted her to preserve by placing a cushion beneath her buttocks. The posture then enabled me thoroughly to fill a larger crevice with the sweet mess. My efforts to ensure that every drop of this was consumed provoked, I believe, just such keen emotions as I had experienced earlier; and while it is of course not in the least difficult to arouse these feelings by the simple exploration of the tongue, I must insist to the reader that the pleasure of combining the taste of good food with the exploration of the body of a lover can provide an experience which no one should deny themselves!

The trembling of the lady's body having twice culminated in a shuddering sufficiently strong positively to displace my tongue from its position upon that spot which can best convey sensual pleasure to the female, I raised my head and lifted an eyebrow: whereupon, Mrs Possett was kind enough to nod, and I, therefore, in a moment placed myself so that I could bring into juxtaposition two areas of our bodies which, whatever other criticism might be made of them as to elegance or beauty (though I dare say that neither particularly lacked either quality) were at least thoroughly clean! – and, moreover, had been so thoroughly lubricated by various means that my entry of her body was almost completely lacking in friction. This, under certain circumstances, can be a disadvantage: but in this case I had been so roused by the activities which preceded the action that friction was the least desirable of stimulants, for it would almost certainly have led to a premature end to the festivities. As it was, I was able for some little time to maintain those movements which, were pleasurable to me, and were made, I believe, more so to Mrs Possett through her lower parts still being elevated by the cushions, thus permitting me to explore with my prick the deepest recesses of her cunny, and bring her, I believe for the third time, to a culmination of pleasure before, with an almost painful constriction of my loins, I myself reached my apogee.

We were both too exhausted by emotion to make any movement for some moments; then Mrs Possett was good enough to congratulate me before asking whether I had eaten sufficiently well. As it happened, my appetite – now the grosser sort had been satisfied – was somewhat recovered, as (she admitted) was her own. The room having a window which looked only on to an enclosed garden, the servants being away, and the weather hot, we were not concerned to resume our clothing, but took ourselves to a sofa inside the open window and reclined there like Adam and Eve among the fruits to continue our supper – even consuming some more of that *blanc mange* which had been somewhat depleted by our former activities.

That done, Mrs Possett offered me the convenience of a bath of water; and led me upstairs to her bedroom, where a large tub stood which was full of cool water – and insisted on helping me to remove those few vestiges of stickiness which remained on my lower body. These were chiefly situated in the bifurcation of my loins, beneath my cods, and her insistence on attending to that spot (which is one ever responsive to the touch) had the result of once more awaking my feelings – which I believe somewhat surprised her, for she had assumed that the completeness of our joint experience over (and under) the supper table had deprived me of my powers for the remainder of the evening.

It is a mistake which has often been made; for even in advanced years – and I was at that time past my thirtieth year – my powers of recuperation were remarkable (no doubt the result of a healthful life and an enthusiastic attention to the pleasures of the flesh, unfamiliarity with which is more than anything else responsible for that lack of vigour which depresses the ladies). On my tool, then, somewhat enlarging between her hands – as she applied to it some soap – she was appreciative and delighted; and on my apologising for the degree of flaccidity which was the result of so recent love-making, asked if she might attempt a complete recovery? – and without waiting for permission brought me to her bed, where an inventive combination of tongue and fingers had the desired result. Our having been to a degree familiar removed any susceptibility to nervousness or shyness, and without further ado she threw her leg over my body, mounted me and rode me with considerable pleasure to both of us until yet another fence had been jumped and the winning post passed – or perhaps I mean, fallen.

We were both now somewhat exhausted and fell into a doze awaking from which I found that complete darkness had fallen, and heard a clock strike eleven, somewhere in the house beyond the bedroom. My companion being sound asleep at my side, I rose quietly and, taking up my clothes, tiptoed, naked as I was, from the room – for not only would it have been rude to awaken my friend from her slumber, but to be frank I did not wish to place myself in the position of having to commit myself to too long or close a relationship, pleasant enough though the interlude had been.

A full moon threw its light through a window and down the staircase as I tiptoed down it. But as I reached the bottom, and was about to pause to clothe myself before leaving by the front door, I heard angry voices whispering nearby – and in a moment, the sounds of a woman in tears. I stepped away from the door as it opened – and through it, a handkerchief pressed to her face, stepped a female figure. I stepped back once more, in order not to be discovered – but unfortunately collided with a small table, and at the noise the woman came forward and could not avoid seeing me, for the moonlight lit the hallway almost as completely as upon a dull day.

The handkerchief taken from her face, in order that she could see, I now recognised the pretty maid who had shown me into the house that very morning – and I believe she recognised me, and knew that I had been there at her mistress's invitation, for she showed no sign of fright, or even surprise (despite my unclothed state) – but once more allowed herself to be overcome by the emotion which caused her tears, for raising the handkerchief to her eyes she again burst into muffled sobs – and upon my stepping forward, all unconsciously threw herself into my arms!

I do not wish to give the impression of taking advantage of a female in distress, but female distress ever involves my emotions, and, moreover, I believe I will be excused simply by invoking the sympathy and understanding of my male readers – and even my female friends may understand me when I say that I found it difficult to be impervious to the charms of a situation in which a young buxom girl of perhaps eighteen, clad in the lightest and thinnest summer clothing, had thrown herself into my arms at a moment when I was divested of my own apparel. Twin breasts, full, soft and appealing were pressed to my chest, a pair of arms were about my neck, a wet cheek was pressed to mine, and a soft voice whispered, 'Sir – oh! – sir!' in my ear. Can I be condemned, I ask, for pressing a kiss first upon the girl's salty cheek, then upon her lips?

The fact that these were so compliant, and that there was no sign of a nervous drawing away – even though the immediate reaction of my body, which was a re-erection of that tool which might have been forgiven for supposing that its work of the night was complete, must have been apparent to her – convinced me that the young lady's distress was not of the deepest nature – a tiff, maybe, with a gentleman friend, some other servant perhaps. That she was ready to be consoled was evident from her continuing to cling to me, and by the fact that when, tiring of standing upon tiptoe to embrace me, she lowered her arms and placed them around my waist, and almost instantly permitted the palms to fall upon the cheeks of my arse, and even pulled me towards her, pressing a thigh between my own, and constricting my prick between our two bellies – and further, now sank to the ground, drawing me after her until we lay upon the doormat by the foot of the stairs.

I was not fully determined upon my next action, the situation being one which (to speak frankly) I had not previously found myself in; but my young friend saved me any necessity to reach a decision for action, by smothering my face and breast with kisses, and, having captured my prick with her hands, covering it equally with loving little puckers of her lips, meanwhile smoothing my cods with her fingers with an urgency which convinced me (had I not already received sufficient hint of the fact) that here was a young lady so urgently in need of amorous attention that for me to attempt to deny her would be to rouse her to a set of hysterics which would necessarily wake the house and lay me open to who-knew-what accusations?

While I had been, as rationally as was possible in the circumstances, considering my next move, the young lady (whose name I never learned) raised herself to her knees, threw up her skirts, and taking my hand in hers placed it upon a full, pouting and lusciously wet cunny. Such a direction I could not ignore; and kneeling in my turn, drew her towards me so that she sat upon my lap – when, before I could act further, she seized my tool and, holding it at such an angle as made the action possible, positively spitted herself upon it. Her pleasure was immediate and considerable: indeed, I had to place my hand over her mouth to stifle those cries with which, as she bounced energetically upon me, she would otherwise have brought her mistress down upon us (who knows with what consequences?). Embracing me not only with her thighs but with her arms, she tore away my hand and fixed her lips to mine, even biting them with a force that drew blood and brought up a swelling which drew curious looks from a number of those with whom I had dealings on the following day – including the landlord of the hotel, who asked with a meaningful look whether I had enjoyed my dinner with Mrs Possett. I ignored the enquiry.

The maid proved less demanding than the mistress, for having brought on her pleasure she was able to satisfy it within a few moments, when she smiled prettily in the moonlight, whispered her thanks, and assisted me to dress, wiping my now somewhat red and irritated tool with a handkerchief before tucking it carefully away inside my trousers with a care which suggested gratitude.

Not necessarily for reasons only of a lubricious nature, I can recommend the interest of Arundel: the castle is certainly worth exploring – while it must be said that the method of payment for an introduction to the custodian is one which, it may be, few gentlemen who retain their powers will object to making. (I should say, however, that the events of which I speak took place some years ago, and upon male visitors finding that they must apply to a female for admission to the place, it will be advisable to show some care in offering to pay in the coin demanded of me; the lady may after all have been succeeded by some less adventurous custodian.)

I now made my way back to Brighton, and going straight to the Albion Hotel took a room there, being delighted to see upon the previous page of the register the name of Mrs Sophia Nelham. Having spent the afternoon resting, I made my way to the rooms noted as occupied by her, and, without knocking, entered and found a charming sitting room. I did not hesitate to look into the next room also – a bedroom at present unoccupied. Clearly my friend was elsewhere: so stretching myself out on the bed, I fell asleep in my clothes, to be awakened, some hours later, by someone entering the room, bearing a lamp.

Chapter Fourteen

Sophie's Story

It now seemed to me that the time which I might continue to spend in Brighton was drawing to an end: I had had a pretty good opportunity of sampling its pleasures, and with August about to succumb to the turning year and become September – though the weather continued to be fine – I began to feel that a return to London would not be disadvantageous to spirits much refreshed by the air and the concomitant delights of the seaside.

There was no sign of Andy's returning to the town; but there was no necessity for my waiting upon this, and I therefore concluded that another week might see my departure, and gave myself over to looking through those parts of Brighton which I had not so far thoroughly explored – one of these being what are called the Lanes.

The new Market House, west of the Town Hall, was erected only some five years ago – a spacious, neat building having some resemblance to that in Farringdon Street, London, but on a more humble scale. West of this building and at the back of North Street is a dense collection of narrow thoroughfares only wide enough for pedestrians, which are called 'Lanes'. A market of miscellaneous character is held here every day in the week, but by far the greatest occurs on Saturday, when in shops of every description vendors endeavour to attract the passer-by by the promise of cheapness. Here too may be seen the anxious wife of the artisan, diligently seeking to lay out her small pittance, which the spectator often wishes were greater, in the most advantageous manner.

These little emporia were fascinating to me – quite as interesting as the larger shops to be found in North Street itself (often inconveniently crowded, through its irremediable narrowness at the summit of the hill). I had formed the habit – finding it interesting as well as useful – of using the Lanes as a form of short cut from North Street towards the sea, and late one night was passing through them on the way back to my hotel.

Brighton is lighted with gas, but very indifferently so; the individual lights in the main streets are large and handsome, but much too few and far between; and in some parts the illumination is confined entirely to the private lights of the shops. Consequently, when these are shut up there is almost total darkness – and this is certainly true of the Lanes, which even on a summer's evening are quite sufficiently gloomy to cause some nervousness to those who suffer from that indisposition (among which, however, I am not to be counted).

As I passed through one of these narrow 'streets' or alleys, I was startled by a female cry of distress which seemed to come almost from over my right shoulder. I looked around, but could see nothing; then the cry came again, this time somewhat stifled, but certainly from behind a door just at my right hand. Without hesitation I turned the handle, the door opened, and I found myself in a narrow passage lit by a small lamp hanging from a dusty fitting.

In the passage two figures struggled, one that of a female, the other that of a man, who appeared slim but powerful. His hand was over the woman's mouth, and she was bent back at an angle, her lower parts thrust against his own in a manner which could only be suggestive of lasciviousness. That she was dissatisfied with her position was clear from her continuing, fruitlessly, to struggle against those arms which pinioned her.

I stepped forward and, without allowing the gentleman the advantage of foreknowledge, delivered a kick of considerable force to the small of his back. Those readers who find such an action from a female improbable might do worse than consult the previous volume[1] in which is recorded how a delightful Siamese boy, Loi – whose almost girlish frame, slim hips and slender waist belied his toughness and strength – spent some time instructing me in a form of unarmed combat, springing from the game of kick-boxing (well known in the interesting city of Bangkok). It is certainly somewhat difficult to employ this means of attack when dressed in the clothing of a Western lady – practising it, on a ship in the China Sea, I was used to wearing only a loincloth, which facilitated ease, though it sometimes led to activities as energetic but less potentially antagonistic than those for which I had adopted the guise.

The blow I delivered was, despite the hindrance of a skirt, still considerable enough to excite the gentleman into dropping

[1]*Eros in the Far East*

his victim with a sharp cry, and turn towards me – when, with
the advantage of the darkness, I was able to deliver a second
blow with my foot in that region where a blow is least
welcome, and on the gentleman bending double, to follow it
up with another, striking him upon the back of the neck with
the edge of my right hand.

He fell immediately to the floor and, holding out my hand,
I was able to assist the lady in the case to step over his body,
and we made our escape.

It had occurred to me that the person to whose aid I had
come was probably a woman of the streets (though no less
worthy of defence, for that); but on our emerging into North
Street not far from one of the lamps, I could see that she was
respectably dressed, and therefore invited her to return with
me to the Albion Hotel, where a glass or two of wine
considerably recovered her from the shock of the assault, and
she was ready, able and willing to inform me of the
circumstances, first introducing herself as Rosabel Esdaile, a
daughter of the Chairman of the Brighton Philosophical and
Ethical Society (a retired lawyer, and a man – as I later
learned – of considerable influence in the town), and the wife
of a young solicitor whose prospects were considerable and
whose respectability was unimpeachable.

'I find it embarrassing to recollect my simplicity,' remarked
Mrs Esdaile, 'in allowing myself to be placed in the
circumstance from which you so kindly rescued me. I was far
too easily led astray by . . .'

'By the gentleman we lately encountered?' I suggested.

'Indeed. Mr Anthony Furness is a young man – though
you might not in the present circumstances credit it – of
extraordinary attraction. His father died two years ago, leaving

him a fortune considerable enough to prevent the necessity of his working for a living; he therefore applies himself entirely to pleasure, and is to be seen at every fashionable occasion in the town. I fear that you had neither the time nor the opportunity to observe him, but even now I must confide that his appearance and manner is remarkable for its elegance, his form equally to be admired, and that it is impossible to see him without wondering what it would be like to be . . .'

Mrs Esdaile here paused, and blushed (as well she might).

'In short, Mrs Nelham,' she said, 'though several of my friends warned me against it, upon his making a set at me at a recent assembly, I unwisely acceded to a meeting.'

She fell silent here, and turned, with considerable nervousness, the wedding ring upon her finger. Observing my glance at this, she blushed once more, and confided that her husband, while she loved him dearly, was sadly deficient in one area of marriage of which she had had higher hopes than he had been able to satisfy; and that she had thought that a single fling (as she called it) with the gentleman of whom we were talking, would at least satisfy for a while the carnal appetite which had begun to cause her considerable irritation.

Upon her signalling to him her consent to a *rencontre*, Mr Furness had suggested, as a meeting place, a set of rooms he kept in the Lanes. This had seemed to her to be a somewhat eccentric venue; but she had agreed to it, and earlier that evening had made her way there. The dark and dirty doorway and dim, cobwebbed passage which I had seen had led to a ramshackle staircase at the top of which, however, was a doorway which, when opened, gave into rooms remarkable (she supposed) in the area, for their luxury. Dimly lit and hung with dark velvet, they seemed designed specifically for vice: the sitting room, if somewhat oppressive through its relative darkness, contained only a table and a *chaise-longue*, a half-open door had revealed a large bed, opulently hung, which the tenant had not troubled to conceal.

Already somewhat regretting her easy accessibility, Mrs Esdaile had allowed herself to be seated and given a glass of wine, when Mr Furness had taken from the table a large volume, and opening it had revealed a set of prints to which he directed her attention. These were at first, if somewhat salacious, at least by respectable artists: here, Mabuse's Deianeira curved her naked legs around those of Hercules, whose club was held at a somewhat suggestive angle; if the gods of Olympus in Frans Floris's picture were engaged in somewhat provocative games, only some were completely unclothed. Other representations – though by the most respectable hands – were more obviously licentious: she had never before seen that etching by Rembrandt entitled *The Bedstead*, for instance, in which a man and a woman were very evidently engaged in the oldest game of all; while in Primaticcio's drawings of women and satyrs nothing was left to the imagination, the appearance of the active masculine organ being most accurately and livelily delineated by the artist.

These drawings were, however, only the prelude to others increasingly libidinous, which gradually became more and more ruttish, until my new friend – at first only pleasantly warmed by them – began to grow positively uncomfortable; and finally, turning a page, her host pointed to a representation of a gentleman with his enormous prick sunk, not into its proper sheath, but into the arse of a slender and beautiful young female (who showed every sign of the experience being a painful one).

'And now, my dear Mrs Esdaile,' he said, 'you would perhaps not be averse to trying something along these lines?' – and taking her hand laid it between his thighs, where an iron-hard and evidently considerable weapon seemed ready to burst from his clothing.

She had now begun cordially to regret accepting Mr Furness's invitation – but was all too conscious that an excuse was unlikely to be accepted. She therefore pretended to be impressed, and passing her hand (with some repugnance) over the limb upon which he had placed it, through a murmured appreciation, gave – as she hoped – the impression of admiration. She then rose to her feet, carrying her hands to her bodice as though to unbutton it; but instead made a dash for the door. Pursuing her, he had succeeded in catching her in the passage below – when in desperation she had cried out, thus attracting my attention, with the consequences we know of.

Mrs Esdaile's narration had left her exhausted and distressed, through reliving her experience. She had been – though this was not the time to say so – extremely unwise, and in my view probably fortunate to escape without injury. About those ladies who permit themselves to enjoy extra-marital affairs with gentlemen of their choice, I have nothing to say; it is impossible to judge them without knowing all the circumstances of a case – and, even so, I would not take that liberty. But a young gentleman, however prepossessing, who upon a first meeting is coarse enough to display an illustration of an act which not every woman enjoys even upon complete familiarity, and by inference suggests that this is the course he would like to pursue, is unlikely to be a pleasant companion. Moreover, any gentleman whose companion – however acquiescent upon first acquaintance – signals her reluctance to proceed further towards the hoped-for conclusion, must respect her wishes or be condemned.

Having comforted her as best I might, and recommended her to confide in her husband her desire for a somewhat more adventurous private life, I bade her farewell and saw her into a carriage.

I then meditated for a while whether I should not enliven my final days in Brighton by teaching Mr Furness a lesson; and decided to do so. In case Mrs Esdaile had in her hysteria overstated the case, I consulted one or two of the gentlemen friends I had made in the town – and both *Señor* Ganivet and Sir Herbert Taylor (indeed, one or two of his friends at the Fitz Club – which Furness had unsuccessfully attempted to join, some months since) confirmed the impression that he was on almost every ground an unsatisfactory character, and best described as a womaniser.

Even while he was at college in Eton, he had got a maid with child and (it was rumoured) disposed of her by accusing her of theft and having her imprisoned; upon his father's death and his enrichment, he had at first contented himself with setting up a virtual harem of young females obtained for the purpose in London, where when he had tired of them he returned them upon the streets. Later he widened the scope of his activities to include a number of young wives and daughters of Brighton – with whom he had initially great success (everyone forced to admit that he was a personable young man), but several of whom he had severely damaged not only in reputation but even in health; for at the age of twenty-four he had tried almost every vice, and driven by familiarity with the more usual forms of love, had turned to more and more extreme and violent ones.

As might have been expected, attempts had been made to subdue him; but as is so often the case, his wealth enabled him to escape retribution – chiefly through bribery (having the law officers in his pocket).

Having decided the gentleman must be put down, I consulted a friend in the town – and someone I found under my nose at the Albion Hotel – and having made certain other arrangements, took a box one evening at the Brighton Theatre, where was to be performed the ballet of *Cinderella*.

The Brighton Theatre is a building in the New Road, unadorned as to exterior flourishes, and with a plain portico; however, the interior is considered to be one of the most elegant outside of the metropolis. The auditorium consists of two tiers of boxes, a pit, and spacious gallery, with a wide corridor to the boxes; their fronts are white, handsomely ornamented with gold and lined with crimson; the drop scene is green and gold. The representations are conducted in so very liberal and skilful a manner that they experience an extensive patronage from those who are accustomed to attend dramatic performance. The scenery and other decorations are splendid, without any limit of expense, while the orchestra is respectable and the usual companies of performers comprise many individuals of talent.

I dressed with care, my *décolleté* sufficiently low to expose to advantage those orbs which my friends have been kind enough to suggest are among my best features; and taking my seat alone in my box saw with pleasure, just before the curtain rose, that as I had expected, Mr Furness

255

strode into a box precisely opposite.

There being a candelabra just above my box, by leaning forward I was able to place myself advantageously, and could not but observe that during the first act Mr Furness's eyes were directed as often at me as towards the stage. Sure enough, when the interval came he was out of his box like a jack rabbit, and in a very short time a footman knocked at my door and handed me his card – upon which I signalled that he was to be admitted.

Upon first seeing him in a reasonable light, I must admit that I was not surprised at the ease with which he had managed to obtain an interview with Mrs Esdaile – or, indeed, with anyone else he fancied, for he was a very proper man: only of slightly more than medium height, but with a superior carriage which made him appear taller; slim but well built, and with a somewhat olive skin and dark, flashing eyes which fixed themselves upon the object of their scrutiny with so intense a gaze that it was impossible to believe that (were oneself the object of it) any other person or thing could be of the slightest interest to him.

He bowed over my hand, and bade me welcome to Brighton as though I had just arrived there (it being, I imagine, his supposition that I could not have been in town long without his being aware of the fact – in itself a compliment). Asking my permission to be seated, he knocked once upon the floor with his cane, whereupon, one of the theatre's menials entered with a tray upon which were two glasses and a bottle of sparkling wine (as it turned out, of French champagne, a drink inordinately expensive, but extremely inspiriting).

And how did I find the entertainment? – he asked; did I not find it much inferior to what I was used to in London?

(Again, the assumption that I could only be from the metropolis was a well-turned compliment.)

On the contrary, I found it charming, I replied.

Ah, but that was surely (he observed) a charitable remark, for he was convinced that in the natural course of events only the very finest shows could receive such a compliment from such a spectator!

While making this comment, he leaned forward and placed his hand over my own, as it lay upon the edge of the box. I was careful not to remove it, and indeed somewhat bowed myself (not, I admit, without the realisation that my doing so further exposed that part of my upper body upon which, from time to time, I had observed his glance to fall).

At this moment, the lights dimmed, and as the orchestra struck up he whispered a request that he might remain in my company during the latter part of the performance – to which I made no reply, except to shift somewhat in my seat as though better to observe the stage, but at the same time placing myself in a closer proximity to him, so that my thigh pressed against his own.

I immediately felt a shudder run through his body – which I must confess I took as another compliment; for I had supposed an experienced *roué*, such as I believed him to be, would have taken such a gesture as his right; the fact that he was still capable of being excited by the presence of a woman seemed to indicate to me that he could perhaps yet be saved; it is the cold-blooded seducer who is most objectionable – warm blood suggests that the heart is also warm.

However, that it was not in this instance the heart that was in the ascendant was almost immediately clear, for Mr Furness's hand soon was lifted from my own, and placed instead upon my thigh; a movement to which I made no objection, rather imitating it by allowing my own palm to fall upon his leg, somewhat above the knee, and to slide upward until I was able to confirm Mrs Esdaile's suspicion that the engine concealed by his trousers was a considerable one; though, again, not unsusceptible to surprise – for such a deliberate gesture made it leap beneath my palm in a manner which I suspected of being painful (through the organ's constriction), for the gentleman winced somewhat, and shifted in his chair.

I whispered my apologies, to which he replied with a somewhat feverish assurance that I had caused him only a temporary inconvenience – which indeed he now went about relieving by (having first somewhat drawn a curtain which obstruct at least the view of those in the next box) lifting my hand from its position at his groin, undoing some buttons which imprisoned his prick, and then replacing my hand – which now fell upon the naked column itself, the skin of which moved over a foundation which seemed to be made of warm ivory, so solid and palpable was it.

My stroking enlivened him still further, and bending towards me he pressed a kiss upon my lips, and drawing down the neck of my gown fixed his own then upon one breast, while thrusting a hand beneath my skirts to discover with perfect freedom (since I refused to adopt the filthy French habit of wearing underclothes) that part of my person analogous to the monolith I held in my own. This so much excited him that he attempted to thrust me to the floor, where – I am convinced – he would immediately have performed the act towards which (I must confess) I had been inclining him.

However, I stiffened my back and taking his arms whispered: 'My dear sir, if you will accept my apologies, I have a rooted objection to coupling so publicly!'

'Why, no one can see us!' he responded (which may indeed have been the case, though I was not entirely convinced that a heavily mustachioed gentleman in the next box was completely ignorant of what was going on).

'All the same, sir, the comfort of my rooms would be more convenient, both as to privacy and allowing more time for a jointure which I am convinced would ripen with the hours.'

With which I rose to my feet. He could do nothing but follow my example. Replacing the bodice of my dress, I leaned forward, pressed my lips to his, and with a final caress of that instrument which still stood out of his trousers at an angle suggestive of a military salute, whispered an address to him, and left the box.

A small carriage which I had commissioned waited for me outside the theatre, and hurried me to an address – which was not that (I might as well say) of the Albion Hotel, but of a set of rooms some way off. There, I greeted a certain person, made certain last-minute arrangements and confirmed others, before changing into a loose robe and taking my seat in a little sitting room. In not too short a space the sound of horses was heard, the downstairs door (which had been left upon the latch) opened, there were footsteps upon the stairs, and the door opened to disclose Mr Furness, who advanced towards me eagerly, and upon my rising to greet him not only embraced me with passion, but threw open my gown to disclose the fact (which delighted him) that I had removed all other clothing.

I permitted him to gaze for a moment at my person –

which the reader will perhaps not condemn me for remarking was at that time not unhandsome, despite the fact that I had passed the age of thirty – before assisting him out of his coat, his shirt, his . . .

It must be admitted that had circumstances been otherwise, and had the gentleman not needed a lesson, I would not have been ungratified by the sight I now saw before me. It is generally not considered proper for a female to admit to an admiration of the male figure: yet have we not eyes? – have we not appetites? May our lips not water at the sight of a promising dish? Mr Furness's body was such as might be expected to gratify any discerning taste; he carried himself well (as I have already remarked) – and far from being shy, was sufficiently vain (as I take it) to show no hint of shame at the vigorous nature of the display which proved his interest in me: his prick stood firmly up against his belly, a little cluster of tightly curled black hair setting off what seemed a whiter skin (wrapped around the organ) than that of the rest of his body. His bollocks below were tightly drawn up – any loose skin which might at another time have suspended them more freely, being taken up in cladding the large column above. No sign of superfluous corpulence was to be seen, the bones of his hips being barely clad, and those of his chest being discernible – though not through a painful thinness, for his breast, which seemed of burnished copper, rather resembled the shield of some Greek warrior, a few jet-black hairs only lying between the paps.

My admiration was such that I almost succumbed to his charm – before remembering that the very reason for my being in his company was that charm was not usually exercised beyond the first moment of meeting, and that if Mrs Esdaile was to be believed, a number of females in the town could testify to the fact.

As he stepped forward to embrace me, I therefore, while not resisting his embrace, put my finger to my lips and quietly informed him that for purposes of privacy, no less than of convenience, we must adjourn to the bedroom.

'Will you allow me a moment?' I said, 'in order further to prepare myself?' – and placing my hands upon his buttocks, drew him even closer to me, so that his prick was briefly compressed between our bellies; to such effect that he was now, I believe, in such a state that he must be amenable to almost any suggestion; and though reluctantly, he released me, whereupon I went through into the next room. A moment later, I summoned him, in a whisper, into the darkened bedroom. Although he moved with remarkable alacrity in the direction of the desired object, by the time he had passed through the door, I had donned a gown laid ready and slipped through another door into the corridor. Meanwhile, Mr Furness, seeing dimly – in the light from the sitting room – the shape of a bed inhabited by a reclining figure, threw himself upon it and vigorously embraced it.

His companion immediately let out a yell – whereupon, almost instantly, there came into the room from the corridor a gentleman accompanied by a footman carrying a lamp. They saw before their astonished eyes – or at any rate eyes which gave the impression of astonishment – a gentleman devoid of clothing, and with his instrument at such an angle as made his intention clear, holding in his arms the wriggling and equally unclothed body of a young man of perhaps fifteen years of age!

The gentleman gave a great roar: 'Sir! – what do you want

of my son?' – whereupon, the boy extricated himself from the embrace of the startled Mr Furness, and ran to his father, who immediately removed his coat and wrapped it around his shoulders before approaching Furness with a furious face and an arm upraised to strike.

The astonished Furness protested and protested – but in vain. The father declined to accept so unbelievable an explanation as that the interloper had been brought into the house by a woman, and spoke of sending the footman for the police – whereat Furness showed signs of considerable concern, for indeed his situation seemed a perilous one. The law's attitude to a corrupter of children, especially of the same sex as the offender, was so rigorous that even his wealth seemed unlikely to be capable of extricating him from his fix.

He made a movement towards the door, but his way was barred, the door closed and bolted against him. Returning to the sitting room, he found that door also closed and barred, and was left to resume his clothing and ponder upon what plot had set him in such a situation, and what explanation he could offer the magistrates for an apparent assault upon an innocent child.

Meanwhile, Sir Herbert Taylor (for it was he who had impersonated the outraged father) retired with a certain Jack Fitton, pageboy at the Albion, and in a room downstairs reported to me Mr Furness's reaction to his predicament. We then sat and enjoyed a cold collation and a glass of wine, allowing that gentleman to stew in his own juice, before we all returned to enter the rooms in which he had been imprisoned, and where he was striding to and fro in a pretty paddy, awaiting his fate.

Upon seeing me, his chin dropped, and he was ready for an accusation: but I was quick to explain the reason for my action, which had had its genesis in his untoward attitude to Mrs Esdaile; and further explained that my friend Sir Herbert and his son (for we had decided to keep up that pretence) would have no hesitation in perjuring themselves should any report reach either him or myself of any trouble Furness might cause the ladies of Brighton in the immediate future. There could be no doubt of the consequences.

Furness gave us his reluctant assurance of good behaviour for the future, and was let go; I have no great confidence in his repentance, for from what I had seen of him he seemed to me to be the sort of man who has allowed his sensual desires such ascendancy that he is now incapable of reining them in. But we shall see.

Thanking Sir Herbert again for his assistance, and indeed for the temporary use of his rooms, I made my way back to the Albion accompanied by young Jack Fitton, who was in high spirits, and did not hesitate to question me, during our walk, about Mr Furness and his activities. My recital of them clearly interested him considerably; and upon arriving at the hotel, on my offering him two guineas (a not unreasonable recompense for his part in the evening's events) he, with the greatest courtesy, expressed his admiration for me, and asked whether he might be allowed to kiss me.

Making sure that we were not in a public place (for it is a cardinal rule with me to be excessively careful in any amorous dealings I may have with servants, not for my own reputation but for the circumstances of their employment), I allowed him the liberty – whereupon, he pressed his lips to mine with an ardour very considerable for a boy of only fourteen or fifteen years of age. On my commenting on the fact, he admitted to no less than twenty years – indeed, almost twenty and one, for his birthday was but two days hence! He believed himself, he said, fortunate in that his appearance allowed him to continue in his present position – the management being pleased to be able to rely on someone of mature years, while his appearance of tender years enabled him to wait upon the ladies staying at the hotel without causing them embarrassment even should he discover them in circumstances which might otherwise upset their propriety.

Jack admitted that his appearance and air of innocence had from time to time persuaded female guests to allow him glimpses of the female form not normally vouchsafed to young men of his real age – but somewhat sadly followed this up by the admission that he had not yet had the courage to follow up such opportunities.

His ardour was such that, being an attractive boy and of such years that I could not be accused of cradle-snatching, I took the liberty of asking whether he would care to accompany me to my room? I must confess that my self-denial in rejecting the attentions of someone as attractive in physique as he was unattractive in manners, viz., Mr Furness, had somewhat raised my spirits – and in satisfying them, if I could offer some gratitude to a handsome boy who had served my plan well, I could see no possible objection to it.

That Jack was willing will surprise no one, and taking every precaution not to be discovered, we made our way upstairs. Once in my rooms, young Jack could not wait for an embrace; but gently persuading him that the bedroom would be more convenient than the sitting room, I drew him to the door, pausing only to light a lamp. Opening the door, I drew him by the hand towards the bed – only to become aware that someone was lying upon it, and to see (with a pleasure which the boy certainly did not share) that that someone was my friend Andrew Archer Esq, MP.

Chapter Fifteen

The Adventures of Andy

I was not astonished, upon waking, to find my friend Sophie had entered her bedroom accompanied by a young gentleman – though I realise that while some readers will accept this statement as a compliment to her charms and continuing interest in the male sex, others (probably consisting of readers unfamiliar with her nature) may take it as the opposite. I was, however, somewhat surprised to recognise her companion as a mere child – for he could not be more than fourteen or fifteen years of age. My friend is not usually particularly drawn to extreme youth, nor does she believe that a coupling between childhood and experience is to be encouraged except under the most extraordinary circumstances.

However, I do not take the position of her keeper, and nothing would have drawn any comment from me on this occasion – at least in the presence of the lad. We greeted each other with pleasure, after which she introduced her friend to me as one Jack Fitton and, she said, a pageboy at the very hotel in which we found ourselves. This, too, somewhat surprised me, for in general Sophie is careful to form no alliance with servants – unless, again, the situation is one which especially favours or positively demands one.

She now apologised to the boy for being unable, as she put it, to reward him adequately for his help; at which he looked much crestfallen. She went on to assure him that his time would come, and very soon – at which he looked not much comforted, but could do nothing but leave, whereupon, my friend leaped upon the bed, embraced me again with a warmth that she would not show in the presence of a stranger, and enquired about my doings.

They seemed to have been nothing, I replied, to her own – and enquired what she was doing with such a child?

'Not such a child!' she replied, explaining that in a couple of days he would celebrate his twenty-first birthday – and going on to give a brief account of her evening's work, suggested that young Jack deserved entertainment, not only on the grounds of his having been of assistance to her, but because no young man should reach the age of majority without a taste of the pleasures to which his years legitimately entitled him.

Surely, I said, it was unlikely that he had not tasted those pleasures? – for few young men of our century grow much beyond their teens without doing so.

He had assured her that such was the case, she replied; perhaps through his appearing of such tender years that only the most rapacious older woman would permit him any familiarity, while no doubt those who were his contemporaries would prefer a companion who seemed more manlike.

We talked long into the night – having first doffed our clothes and rendered ourselves comfortable, by which I mean in that state of nature which permits a man and a woman that feeling of familiarity and freedom which can be achieved in no other form of dress (while not leading necessarily to physical familiarity, unless that becomes desirable or inevitable). Our respective adventures lost nothing in the telling – and I must confess that the narratives of which we delivered ourselves were sufficiently warming to rouse us to an embrace, which without being unduly passionate culminated in our falling asleep without any of those regrets which must be the result of unsatisfied desire.

Waking next morning, we sent for some breakfast, and I instructed the servant who brought it to have my luggage sent up to Mrs Nelham's rooms, which I would now be sharing. The man did not in the least stare at this (or indeed at our being found together in the same bed), for this town has been for the past twenty years a resort of those who wish to take an intimate holiday together, either with their lovers or with someone else's, without the inconvenience of having to cross the Channel, and in such privacy as will not result in a challenge from any party who considers himself or herself wronged.

Over breakfast, we discussed the party which Sophie was determined to hold for young Jack. It seems that some confidence or another had had the result of persuading her that she could provide an entertainment which would please him, and might result in a lasting liaison – though, she said, she would not object to inviting a few other gentlemen friends, in order to bid them farewell before we left Brighton, and asked whether I thought that a couple among my recent female acquaintance would object to being present. It might not be impossible that such ladies and gentlemen would benefit from being introduced to each other.

The next two days were spent in making arrangements for

the party – and lest anyone should think this a superfluous occupation, being made on behalf of those we scarcely knew, they are not aware of the pains which both Sophie and I are willing to take on such occasions – for we are by way of being perfectionists, and any such undertaking must be planned with the utmost care.

Our first task was to discover a setting for our party. I was somewhat perplexed at this, for although in London I knew a number of houses where such activities as we planned would by no means be considered surprising, my knowledge of Brighton was not sufficiently complete to enable me to judge who might or might not be scandalised by what we planned; and certainly no public rooms could be considered, for though by no means troubled for my reputation, I was not eager to go out of my way to offend the susceptibilities of hoteliers or landlords.

The problem was, however, soon solved, for Sophie, was able to take advantage of her acquaintance with Sir Herbert Taylor, who placed at our disposal the rooms of the Fitz Club, set up in memory of Mrs Fitzherbert, the friend of the late King; these proved admirable for our purpose, with only the slightest modification required – such as the provision of tables for one of the rooms, in which we would set out food and wines. The room in which the chief entertainment of the Club took place was absolutely what we required.

The venue fixed upon, we immediately sent out invitations to those of our friends we wished to entertain; and received from each of them an enthusiastic acceptance; my two particular friends not in the least objecting to travelling from Eastbourne in response to what I suggested. In the meantime, young Jack was at a pitch of excitement, and lost no opportunity to enquire as to the nature of the entertainment being planned for him – Sophie having informed him that we wished to pay him tribute upon his reaching the age of majority. If at first I had had some doubts of the wisdom of providing him with such a relatively expensive introduction to manhood, I soon grew fond of the young fellow – apart from his having been of use to Sophie in her putting down of the egregious Mr Furness. On my conversing with him in private, it proved indeed to be the case that he was entirely inexperienced in connection with the female gender, this being the result of his inordinately youthful appearance.

That Jack was ready for a proper introduction to womanhood was evident, however, if only in the sheep's eyes he continually cast upon Sophie.

The day of the boy's birthday having arrived, we were awakened by him early in the morning – he having bribed the chambermaid to permit him to bring us our breakfast, which as usual we took in bed. It was clear to us both that the chief reason for this was his wish to be greeted first by Sophie, who (as could be told by his covert and even overt glances of admiration) had become something of an ikon to him; and his pleasure when, upon his approaching our bedside, she sat up and invited him to take a kiss, seemed alone almost sufficient recognition of his reaching years of indiscretion – especially since my friend was careful to take no trouble to cover herself, allowing the boy to admire breasts which were as pert and pretty (I dare say) as those of any woman of half her age.

On his proving unable – despite my presence (which only a very little deterred him) to resist placing his hand upon one of those delightful globes, my friend, however, gently deterred him, with the advice that he should wait a few hours – whereupon, his eyes opened wide in speculation, and reluctantly and wordlessly retiring from the bed, he drew the curtains and with a final glance at Sophie, made a somewhat uncomfortable bow, the elegance of which was constrained by some inconvenient obstruction within his breeches, and left.

He had been told to make himself ready by six o'clock, and at that time – he having been permitted by his employer to absent himself from his duties – I escorted him on the short walk to the premises of the Fitz Club. He had no idea where he was going, and if some notion of the purpose of the evening had occurred to him, he kept it to himself, though his eyes seemed to shine with anticipation, and he was more than somewhat nervous.

I had not been able to restrain myself from hinting that his state of innocence might not now be long maintained, and I believe that he was ready for whatever came; though upon our entering the main room of the Fitz Club his expression seemed to declare that he had had no notion of the luxury which now confronted him.

This consisted of no fewer than three ladies, all in a state of complete undress, and reclining upon the large mattress which virtually formed the floor of the room (as Sophie has already described earlier in the present volume). In the centre, my friend herself lay face downward, but her chin propped in her hands, so that her breasts were partly exposed, though the chief charm upon view was her long back and full, pear-shaped bottom, luscious enough to cry out for a caress. Upon her left, Mrs Carclase lay upon her back, her head towards the door, her fine breasts, even in repose, displayed to advantage, and one hand lying idly between her thighs, only a few curls escaping her palm to suggest what pleasure she concealed. Finally, upon Sophie's right, Mlle Beauregard had adopted a pose which, while it might be condemned as too free, had its attractions for a young man unfamiliar with the female form – for she lay back, her upper body supported upon her elbows, and her legs thrown apart to reveal the chief mark of her womanhood without the least concealment – the moss which lay between her thighs thrust aside by two lusciously full lips which seemed to pout in the most promising abandon.

Young Jack staggered and, I believe, almost fell, partly no doubt with surprise, but I am sure with equal delight. Turning to me, his lips seeming to frame a silent question, upon my smiling and nodding, he threw himself forward and falling to his knees planted a kiss upon Sophie's lips – without even taking the time (as a more experienced fellow no doubt would have done) to remove his shirt.

This omission, however, was speedily remedied, for while Sophie, placing a hand at each side of his face, retained his lips upon hers, Mrs Carclase set about unbuttoning his pantaloons and drew them about his knees, while Mlle Beauregard, equally adept at unbuttoning, disposed of his shirt. This done, while Sophie continued to receive the boy's panting kisses, the two other ladies lavished their caresses upon his small, firm arse, jutted upward by his being upon all fours, and to them the most delightful sight, so that each with avaricious pleasure consumed that cheek which fell to her, not neglecting at the same time to tickle that apparatus which, though out of sight, responded (I had no doubt) with enthusiasm to their touch.

Jack was by now, I believe, somewhat eager to take a more active part in the proceedings than he had yet been permitted to do, but this was restricted to Sophie's (by sitting up) permitting him to transfer his lips from her own to her bosom, at the same time encouraging her companions to turn him so that he lay upon his back rather than his face – exposing as he reclined upon her bosom a prick which, experienced or no, clearly had the potential to give and receive pleasure, both from its being of more than average dimensions, and being engorged to an advanced state of rigidity – which did not prevent the two other ladies from attempting to enrage it still further by at once setting to work upon it, one upon each side, so that no surface of that part of his body was neglected – belly, sides, prick and cods all receiving the compliments of their tongues and lips. Sophie, meanwhile, drawing his head back upon her shoulder, stroked and played with his hairless breast and paps, flicking at them with a teasing motion which I recognised as provoking (having myself experienced it upon many occasions).

That the boy was able to stand such treatment for more than a moment promised well for his mistresses in future years, for I am sure that at his age and with his lack of experience, I would have reached my apogee long since. He was, I believe, determined not to do so before ceasing, technically, to be a virgin; and three or four beads of blood now appeared upon his lower lip, where his teeth inflicted such pain as would enable him to retain his self-control – while his hands hung motionless at his sides, unoccupied (I fancy) lest the pleasures they might discover should please him beyond endurance.

Seeing that the acuteness of his pleasure was (though

delightful) no less than distressing to him, I signalled to
Sophie, who tapped her colleagues upon the shoulders. They
immediately left their work, merely lying one upon each side
of him as he reclined between Sophie's thighs, his back
against her bosom.

Jack now looked somewhat confused, and even a little
troubled; but seeing me step aside, fixed his eyes upon the
door behind me – which opened, and through it stepped a
fourth female: but one whom he knew. This was a
chambermaid at the Albion Hotel: one who noting Jack's
admiration of Sophie had at first been discourteous to her,
but upon being reassured had confided in her her admiration
for the boy, long concealed from him for fear of rejection –
and had been taken into the secret of the party and awarded a
major role in the proceedings.

If Jack had previously taken no notice of her, it had not
only been because he considered her too young for admiration
(being between seventeen and eighteen years of age) but also
because he had always seen her in the somewhat unromantic
garb which she was forced to wear for daily use. She had
eschewed this on this occasion; and indeed – having been
persuaded by Sophie that she would not lose by it – had
adopted the same clothing as the other ladies: viz., a complete
absence of dress.

Her first objection to being present had been that she had
grown tired of Jack expressing his admiration for the female
guests at the Albion, all of whom had naturally been somewhat
older than herself. However – as Jack's present expression
confirmed – she need not have had any concern; her figure
was remarkably mature for her years. A mass of red hair fell
to her shoulders, almost to her breasts, which far from being

negligible in form, were full but well shaped, being firmly uplifted so that the nipples pointed ever so slightly outwards, the weight of flesh beneath them falling into the most delicious curves; her waist was small, but her hips swelled to a proper declaration of womanhood, and below a charmingly round, small belly a splash of red hair announced (though somewhat at the same time concealing) a target at which any man would have been pleased to aim.

The three ladies now rose to their feet, bringing Jack with them; while I stepped behind the young lady and (without the slightest impropriety, for I was still fully clothed) persuaded her to take a step forward, when in a moment the two young people were in each other's arms. As the boy sank to his knees, taking her with him to the floor, the four of us left them, retiring to the neighbouring room – where *Señor* Angel Ganivet and M. Charles Tronc, two musicians with whom Sophie had established an acquaintance, were waiting. They were evidently not displeased at the sight of the three naked nymphs – but were sufficiently in control of their emotions to content themselves with pouring wine and acting as gentlemen should in serving the ladies before inviting them to serve themselves.

The evening was sufficiently warm, fortunately, for informality to be a comfort; the gentlemen had (while the above described entertainment had been underway) removed their street clothes and clad themselves in dressing-gowns; but on the ladies declining to avail themselves of similar garments (they said, through the heat; but I doubted not through the raising of their spirits by their recent kindly activities) the gentlemen soon removed their own, while I too without undue tardiness placed myself upon equal terms. It must be said that though we made a good meal, enjoying several glasses, our minds were as much upon flesh as upon fruit. Mrs Carclase had clearly at first sight set her heart upon entertaining M. Tronc, and was now seated upon his knee (he taking the precaution of making himself comfortable by ensuring that his prick – which was naturally not unaroused by her propinquity – rose between her thighs rather than being confined beneath them), and they were mutually engaged in an exchange of tongues while their fingers explored such parts of each other's persons as were capable of being reached by them.

Mlle Beauregard had at the same time seated herself upon the floor and lay back between the thighs of *Señor* Ganivet, where her cheek was inevitably caressed by his own weapon, to which from time to time she paid the compliment of saluting it with her lips – while playfully at one point pouring a glass of wine over its dome in order that she might lap it as it ran down the column, from whence it fell from his bollocks upon her shoulder and ran between her breasts.

Sophie was (as always concerned for my comfort) good enough to enquire whether I was not jealous at the sight. My reply was that she would not have supposed that I had not already made myself familiar with the two ladies, whereas she and I had been for some time out of each other's company; and that while, as she knew, I was never opposed to adventures abroad, returning home was a greater pleasure. But we had (she remarked) several times during the past three evenings enjoyed each other's company.

And did she suppose (I responded) that this had left me incapable? – and conveyed her hand to that part of my body whose condition could not leave her in doubt of the fact;

whereupon, she took my hand, and, rising, announced that the two youngsters had been left long enough alone, and led the way into the neighbouring room – where though it might have been supposed that they were temporarily exhausted, they proved to be engaged in a form of activity which I will not be so impertinent as to describe in detail, but which employed both pairs of lips in the activity of kissing, though not in juxtaposition to each other: it amused us all to see that, young and inexperienced as they were, our friends had nevertheless been able, through a natural ability, to contrive a position in which this could be done with ease.

Our companions were at first somewhat shy of the idea of joining so much younger a pair; but as I pointed out, the youngsters could only profit by our example – and in no time we were all expressing our passions in the manner preferred. The rooms being ours until dawn, the time passed in leisurely delights, Mlle Beauregard and Mrs Carclase being complimented by both gentlemen in turn; and being so good as to instruct Jack and Betty in as many postures as would keep them in rehearsal for some time.

Sophie and I were not slow in proving once more our love and admiration for each other; but in the early hours – the others having fallen into a sleep – took the liberty of slipping back to our rooms and taking some time for genuine rest before joining the ten o'clock coach for London, our summer excursion to the coast having proved, if unprofitable for those who had suggested it to me, entirely delightful in every other way.

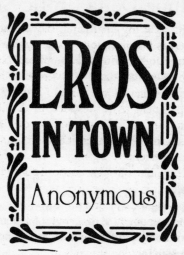

Headline Delta Erotic Survey

In order to provide the kind of books you like to read - and to qualify for a free erotic novel of the Editor's choice - we would appreciate it if you would complete the following survey and send your answers, together with any further comments, to:

> Headline Book Publishing
> FREEPOST 9 (WD 4984)
> London
> W1E 7BE

1. Are you male or female?
2. Age? Under 20 / 20 to 30 / 30 to 40 / 40 to 50 / 50 to 60 / 60 to 70 / over
3. At what age did you leave full-time education?
4. Where do you live? (Main geographical area)
5. Are you a regular erotic book buyer / a regular book buyer in general / both?
6. How much approximately do you spend a year on erotic books / on books in general?
7. How did you come by this book?
7a. If you bought it, did you purchase from:
    a national bookchain / a high street store / a newsagent / a motorway station / an airport / a railway station / other........
8. Do you find erotic books easy / hard to come by?
8a. Do you find Headline Delta erotic books easy / hard to come by?
9. Which are the best / worst erotic books you have ever read?
9a. Which are the best / worst Headline Delta erotic books you have ever read?
10. Within the erotic genre there are many periods, subjects and literary styles. Which of the following do you prefer:
10a. (period) historical / Victorian / C20th / contemporary / future?
10b. (subject) nuns / whores & whorehouses / Continental frolics / s&m / vampires / modern realism / escapist fantasy / science fiction?

10c. (styles) hardboiled / humorous / hardcore / ironic / romantic / realistic?

10d. Are there any other ingredients that particularly appeal to you?

11. We try to create a cover appearance that is suitable for each title. Do you consider them to be successful?

12. Would you prefer them to be less explicit / more explicit?

13. We would be interested to hear of your other reading habits. What other types of books do you read?

14. Who are your favourite authors?

15. Which newspapers do you read?

16. Which magazines?

17. Do you have any other comments or suggestions to make?

If you would like to receive a free erotic novel of the Editor's choice (available only to UK residents), together with an up-to-date listing of Headline Delta titles, please supply your name and address:

Name...

Address...

....

....

A selection of Erotica from Headline